MALIBU BURNS

MARK RICHARDSON

For my dad

If you understand a painting beforehand, you might as well not paint it.

—Salvador Dali

ACKNOWLEDGMENTS

Continued gratitude to Rob, Al, and Greg for your feedback and ongoing support. A special thanks to Tracy Richardson and Elizabeth White for your editorial expertise.

With love for Jenn. You're the tops, babes!

PART ONE

SAN FRANCISCO—MARCH 17, 2049

A SNAKING EMOTION

MALIBU MAKIMURA WAS DRAWING THE FINAL TOUCHES TO a woman's portrait when she felt the creeping sensation of someone else's emotion. Her lower half twitched as the emotion hit her feet and slithered up her legs, just like how a snake feels vibrations on the surface of the earth. Only a snake's sensory capabilities are more dependable than her psionic powers, which were annoyingly unpredictable.

Malibu focused on this feeling as it methodically slithered its way up her leg. The word sinister sprang to mind. Was that even an emotion? No, it probably wasn't. Still, sinister was the word that best described what Malibu felt.

Malibu leaned back in her chair, spun the pencil between her fingers, and focused on trying to shake loose from the alien feeling. She shook her body, head to toe.

No dice—the emotion held firm.

In fact, it continued its upward climb. It no longer felt like a snake, but an octopus wrapping its tentacles around her limbs, her neck, suffocating her.

"Are you okay, dear?" asked the older woman whose portrait Malibu had been sketching. The pancake makeup on the woman's face had been packed on extra thick, her cheeks colored red, her eyebrows shaved and painted on like big, wide, black rectangles. She looked pitiful and clownish.

"I'm fine," said Malibu, which was suddenly true. The alien emotion, although still poisonous in nature, felt weirdly seductive as well, and almost as if Malibu was pulling the sensation toward her. She could sense the emotion slip through her skin and seep inside and spark to life something savage and angry that had been dormant.

Yes, hissed Malibu's inner voice, a presence she was loath to acknowledge. It welcomed the feeling, found nourishment in its villainous nature.

"Can I take a peek?" the woman asked, meaning the portrait.

"Not yet. It's not quite done."

Malibu returned her focus to her work. She drew carica-tures, although not the goofy, comical types you'd see drawn at tourist hot spots. Malibu's drawings were surrealist abstracts, a blend of Picasso and Dali. She liked what she had done with this one. The eyes were particularly cool. One was placed high on the head, and the other down near the cheek. The contrast worked. Overall, she made a point to have the woman come across as interesting and not ridiculous; Malibu could be thoughtful that way. The portrait was more or less finished, but on a whim Malibu added one more feature—a knife. Working quickly, she drew it so it looked as if it had been recently plunged into the side of the woman's head. Small traces of blood covered the part of the knife that touched the head. Perfect.

Malibu picked up the canvas and turned it to give the woman a look at what she'd drawn. The woman's eyes narrowed and then widened. A horrified expression spread across her face.

"That's me?" she asked.

"Uh-huh."

"But it doesn't look anything like me." The woman's thin lips narrowed into a line.

"It's your essence."

"My essence?" Her lips pursed, the makeup around them cracked.

"Think of it this way," Malibu said, trying to add a professorial air to her voice. "We all exist in different realms simultaneously, parallel worlds. I focus on breaking down the doors that separate those realms of existence and capturing different elements of who you truly are. That's what I draw, those different elements."

It was a practiced speech, one designed to make the subject feel like a mystery was being unveiled. Years earlier, Malibu had read part of an essay on Charles Manson that discussed his obsession with the Beatles' *White Album*, how he believed its songs had a hidden, deeper meaning, a meaning the Beatles themselves were unaware of. As if an unknown force was able to use the pop group to channel its message. Malibu obviously didn't approve of the murderous path Manson and his family had followed, but she was drawn to the multi-world imagery. Mainly, though, she'd found the speech helped to pacify unhappy clients.

"I...I see," the woman said. She leaned forward to get a closer look. A sense of understanding seemed to wash over her face. Her eyes brightened, sparkled, and the painted-on eyebrows were lifted higher on her forehead. "I love it!"

"I'm so happy." The malevolent feeling wrapped its tentacles more tightly around Malibu's body and squeezed. It felt hard to breathe.

"The knife is so..." The woman trailed off, smiled, as if happy to have been let in on a delicious secret. The woman dug into her enormous purse and pulled out five shekels. She placed the coins into Malibu's hand, took the drawing, and hurried toward the exit.

Malibu worked at the Kit Kat Club, a women-only night-club on Green Street, two blocks off Broadway, situated on the edge of North Beach. She had been employed there for three weeks; hired by the club's owner, the multi-jowled, wig-wearing Hilda Martinez. Hilda had played a hunch and brought Malibu on board in the hopes her off-center artistic talent would appeal to the club's refined clientele. Sadly, the experiment hadn't paid off. There was scant customer demand for portraits. The well-heeled women who frequented the club for the most part didn't want their portraits drawn; they wanted to cut loose. Malibu had caught murmurings within the ranks that Hilda was reconsidering her decision and Malibu's days were likely numbered.

The base pay at the club was dismal, and the cocktail wait-resses, bartenders, and other young women who worked there were all expected to survive on tips. To drum up business, most wore eye-catching getups: miniskirts, Daisy Duke shorts, fishnet stockings, cleavage-flashing tops, stiletto heels, and extra-fragrant perfume designed to climb up a customer's nose, tickle the inside, and solicit an animalistic reaction.

Malibu didn't consider herself a prude, and although she was nineteen and could have pulled off one of the risqué costumes, she had always been on the mousy side, and frankly didn't feel comfortable advertising herself that way. When working, she opted to wear dresses that fell to just above the ankles and thin cardigan sweaters. Like her drawings, the outfits failed to generate any significant customer interest. Really, she was something of a bust.

On her first day working at the club, Malibu had gathered that the real action was found in the back rooms. What happened there was never discussed, but it was not hard to guess.

Malibu fiddled with the five shekels she gotten for her portrait, juggled them in the palm of her hand. A few feet away, a Persian girl in a belly dancer outfit sashayed toward a table where a sad-looking woman decked out in bling-bling jewelry sat alone. Malibu could hear the girl whisper in the woman's ear: Would you like a private party? The woman stifled a smile and nodded. Malibu watched as the belly dancer took the woman by the hand and walked them to a side door.

Perhaps it was inevitable Malibu would find herself slipping into a more racy outfit and going down that route as well. After all, a girl needs to survive and her options were limited. And since the tragedies with her parents, she was on her own. Now surely the backroom shenanigans paid much more than five measly shekels. Besides, she would do almost anything to avoid returning to the homeless encampment.

So...

The black-hearted alien emotion gave her neck a squeeze, as if protesting that it was being ignored. Malibu dropped the shekels into the side pocket of her sweater. She let her eyes roam around the room until they landed on a woman on the opposite side seated at a round table sipping a cocktail. She wore a leopard-spotted dress. In the filmy light, it was hard to gauge her age. Forties? More likely fifties, but she was put together in such a neat package, gave off such an air of authority, that her age seemed irrelevant. One of her legs was hooked over the other at the knee. The foot in the air wiggled. Her tortoise-shell glasses sat perched at the end of her nose. As Malibu's eyes lingered, she felt the emotion become fiercer, overwhelming, and the voice inside her grew louder, as if the two entities fed off each other.

The woman turned her head and looked directly at Malibu.

She pushed her glasses back to the bridge of her nose, appearing to try and get a clearer look. Forcing the presence inside her down, Malibu blinked and diverted her eyes, as if it was deadly to look at the woman for too long, as if she'd snuck a peek at the sun and now her pupils burned.

Leaving her art stand, Malibu walked behind the bar where Hilda was hand-washing glasses.

"Do you know her story?" Malibu asked Hilda. "The one in the leopard-print blouse."

Hilda's wig that day was a bright purple. She wore an extra-large black kimono with red polka dots draped over her rotund figure. Hilda lifted her eyes and glanced at the woman. With a frown, she said, "That's Luciana. She works for the Chairman. I suggest you steer clear."

"The Chairman?" Malibu snuck another peek at Luciana, welcomed the burn, and wanted to feel it even more. As if listening to her plea, the dark emotion practically strangled her. She coughed.

"Steady," Hilda said, and patted her on the back. "That's right, the Chairman." She didn't elaborate. She'd finished washing the glasses and had started using a fresh towel to dry them.

The Chairman. It sounded cartoonish, a name you might give a crime boss featured in a comic book. Malibu didn't know who the Chairman was and she frankly didn't care. Her mind was fixed on Luciana. "So was she his moll or something?"

Hilda shrugged. "Doesn't fit the profile. People say she's a witch, that she can control the weather, crazy shit. Like I said, it's best to stay clear."

"Control the weather?"

Hilda shrugged again.

Malibu continued to look at Luciana, who now had her head tilted back and seemed to have let her mind drift elsewhere, maybe contemplating the meaning of the universe. The sinister emotion shifted again, and now it felt like a black cloud that hung all around her. In this form, it was slightly easier to breathe.

Hilda tried to slip around Malibu so she could reach a clump of dirty glasses on the opposite side, but the area behind the bar was tight and her body was so wide the two women were momentarily stuck at their midsections. Malibu sucked in her stomach, which allowed Hilda to squeeze through.

"A witch. That's crazy. I bet she helps with gambling, drugs, extortion—that sort of thing," Malibu offered.

Hilda frowned. She made a wheezing sound as she labored to catch her breath after the recent brief exertion. "You watch too many movies."

Malibu couldn't argue with that. She was a movie buff, always had been, as far back as she could remember. Malibu saw a man approach Luciana's table. She'd never seen a man in the club before, and she half expected him to burst into flames. He looked to be in his early sixties, with a shiny bald head and a thick neck. His face had a grim, serious expression, his mouth locked in a frown. He wore a black suit, white shirt, black tie, and white gloves. He was the spitting image of Max in *Sunset Boulevard*, a movie Malibu had watched dozens of times despite it being nearly one hundred years old.

Max, as Malibu thought of him, bent at the waist and whispered into Luciana's ear. As he spoke, Malibu felt the black cloud that had been lingering around her evaporate. Luciana took another sip of her drink and placed the still half-full glass down on the table. She stood as Max dropped some shekels on the round cocktail table. Malibu watched as Max cupped Luciana by the elbow and led her out the exit.

. . .

Malibu left the club at exactly sunset—7:48 p.m.—slipping on a trench coat and walking outside. Fog had rolled in and coated the streets and buildings with dew. It was twilight, and the remaining sunlight slipped between the large wisps of fog, the light becoming splintered and scattered and as it reflected off the damp streets.

Malibu walked to Chinatown, onto Waverly Place, to the unmarked entrance of a Memory Station den. The place was a relic, one of the few dens that still existed, built at a time when such establishments were common. Before most people—those who could afford them, at least—had consoles installed in their homes. Malibu gripped a handrail as she walked down a steep and narrow stairwell, pushed open a door. A gusty wind blew down the stairs and followed her through the entrance.

A lonely looking man sat on the floor, shoulders slumped, head down, eyelids heavy. As the door slammed shut, he pulled his gaze up at Malibu. He wore wingtip shoes that looked like they were a million years old with holes on the bottoms and no shoelaces. With drowning eyes, he asked Malibu, "Can you spare a shekel? I want to see my daughter again. I want to see my wife."

Malibu reached inside her trench coat and pulled a coin out of the pocket of her sweater. She walked to where the man sat and placed the dirty coin on his open palm. His hands looked rusty and covered with grease. He squeezed the coin tightly, his eyes bugged out of his head. He sprung to his feet with surprising vigor and hurried to a counter where an old Chinese woman sat leafing through a magazine. The woman's hair was gray and thinning, coarse and wild, like a used Brillo pad.

"One hour, one hour, one hour," the man said as he smacked the coin loudly down onto the counter.

The woman picked the shekel up off the counter with her

thumb and forefinger, as if she were lifting something distasteful, lifting a turd. She nodded toward a hallway. "Room three."

After the man brushed past her, Malibu went to the counter and said, "I'll take an hour as well." As she spoke, Malibu touched the old woman's hand and got a glimmer of her thoughts. She had only seen the thoughts of one other person, her father. It was jarring to have it happen again, and with a stranger. What had triggered the insight, what had caused the thin fabric that kept their two realities apart to dissipate? Malibu could only guess. The woman's mind was focused on the prosaic realities of life—rent, food, family. Before Malibu could get a fix on anything more substantial, the psychic vision stopped, like a wall being put in place.

"Room number nine," the woman said as she pulled her hand away from Malibu's touch.

The hallway was covered with a filthy, threadbare carpet. The door to room nine was open. Malibu entered and closed the door behind her. Inside the walls were yellow, the paint badly chipped. There was a recliner and above it a console, which looked like an old-style hair dryer, the kind you used to see in vintage black-and-white movies. The red power light was on. Malibu sat in the chair and pulled the console down over her head. She imagined she could feel it synch with her cortex, a marriage of mind and machine. Where in the brain were memories stored? It was a question Malibu had asked before, but never bothered to investigate.

Within seconds, she was thrust into a sleeplike state, eyes shut, eyeballs flicking left and right.

But she wasn't asleep, and she could still maintain control of her conscious thoughts, enough to let her mind sort through a catalog of memories until she landed on the right one. It was a memory she had returned to again and again. She felt it marked a turning point in her life, at least with how she interacted with her father. With each review, what struck Malibu was how many new details were uncovered, how the scene came into sharper focus. When living through an event, it seemed she could only process so much. Images, like a movie, danced across her mind.

Santa Monica beach. October.

Despite it being the early weeks of fall, the rays of the sun hit like a hammer. Malibu watched her sixteen-year-old self as she splashed in the Pacific Ocean, just a few feet from the shore. At the edge of the water was her mother, a smile spread across her face. Malibu noticed that her mother's toes were dug into the wet sand and her arms were slightly pinked, shoulders freckled. Her blonde hair fell from under a wide-brimmed hat, and in her oversized sunglasses and black two-piece bathing suit her mother sparkled like a movie star.

Farther up the beach, her father sat upright on a beach towel. Unlike her mother, he wore no hat or sunglasses or any protection from the sun. Even though he was sitting down, Malibu could see that he was trim, his stomach flat and as firm as a surfboard. He was reading a book and his face wore a serene expression. The same expression Malibu had seen in all the pictures taken of her father as far back as his days as a boy in Japan. His hair was long, falling down to his shoulders. Crow's feet had formed around the edges of his eyes. He wore a leather necklace with a shark tooth dangling at the end. He looked more like a surfer than the physicist professor he was.

The book he read was a memoir written by Timothy Leary, the 1960s Harvard professor and LSD pioneer. Malibu's father had recently become obsessed by the consciousness-expanding powers of the drug. He had read countless scientific journals on the topic of psychedelic drugs and testimonials from people who claimed LSD had delivered mystical experiences that allowed them to shed the shackles of the material world and experience something more profound, more spiritual. Malibu's father believed the drug might offer a path to better connect with his daughter, to reach her on a level where she existed but he could not reach.

Earlier that day, he had gotten a tab of LSD from a colleague at the California Institute of Technology who had recently reinstituted an LSD testing program. It was a small dose, only a hundred micrograms. "Since it's your first trip," the colleague had said, "I suggest you go easy. Ideally, you should be accompanied by a guide, someone who can step you through the process."

Malibu's father assured the colleague a guide was unnecessary. He had picked the beach for his first time because he knew it was a place where he felt particularly comfortable. Without telling his wife or daughter, he had placed the tab on his tongue and washed it down with a sip of water an hour before the Memory Station-generated memory Malibu was watching had begun. The tab was a small square of paper with a picture of Yoda on one side. As soon as the day-glow effects began to kick in, Malibu could recognize the difference in her father's thought processes. His thoughts were always delivered in a clear signal, one she could tune in to like a radio station. Although she'd become somewhat accustom to the experience, the fact she could read his thoughts shook Malibu—mind and soul. Mindreading should be impossible. Right?

The Memory Station allowed Malibu to access the memory of her entering her father's mind just as the drug kicked. His thoughts expanded and became beautifully bizarre. She could sense him fighting the more extreme effects of the drug, while also allowing himself to be carried down a river of shifting consciousness. It was all a bit much for a sixteen-year-old girl to handle; still a bit much for a nineteen-year-old, although the repeated viewings had tamped down the impact.

"What am I thinking of?" her father asked.

Malibu felt the question float through time and space and crash into her mind. Her father had placed the book down and looked across the stretch of sand to where she splashed in the water.

She saw an image of a kangaroo as vividly as if it were hopping in front of her. "A kangaroo," Malibu thought in response.

"Now?" he asked.

"Our dog, Sadie."

"Now?"

"I don't want to do this anymore," she thought. "Let's give it a rest."

Her response fell on deaf ears. Malibu's father continued to lob her questions, to prod her. His scientific mind was eager to gather more data. But after a few minutes, he stopped. Malibu detected that his mind had traveled further along an unsettling and strange and circuitous path. Colors had become more vibrant, sounds more alive, his feelings more intense. All of his perceptions were heightened. And in way, Malibu's perceptions were heightened as well. She could access his experience, while also keeping a foot firmly planted in her drug-free mind.

Malibu's mother waded into the water, as her motherly instinct told her that her daughter needed a distraction. With one hand, she pressed her floppy hat down onto her head, while with the other she splashed Malibu. Malibu splashed her back, eliciting a screech.

"Come join us," her mother yelled and waved.

To Malibu's surprise, her father did, pulling himself off the towel and running to the water, his mind still trapped in a hallucination. He leapt into the ocean cannonball style, beads of water landing on both Malibu and her mother.

Under the console, Malibu's eyeballs twitched faster beneath her closed lids.

As she observed the memory, Malibu became overwhelmed with a sense of loss, so she pulled back from the scene. The Memory Station was equipped with Artificial Intelligence (AI) that allowed her to manipulate the memory so she could take different perspectives from the one she'd actually experienced. The AI effectively rebuilt that memory, like a video game, allowing the viewer to get a deeper perspective than real life. Malibu lifted her vantage point upward, established a bird's-eye view. She looked down below where she and her mother and father splashed and laughed. Off to the side, she could see Santa Monica Pier, Los Angeles farther in the distance. A pelican skimmed across the water. She pulled her perspective even higher so that all the people looked like dots, like ants scurrying along the shore.

She stayed at that godlike perch as the time in her hour clicked by.

MALIBU MEETS MAX

THE NEXT DAY, MALIBU PULLED ON ANOTHER OVERSIZED dress and went back to work at the Kit Kat Club. She was working the night shift, so the place was hopping. The small, round cocktail tables were filled with tipsy women, while frisky young waitresses wearing high heels and fishnet stockings glided around the tables like river water flowing past rocks.

After about an hour, Max from the previous night pushed through the front door. He stood out like a sore thumb. His very presence changed the character of the room, as if the universe itself had been tilted on its axis. Still, no one bothered him—he was just ignored. Max wore a nearly carbon copy outfit to the one he had donned the day before—a dark suit with a white shirt and white gloves—only this time he had on a bow tie. His lips were still pushed down into a frown.

He approached the back of the room where Malibu had set up shop. "Will you draw my picture?" he asked.

"It takes some time."

"I have time." He sat down as Malibu flipped to a blank sheet of paper. "I'm Max," he said.

"Of course."

"Of course?" he repeated, twisting the words into a

question.

"You're the spitting image of Max from *Sunset Boulevard.* It's like you stepped off the screen. Even your outfit is just like the movie."

"Like the movie?" Max again took the words and bent them into a question. As he spoke, Malibu could detect an Austrian accent.

"It's uncanny. Have you seen it?"

"*Sunset Boulevard?*"

"That's right."

Max's frown dipped lower. He shook his head. "Never heard of it." He sat with his legs pressed together and his feet planted firmly on the ground. His back was rod straight. He didn't look at Malibu but stared off into the distance, as if he was observing a scene only he could see.

"I'm jealous," she said.

"Why is that?"

"It has the biggest impact when you watch it the first time."

"Is that so?"

Malibu nodded. "Emotionally, yes. But there are benefits in watching something over and over. You pick up new details each time. It becomes richer. But the first time always packs the biggest wallop."

"Can I buy you a drink?" Max asked.

"I don't drink."

"Not while you work?"

"No. Not just then. Never. It's not by choice. It's an Asian thing. I'm allergic. Just one sip and my neck turns red, it's hard to breathe."

"I see. I won't drink either then."

"Suit yourself."

There was a lull in the conversation while Max let Malibu focus on the portrait. The drawing went surprisingly well. She typically used colored pencils to capture different moods, but with Max everything was black and white. Malibu was able to tap into the essence of Max. Although, was it really the Max sitting next to her, or Max von Mayerling from the movie? She even caught herself adding a director's megaphone to the drawing, but stopped herself before committing it to the paper.

"Is your last name von Mayerling?" Malibu asked.

"It's Strobl."

"Austrian?"

"That's right."

"Close enough."

"When was this *Sunset Boulevard* released?" Max's eyes were still fixed in the distance.

"1950."

"So you like older movies."

"Vintage Hollywood, yeah. I got the bug from my mother. She was a film buff. She grew up near Hollywood. Her grandfather actually worked in pictures, back in the day. He knew Billy Wilder, the director of *Sunset Boulevard*. My grandfather was a friend of Humphrey Bogart. They used to play chess together." Malibu bit her lower lip to stop herself from talking. She didn't normally like to reveal too much of herself. But she felt strangely connected to the man next to her, as if he was someone she knew intimately, as if he was a friend.

Max pulled his eyes from whatever he was looking at, and without turning his head, gazed sideways at Malibu. As he did, an image popped into Malibu's mind, just as it had when she touched the Chinese woman at the Memory Station den. She saw Luciana sitting in a wing chair, petting a black cat that rested on her lap. It felt like Luciana was starring back at her. The image continued to unfold. Luciana stood and seemed to step from wherever she was and into the club. In Malibu's mind, Luciana took her by the hand and led her to one of the back rooms. The psychic vision—if that's what it was—dissolved, leaving Malibu feeling shaken. She paused and took a few deep breaths through her nose.

"I'm not going to sleep with that woman," Malibu said to Max. "I don't care how much she pays."

To Max, the comment came completely out of the blue. It might as well have been dropped down from Mars. "Sleep with who?"

"Luciana."

"Why would you say that?" He frowned so deeply that it looked painful.

"I just want to make it clear," Malibu said, feeling a tad self-conscious.

"Have you done that the type of activity before? Slept with a woman for money?"

"No. I haven't. But it's sort of baked into the cake here. With all the others, at least."

Max's mouth turned upward; not to a smile, but landing on neutral. "You need not worry about your virtue. Luciana has other plans for you."

"Other plans?" As Malibu spoke she kept drawing. She added a leopard-skin etching to the background of Max's portrait, as if the essence of Luciana was wrapped around his head.

"She wants you to work for her."

"Doing what?"

"You'll have to ask her yourself." Max reached into the pocket of his jacket and pulled out a white business card. "Here," he said as he placed the card on the rim of the easel.

Malibu looked down and saw an address printed in black letters: 36 Pacific Avenue. Malibu was roughly familiar with location. Presidio Heights, at the edge of the former Spanish military base.

"Madam lives there," said Max. "She wants to see you tomorrow night. Can you come by at eight?"

"I'm working."

"Skip work. Luciana pays much better."

"I'll think about it," Malibu said, although she had already decided to go. In fact, she felt pulled toward the home, as if she were a kite at the end of a long string and Luciana was slowly but inexorably winding the string back, drawing Malibu toward her.

They drifted into silence again. The noise around them grew louder. Women laughed and ice cubes clinked. Malibu shifted her head to the side so she could get a different perspective on her work. She added a few final touches to Max's bow tie, then in a singsong voice said, "Voila. I'm finished." She waved her hand theatrically and turned the easel so Max could see the drawing. Just as she had the other day, she made the eyes in the portrait disjointed—one up, one down. One eye was shut and the other wide open. Max's nose was bent impossibly to one side. She had drawn a line down the middle of his face and shaded one half gray. Leopard spots danced all around. What really popped out were the lips, which were exaggeratedly large and bent, naturally, downward.

Max observed the portrait with the same faraway look in his eyes he had employed before when gazing off into the distance. He didn't offer any expression at all, not a narrowing of the eyes or a nod of his head. His facial expression did not change. It was a bit deflating. He stood and dug a handful of shekels out of his trouser pocket and deliberately stacked them on the table next to Malibu's easel.

"We'll be waiting for you tomorrow night," he said. He took the portrait out of Malibu's hand and rolled it up, tucking it along the side of his body, under his arm. He marched toward the door with the purpose of a man who had a place to go.

THE CHESTERFIELD

The Chesterfield Cinema on Market Street had been built back in the 1970s when porn movie theaters became the rage. It had never completely stopped operation, but the flow of business dropped to a trickle with the boom of online porn just before the turn of the century and beyond. Why bother with the hassle of schlepping downtown when you could handle your business in the comfort of home? But the outlawing of the Internet ten years earlier had served to rekindle interest in places like the Chesterfield.

"It's a scientific fact that sometimes a man has got to shoot his load," Hank McDonald, the cinema's owner, told Malibu the day she applied for the sole one-bedroom apartment above the theater. "If he doesn't, the jizz will just build up inside him until it practically bursts out of his eyeballs. You ladies will never understand."

By that tine, Malibu had already spent one week working at the Kit Kat Club, where she'd seen her share of fever-eyed women hand over ridiculously large numbers of shekels to miniskirt-wearing party girls, so she thought she did under-stand. But she didn't argue the point with McDonald; Malibu desperately wanted the room. It was the cheapest she could find, and after living at a homeless tent camp on Martin Luther King Way near the old crumbling baseball park, she wanted a real roof over her head.

Normally, when her shift ended Malibu would walk home. But since Max had given her so much money, she decided to catch a ride. Personal ownership of cars had been banned at the same time as the Internet, but there was a fleet of self-driving commuter cars that zipped around the city. They were electric four-door sedans, painted black and yellow like old-time taxis. The wait for a car was never long. Their AI was so refined the cars could predict where and when a passenger would need a ride and magically appear at that spot, no matter where it was in the city. It was creepy but so convenient.

Just outside the club's entrance, a car pulled up to the curb and Malibu slid into the back seat. "The Chesterfield Theater," she said.

"Two shekels," the car responded. The voice was a deep, male baritone with what seemed to be a Russian, or at least Slavic, accent. All the robotic commuter voices were unique, as if by customizing them this way lent an air of humanity. Malibu deposited two coins in a metal slot and the car sped off noiselessly.

They drove from North Beach through the Financial District to Market Street. The sidewalks were empty of people and no cars were parked along the side of the roads. It was what Malibu was accustomed to, but she had seen old photographs of San Francisco and imagined that to an old-timer the barrenness would look odd, almost postapocalyptic.

The car turned right on Market, drove a few more blocks, and dropped Malibu in front of the theater. She stepped onto the sidewalk and was hit by sheets of fog. It was thin enough that it allowed Malibu to make out the outline of the full moon, which hung high in the sky like an eerie white skull. At the entrance to the theater, a woman screamed at a man who was lying on the ground. She repeatedly hit his head with what looked like an old pillow. The man didn't bother to cover his head, but just accepted the blows as penance for some unknown crime. Directly above them the neon lights of the theater shone brightly red.

McDonald had given Malibu a key to a side entrance, which she typically used so she could avoid the lecherous eyes of the men who frequented the theater.

After climbing the stairs and entering her apartment, Malibu deposited the haul of coins she'd acquired that night into a shoebox she kept covered by a blanket under her bed. The box was now half full. She reapplied the blanket and pushed the box as far as she could under the bed. It wasn't an optimal security method, but it would do for now.

The apartment had one window, which looked out onto Market Street. Through it, Malibu saw the red glow from the theater's marquee reflected in the fog. She stood at the window for a moment and watched the fog dance. She stepped back into the room, pulled off her dress, and let it drop to the floor. She dropped her panties and unsnapped her bra. As she stood naked, the vision of Luciana taking her by the hand and leading her to a back room replayed in her head. She didn't find Luciana particularly appealing, so it was a strange thing to replay. Maybe she thought about it now because the vision had been so unexpected? Naturally, you need to reexamine a vision closely to make sure it its fully understood. The scene unfolded as if a director inside her head had ordered the footage to roll. As it played, she lightly brushed her nipples with her fingertips and a shiver ran up her spine.

Malibu went to the bathroom and turned on the water. She watched as it fell from the showerhead and swirled around the rust-colored drain before plunging out of sight. It took an ungodly amount of time for the water to heat up, and as Malibu waited goose bumps spread across her forearms. Eventually, it warmed enough to allow Malibu to step under the stream of water and take care of business. Once done, she toweled off and pulled on a pair of sweatpants and an oversized hoodie with the words University of Santa Cruz printed in purple lettering that framed a yellow, wide-eyed, cartoonish picture of a banana slug. She stepped into a pair of fuzzy slippers. Using a small Bic lighter, she lit a large, round, purple candle that stood on top of a dresser and two long sticks of incense. She paused a moment to watch strands of smoke rise off the sticks, before turning and walking to her bed, where she flopped down onto the mattress. She turned her head toward the yellow lights on the bedside clock, which blinked 10:09 p.m.

On the wall next to her bed was a self-portrait. Malibu had painted it the day she moved into the apartment. She had used a particularly large canvas, so it felt like the image she'd created of herself loomed over Malibu, as if it were judging her. In the portrait, her hair was jet-black, like it was in real life, but streaked with purple highlights. She had divided her face into four quadrants, painted red and yellow, green and orange. Her lips were purple. She'd made her eyes narrow and markedly Asian looking. The pupils were directed toward the side, with her gaze focused on an outsized apple. Malibu had included the apple on a whim, having recently visited the San Francisco Museum of Modern Art, where she had seen a collection of Degas still life paintings. Inspired, at the last minute she'd added the apple, coloring it red and yellow and orange. It looked so real it felt like it could fall off the canvas. The apple was so plump and ripe that Malibu could practically taste it as she gazed at the painting.

As she considered the apple, Malibu found her mind

drifting back to Luciana. Again, she shivered. Malibu felt a bit feverish, unmoored.

To steady her nerves, Malibu fell into a type of meditation her father had taught her years earlier. She closed her eyes, breathed in through her nose until her lungs expanded to their full capacity, and then slowly let out a long stream of air through her mouth, repeating the process four or five times. Find a happy place, her father had instructed, and put your mind there. She selected a beach in Mexico. Not that she'd ever been to Mexico, but she imagined one day she would go. Malibu liked beaches. She could see herself wearing a flower-topped tankini, and she walked on sand so hot it singed the soles of her feet. It got so uncomfortable, she hopped herself over to the shade of a palm tree, where she gazed out at the ocean. Two tiny lizards ran up the tree. A pelican dove into the ocean, caught a fish. Pelicans had a good life. They lived near the beach and carried their food with them.

Off to the side, Malibu heard a scraping noise. There was a resort hotel where two women with long rakes carved the sand into swirling patterns. One of the women stopped raking and looked directly at Malibu, a lascivious smirk plastered on her face. Malibu lifted her arms upward, stretched to one side and then the next, and thought: Soak it in, sister. Just know that I am out of your league.

Still meditating, Malibu left the shade of the tree and hurried across the hot sand until she reached the wet sand on the edge of the water. Her feet cooled. A warm breeze blew across the ocean as water slowly licked her feet. She stood and gazed toward the horizon and imagined the sun sinking into the sea.

The little exercise worked. Malibu felt relaxed but not sleepy. She climbed out of bed, headed down the main stair-case, and to the lobby.

The Chesterfield had a surprisingly opulent lobby. It had a high ceiling with a large, crystal chandelier that delivered a soothing sheen of yellow light throughout the room. The carpet, which looked expensive and recently installed, was a rich shade of blue with a yellow, swirling pattern. There was a long counter where customers could buy popcorn, soft drinks, and other standard movie items. Malibu imagined Hank had thrown a lot of money into refurbishing the old joint. The only telltale sign it was a porn theater was the inescapable stench of stale cum that hung in the air like a disease.

As Malibu walked across the carpet, she brushed past a man who wore a long trench coat. She imagined he had a wad of Kleenex stuffed in his pocket. She nodded toward the plump black woman who stood behind a counter and said, "Hi, Margarita," as she passed. Eventually, Malibu arrived at the front desk, where Hank sat on a tall chair. He was a white man in his fifties. His head was shaved but he wasn't completely bald; a thin layer of stubble remained. He had an equally thin beard that only covered his chin. His shoulders were stooped slightly and his left hand had a small tremor. The expression on his face was a peculiar mask, offering a lack of recognizable emotion. Hank was studying a little chessboard.

"Playing with yourself?" Malibu asked, using a line she recognized typically had a different meaning in a porn theater.

Hank didn't look up.

"Who's winning?"

He tilted his head back. "Hi."

"Who's winning?" she repeated.

"Oh, I'm just studying an old game. Fischer vs. Larsen, 1971. French defense. Fischer won."

"Naturally."

"Did you know Fischer lived to be only sixty-four years old?"

Malibu nodded. She did know because Hank had told her this little nugget before. She'd never heard of Bobby Fischer until she met Hank, but in the short time she'd known Hank, he must have mentioned the grandmaster at least three times.

"Sixty-four years. That's one year for every square on the chessboard. There's something poetic about that, don't you think?"

"Are you boring Miss Malibu with stories about that crazy chess player again?" Margarita had moved down the counter so she could eavesdrop on their conversation.

"Don't you need to get someone a popcorn?" Hank scolded.

"Popcorn, popcorn," Margarita mocked. "No one has bought a popcorn in this Devil's playground since Ivanka Trump was president. Popcorn." She shook her head. "Would you eat food here?" She looked at Malibu. "Need to get some type of Goddamn disinfectant first. Popcorn."

"Did you get in any new films?" Malibu asked Hank. In addition to receiving all the latest porn flicks, he would also request vintage movie reels from his distributor. Like Malibu, he was a bit of a movie buff. The two of them had watched a couple of movies together in a private projection room.

"Yeah, a few. *Horny Stepmom Teaches Son a Lesson* sounds like a winner." He shot her a wink.

She shook her head. "You know what I mean."

"Ever heard of *Eternal Sunshine of the Spotless Mind?*"

"No," Malibu admitted. There were few movies—at least good ones—prior to 2010 she had not seen. Malibu had been a lonely kid, and for companionship, she devoured movies. She considered them her friends. In another lifetime, she would have been a movie director.

"Jim Carrey. Kate Winslet. It's supposed to be damn good. How about we give it a whirl?"

"That would be great."

"Margarita," Hank yelled out of the side of his mouth. "I need you to look after the ticket counter."

"How can I look after the counter when I need to dish up popcorn?"

"You just said no one buys the popcorn."

"Miracles do happen. A person can't be in two places at once."

"Quit your bitching. I'll give you time and a half."

That seemed to soothe Margarita's ruffled feathers. "Awright."

"I'd like some popcorn," said a man who'd just walked in the front door.

Hank pushed his chair back and stood up. "Customer, Margarita."

She huffed her way to the ticket counter. "What do you want a damn popcorn for?" She didn't give the man a chance to answer. "Need to buy a ticket first."

Hank left Margarita to handle business. He lifted a panel on the counter, opened a walkway, and waved for Malibu to follow. He led her through a doorway and into a back room where there was a small sofa, a coffee table, and a projector. She settled onto the sofa, grabbed a blanket that had been draped over the armrest, and covered herself. Hank slipped a tiny memory stick in the monitor and joined Malibu on the sofa, keeping a respectful distance. He stretched his legs out and tried, unsuccessfully, to stop his left foot from shaking. Malibu watched about half the movie before she drifted off to sleep.

The next day, as she reflected back on the flick, she found she couldn't remember anything she had seen, as if it had been erased from her memory.

PART TWO
PALO ALTO, CALIFORNIA— SEPTEMBER 9, 2048

MALIBU IN THE LOONY BIN

Sleeping was nearly impossible.

For starters, the door to Malibu's room was left open, allowing light from the hallway to flow in, which was annoying. Plus, every fifteen minutes a nurse would come into the room and shine a flashlight on Malibu's face. But worst of all was Malibu's roommate, a heavyset, grim-faced Samoan. Not only did she snore like a dying chainsaw, but she also emitted a foul odor. The room was small, and the stench was so overpowering it caused Malibu's eyes to water. The roommate stayed in bed most of the time, completely covered by a blanket. She lay on her back with her knees propped up so she looked like a large, blue-blanketed mound. She'd emerge from her cocoon only for breakfast, lunch, and dinner. If she had to leave to crap, Malibu never saw it.

The morning after Malibu had been admitted to the hospital, the sun shone through the tiny window and signaled the day had begun. Malibu was happy to climb out of bed and escape to the hallway.

"Let me check your vitals," said a nurse. She wore the standard-issue blue scrubs and pushed a cart with a computer monitor on top. "Take a seat." She nodded toward a chair pressed against the wall.

Malibu sat down and extended her left arm. Like all the patients, Malibu wore a two-piece uniform—pants and shirt—not too dissimilar from what the nurses wore, but a lighter shade of blue. The pants had an elastic band, but no tie string, which was a suicide risk. The patients also wore yellow socks.

The nurse wrapped a black strap around Malibu's arm and sealed it in place with Velcro. She turned the device on so the strap puffed up. After about half a minute she said, "Normal." She pulled the strap free so the Velcro made a ripping sound. "Now let me take your temperature." That was normal too. "Let me check your meds."

The nurse clicked onto the monitor until she found Malibu's file. She then poured five pills into a tiny plastic cup, which she gave to Malibu. There was a pitcher of water on top of the cart. The nurse poured water into a paper cup and gave that to Malibu. Malibu placed the pills individually on her tongue and washed them down. The last pill was so large, Malibu could feel it expand the sides of her throat as it slid down.

There were ninety-six steps from one end of the hallway to the other. Malibu would walk each step in a trance, her head down, focused on her sock-clad feet as they slid along the linoleum floor.

The patients' rooms were all on the northern side of the hallway. Almost everyone stayed in his or her room, although one other patient did march along the hallway with Malibu. He was a toothless old man named Kenny. The first few trips along the hallway, Malibu and Kenny didn't acknowledge each other —ships passing in the night. But eventually they would high-five when their paths crossed. No words were spoken, just arms raised and palms slapped.

The doors to the patients' rooms were required to remain open. Malibu could peek inside and see people spread out on their beds. There was nothing else to do but walk or sleep. No magazines to read or TVs to watch or music to listen to. It was a poorly designed setup if the goal was to make people less crazy. The patients' minds were given too much time to roam. Outside one of the rooms stood two bodyguards—big men in black uniforms. The patient inside the room was a morose white guy with scary-looking tattoos inked across his face. It wasn't clear to Malibu if the guards were there to protect him from himself, or to protect everyone else from him. She made a mental note to steer clear.

In the middle of the hallway on the southern side of the building was a group of desks where the nurses sat. In addition to the nurses, there was also one robot, blue uniform and all. He was designed so well that he looked nearly humanlike. Malibu never saw him move. Really, he was almost like a statue. But it was clear he was recording everything that happened on the floor; his unblinking eyes missed nothing. Even the nurses seemed wary of him.

Also along the southern side were the shower room and a locked office with no windows where psychologists and others doctors could hide away. Next to that was a visitors' room with a rectangular table and four chairs. Sometimes Malibu would look through the glass windows of the visitors' room and see patients meeting with friends and family members. No one ever came to see Malibu.

On either end of the hallway were locked doors. At the end of her ninety-six-step trek, Malibu would lightly kick a door, spin around on her heels, and restart her journey, the numbers ticking by in her head.

One, two, three...

After a dozen or so trips up and down the hallway, she stopped counting and instead focused on the number ninety-six. It was an interesting number. If you flipped it upside down it looked the same way. Days after his first acid trip, Malibu's father had dragged her to a new age guru, a numerologist, a woman who believed there was a mystical relationship between numbers and events.

Her name was Annika Eagle Feather. She was white, so obviously she must not have been given that name at birth, but rather picked it up somewhere along the line. The day Malibu saw her, Eagle Feather wore a black, sleeveless dress and a black, leather choker necklace. Big hoop earrings dangled from her ears. Black tattoos ran down her arms and a large tattoo of a star with a circle around it was imprinted on her breastbone, the tattoo clearly visible in the low-neck dress that advertised an uncomfortable amount of cleavage. Her hair was a wild mass of blonde curls that fell below her shoulders; the roots were black.

Malibu sat in a beanbag chair, the room lit by candlelight, as Eagle Feather made a show of doing a detailed analysis of Malibu's numerical values. She wanted to know Malibu's birth-date, assigned a value to her name, and asked a series of prosaic questions. Malibu felt a bit uncomfortable when she asked if Malibu remembered the day of her first menstruation (she didn't). Eagle Feather built a numerical chart for Malibu, which essentially boiled down to one number, the number nine.

"The number has a special value to you," Eagle Feather told her.

"Do you hear that, honey?" her father asked. The day before, he had gotten a small rainbow-color peace sign tattoo on the inside of his right wrist, which Malibu could see clearly from where she sat.

"The number nine?" Malibu asked.

"That's right," said Eagle Feather.

"John Lennon believed the number nine had particular significance to him."

"Is that right?"

"Uh-huh. He said it followed him everywhere." Malibu broke into a chant, using a mock Liverpool accent. "Number nine, number nine, number nine..." She paused, smiled. "That's from a Lennon song. 'Revolution 9.'"

"I see," said Eagle Feather. "I'm not really familiar with John Lennon or The Beatles. They were before my time."

"What do you think, dear?" Malibu's father asked her.

She shrugged. "It works for me. Number nine. I can live with that."

What she didn't tell her father or Eagle Feather was that an image of the number nine had suddenly landed in Malibu's head. She could see the number spin around and dance, fade and brighten.

Malibu thought about that day with her father as she marched up and down the hallway of the Stanford inpatient mental institution. With each step, something shook free and sparked to life and she could see the number nine as it twirled in her head again. Her heart ached as she remembered her father and pondered on the peculiar twists of fate that had landed her in the loony bin. She felt as if she had no hope to live a normal life, whatever was considered normal these days. She was only eighteen years old, soon to turn nineteen. Her mother was dead, her father who knows where.

She felt anger gurgle inside her. She successfully pushed it down, although not completely. She still had control, but could feel the anger gaining strength. Malibu continued to walk, focusing on each individual step, one after the other. As she walked, it struck her that the number ninety-six, if looked at in a certain light, was actually two nines—you just needed to spin one number upside down.

On her fourth day at the institute, Malibu met with a psychologist, a kind man with intelligent eyes and perfect half-moon cuticles. He told her she could spend two hours in the voluntary portion of the hospital. "It's a step toward your eventual release," he said, with a comforting smile. "We think of it like a decompression, like a diver slowly ascending from a deep dive."

Kenny, her toothless high-fiving partner, was allowed to go as well. A nurse unlocked the double doors at the end of the hallway and Malibu and Kenny walked through.

Through the door, reality felt distorted, the way it does when a snow globe is shaken. It was less oppressive, even a bit cheery. For starters, in the voluntary section, there were no guards. All the patients wore street clothes. Malibu and Kenny, however, still wore their light-blue pajamas and yellow socks. Potted plants were scattered about and there were cut flowers in vases. There were two sofas, where a small group of women sat talking. In front of the sofas was a coffee table with a pitcher of iced tea, paper cups, and a plate full of sugar cookies. The women nibbled on the cookies and sipped the tea. They looked so normal and so well adjusted. It seemed impossible they should be in the hospital.

Pushed against a wall was a piano. Kenny sat on the piano bench and played a funky jazz number, while Malibu plopped down on a comfy chair nearby and listened. Kenny was surprisingly good.

After about twenty minutes, Malibu asked, "Kenny, do you know any Beatles songs?"

He pulled his fingers off the keys and turned his head

toward Malibu. He had a five-o'clock shadow, hair that fell below his ears, and a kind face. "Maybe. I'm not sure. I used to know the song 'Piggies.'"

"That's an obscure one."

"Let's see..." Kenny started playing the tune. He broke into song, his voice rough, like sandpaper.

> *Have you seen the little piggies crawling in the dirt?*
> *And for all the little piggies, life is getting worse*
> *Always having dirt to play around in*
>
> *Have you seen the bigger piggies in their starched white*
>   *shirts?*
> *You will find the bigger piggies stirring up the dirt*
> *Always have clean shirts to play around in.*

Kenny stopped playing. "Did you know Paul McCartney died in 1968?"

"Are you sure?" In addition to movies, Malibu also loved old pop music and was a Beatles aficionado. Naturally, she'd heard the stories about Paul's death.

"It's a well-known fact," Kenny continued. "At least if you're paying attention. They tried to keep it buried from the public. The Beatles and their manager. Paul died in a car crash." He paused, continued. "They even reference it in song. 'He blew his mind out in a car.'" Kenny sang this last bit.

"Is that so," Malibu said, a skeptical tone in her voice. "Then how is it there's video footage of Paul? And photographs? All after 1968, the year he supposedly died?"

"That was a double. The Beatles didn't want everyone to know he died because they were afraid it would hurt record sales. What's ironic is the band split two years later anyway."

As he spoke, Malibu noticed Kenny didn't open his mouth

very widely. She imagined he was embarrassed by the fact he had no teeth. He had an accent Malibu couldn't quite place, a California twang.

Kenny held a number of other conspiratorial opinions, including that the 1969 moon landing was hoax, and that the Earth is flat. "There is a dome over the Earth," Kenny explained. "A plastic dome. Rockets have been launched, but they hit the dome and fall down."

Malibu didn't want to argue with Kenny, so she steered him in a different direction. "Why are you in here, Kenny?"

"I admitted myself."

"Oh yeah?"

"Some people are trying to kill me."

"Trying to kill you. Why?"

"Don't know. Some people are just angry. I can hear whispering at night when I'm trying to sleep. They yell at me. The other night, when I was in my sleeping bag, I had to get up and run as they chased me. That morning, I admitted myself. I don't want to be released. It's safe here, and they feed you."

"Are you homeless, Kenny?"

"Uh-huh. I used to sleep in the doorway of a law office, but about six months ago I was kicked out. Now I live in a tent city in San Jose. I hate it. I'm really afraid for my life."

"I'm sorry."

"Why are you here?"

"Suicidal ideation."

"You tried to kill yourself?"

"Not exactly. I mean, I thought about it."

Malibu had done more than think about it. When she first moved to San Francisco, she uncovered a man who trafficked in illicit goods and services. He worked in Daly City. She visited his tiny shop and inquired about buying a handgun, which she planned to either place against her temple or inside her mouth

—Which method was more precise?—and be finally done with it all. But the gun would have cost twenty shekels, far beyond what Malibu could afford at the time. So instead, she bought a pack of cigarettes, shook one free, lit it, and took one hit before she was thrust into a coughing fit so intense her body spasmed wildly and she had to lie down on the ground to recover.

After pulling herself together, she had a commuter car drop her near one end of the Golden Gate Bridge. She walked to the middle and climbed on top of a railing. She held on to a cable and looked over the side, working to muster up the courage to jump into the icy Pacific, to jump to eternal freedom. She believed she had the fortitude to take the leap, but something inside her resisted, something inside her fought to live. When she tried to lift her foot, that internal force would pull it back down. She'd felt inklings of the force before, but it had been weak, voiceless. Even now, all it could do was fight, not argue for its case. But its will to live seemed to be strengthening it. As Malibu and the force battled for control of her body, she gazed out across the bay to Alcatraz. It was midday, but the neon light was already on. *Casino*. It looked horrifyingly menacing and beautiful. If she didn't take the plunge, she would make sure to travel there one day.

The struggle ended when two Union Members, a human and his androidic partner, arrived where she stood and walked Malibu off the bridge. Union Members were a federally run police force, which had replaced most tradition police organizations around the time that Malibu was born. Malibu imagined that the name was designed to sound less threatening than police, although it had the opposite effect on her. Typically, Union Members traveled in pairs—one robot and one human. As they led Malibu to safety, the human tried to be comforting, although he seemed disinterested. The robot never took his soulless eyes off her.

"You're lucky they took you here and not to San Francisco," Kenny said after Malibu told him the story about her trip to the bridge. "It's rough there." He paused, as if recounting a bitter memory. "So why did you want to kill yourself?"

"It runs in the family."

To Malibu's surprise, Kenny started to cry. Tears welled up in his eyes and rolled down his cheeks. "Promise me you won't try again."

"I promise," Malibu said, touched.

Just before their time in the voluntary section ended, Malibu noticed a small stack of books on a coffee table. She sat on an open cushion on the sofa and examined the options. Most looked like romance novels—the bodice ripping types—but there was a tattered copy of *Moby Dick*. She picked it up and started to read it.

"Malibu, Kenny, it's time to go," a nurse said.

"What do you have?" the nurse asked Malibu as they were about to pass through the door that separated the two sections.

Malibu lifted the paperback. "Just a book."

"You're not supposed to bring anything across."

"It's just a book."

"I know. But rules are rules. You have to put it back."

"I'm going crazy in there. There's nothing to do. The goal is to make me better, right?"

The nurse opened her mouth as if about to speak, but kept quiet. She frowned a little, and then nodded her head toward the side, indicating that Malibu and the book should pass through. There was still compassion in the hateful world.

That night, well past midnight, as her roommate snored like a flu-stricken grizzly bear, Malibu cracked open *Moby Dick*. The book smelled old and dusty; the paper brittle to the touch. There was just enough illumination seeping in from the florescent lights in the hallway for Malibu to make out the text. She didn't read from the start of the book, but instead skimmed sections.

One page in the middle of the book was dog-eared. Malibu flipped to it and found a passage highlighted in yellow.

> *What the white whale was to Ahab has been hinted; what, at times, he was to me, as yet remains unsaid. Aside from those more obvious considerations touching Moby-Dick which could not but occasionally awaken in any man's soul some alarm, there was another thought, or rather vague, nameless horror concerning him, which at times by its intensity completely overpowered all the rest; and yet so mystical and well nigh ineffable was it that I almost despair of putting it in a comprehensible form.*

Malibu read the section three times. She moved her thumb as if about to flip through the remainder of the book, but instead let her eyes scan the highlighted text again.

We all have our white whales.

Unable to keep her eyes open any longer, Malibu shut the book, yawned, closed her eyes, and drifted off to a fitful sleep.

The next day, one of the counselors, a woman in her late twenties, organized an art group in the visitors' room. Five patients, including Malibu and Kenny, participated. Scattered around the table were small plastic containers of Play-Doh, watercolors and paintbrushes, Crayons, and paper. The room felt oppressive. Unlike in the voluntary room, there were no cut flowers and only artificial light. The patients in their blue uniforms looked sad and ridiculous. Their faces were expressionless, but their eyes were manic. In the struggle between despair and hope, despair was the clear winner.

The whole scene made Malibu angry. By now, she was slowly beginning to recognize there was rage brewing inside her that she did not fully own, but still maintained enough control to tamp it down and keep it hidden. She knew she had to behave in order to be released from the hospital, so she masked her anger behind a happy facade.

"Studies have shown that when we use our hands it frees up our minds," the counselor said. She spoke in measured tones, enunciating each word, as if she were speaking to children. "I want you to pick a Play-Doh container. Choose a color."

Four of the patients did as instructed. The fifth, an older Latino woman, just stared into space. The counselor glanced her way but didn't say anything to her.

"Now open the container," the counselor continued. "Pull out the Play-Doh. Move it around in your hands." She looked around the table. "Open other containers if you want to. Build something."

Malibu didn't open the container, just held it in her hand. "Can I paint instead?" she asked.

"We're sculpting right now."

Malibu felt the woman's emotions rise off her. How long had it been since her psionic abilities had kicked in? *Too long*, she was surprised to hear herself think. It felt good to have them reemerge. What the woman was feeling was a putrid combination of contempt and righteousness. She looked at Malibu as a pitiful case.

Malibu, shrugging off the woman's ridiculous emotions, offered up a phony smile and said, "I get that, but I want to paint. I'm more of a painter."

"There are times when you have to follow instructions. This is one of those times." Her voice was dripping with condescension.

The older Latino woman spoke. "He said to check the clothes hamper." The sentence started softly, but increased in volume. "I did, and it was there." She repeated the phrase two more times, and then she stood up and started to yell. "It was in the clothes hamper! It was in the clothes hamper!"

The counselor stood, grabbed the woman by the shoulders, and gently encouraged her to sit down. "You can't yell in here." She plucked a purple Play-Doh container off the table, removed the lid, and placed the clay in the old woman's hands. It seemed to soothe her. The woman stopped yelling and started to gently rub the clay between her palms.

Malibu used the distraction as an opportunity to grab a piece of paper, a paintbrush, and a plastic tin of watercolors. She dipped the paintbrush into a glass of water, rubbed the bristles in the color purple, and started to paint. It was a portrait of Kenny. She glanced his way. He was rolling his Play-Doh into the shape of a snowman. Malibu worked quickly. The portrait was less abstract than most of her work, more realistic, as if she could clearly see the true Kenny. His eyes were a bit too wide, his mouth too narrow, but other than that it was a spitting image. She made a point of highlighting his toothless grin.

Satisfied that the older woman was pacified, the counselor settled back down into her chair. Once in place, she glanced in Malibu's direction. When she saw Malibu was painting, her eyes narrowed. "I told you that we were—" She stopped in mid-sentence as she got a glimpse of Malibu's work. "That's quite good."

Malibu felt a grudging respect rise off the woman. Malibu didn't respond, but kept on working.

"Is that Kenny?"

"It is."

"You're painting me?" Kenny asked. "Can I see it?"

"Not yet. When I'm done."

"You've painted before?" the counselor asked. Her voice still held that talking to a child tone.

"Obviously," Malibu snapped. She checked herself, worked to center her emotions, and said in a more measured tone. "Yes, I have spent a lot of time painting. And drawing."

When Malibu finished, she turned the picture around so Kenny could see it. He smiled and said, "Can I keep it."

"Sure. I made it for you."

He took it, placed it on the table and studied his image. "When we leave here, can we keep in touch?"

"Of course," Malibu said, knowing as soon as she spoke that the words were a lie. She would leave here and never return and never maintain any connections at all.

SHRUNKEN HEADS

GROWING UP, MALIBU LIVED A FEW MILES FROM SANTA Monica Beach. Even at a young age, her parents used to let her ride her bike to the pier. She'd happily zip down the backstreets and cross the covered bridge over Pacific Coast Highway. The sun seemed to always shine warmly in a cloudless sky, and the ocean air was crisp.

Typically, once Malibu arrived at the boardwalk, she would buy a corndog, wolf it down, and then stroll around Ocean Front Walk and people watch. It wasn't as freaky as Venice Boardwalk, but for a preteen, it was eye opening: skateboard punks, homeless people, girls in bikinis, muscle men, costumed performers, old men playing chess, all mixed together.

Inevitably, she would climb the wooden staircase up to the pier. Most kids her age liked to take the rides or go to the video arcade, but Malibu would make a beeline for a tiny museum that was tucked between a psychic fortune-teller's shop and a warm pretzel concession stand. It was called *Wonders of the World*.

The museum was just two rooms. It cost a couple of bucks —this was before dollars were replaced by shekels—to enter and was usually empty. There were no windows and it was always a few degrees warmer than outside, the air a bit stale. Stored on shelves behind glass were "Strange and Unique Artifacts," each item ostensibly gathered from around the world. There was Dracula's tooth (a blood-stained incisor), a clump of fur from the Abominable Snowman, a stuffed duck-billed platypus from Australia, and assorted dinosaur bones. But Malibu's favorite item was a shrunken head.

Shrunken Woman's Head from Deep in the Amazon Forest, the caption read.

The head was impaled on top of a wooden stick. The skin was a rich bronze color, like coffee with cream. The eyes were shut and misshapen, the lips exaggeratedly fat, the nose twisted to the side, and the hair long and coarse, as if it had been taken from a horse's tale. Malibu imagined her interest in abstract art was somewhat inspired by the shrunken head, how the people who had shrunken the head had been able to manipulate reality. Art could do that too.

Malibu was also drawn to the head for another reason. Her mother was a Freudian psychiatrist, and Malibu had heard her referred to on a few occasions as a "head shrinker." As a child, at least until she was old enough to know better, Malibu had taken that description literally. Inside the museum, as she stared at the disturbing image of the shrunken head, Malibu imagined that her mother had boxes full of heads she had shrunken stored in her office.

On her last day in the Stanford hospital, as she sat in the visitors' room finally back in her street clothes, Malibu's mind randomly drifted to the shrunken head. She hadn't thought about that damn thing in years. It's strange how the mind works, how a neuron fires to life a buried memory. Why now?

"I lost you for a minute there, Malibu," said the kind doctor with the perfect cuticles. He and Malibu sat alone at the table. "Care to tell me what you're thinking about?"

"A shrunken head."

He laughed. Malibu liked the man and wished he would give off an emotional cue, but sadly, he did not.

"I don't want to shrink your head. I'm worried about you. I am worried about your safety."

"I know." Malibu was sure that was true, although in reality, not much had been done at the facility to help foster better mental health. It was more of a place to keep her from harming herself.

"Are you sure you're okay to leave?"

"Yes."

"Okay. There is some paperwork you need to sign. You won't be able to buy a gun for five years."

"Fine."

An hour later, she was released. Once outside the hospital's sliding glass doors, Malibu paused, looked upward, and let the sun beat down on her face. Freedom! She would never be back. Besides, any desire to kill herself was gone. *That was a stupid idea*, she heard one part of her say. It was a tiny voice. Actually, maybe it was her voice? She'd been in the crazy house too long and was talking to herself. It would pass. Still, she argued back, I was at a low place. And then the voice, still tiny but forceful, said, *You'd be fish food if not for me.*

PART THREE
SANTA MONICA, CALIFORNIA—SEPTEMBER 9, 2046

WHEN THE SANTA ANAS BLOW

THE FIRST TIME IT HAPPENED IT WAS LIKE A WHISPER.

It was a scorching late summer day, the Santa Ana winds blowing westward from the inland desert toward the coast. Malibu's mother called it earthquake weather, which caused Malibu, who was sixteen, to think of the earth ripping open, buildings tumbling, her world falling apart. Life can change in a snap. Malibu's family lived twenty blocks or so east of Ocean Avenue, close enough to the Pacific that on most days she could feel an ocean breeze. Not that day. The hot, inland wind caused the hair on the back of Malibu's neck to bristle. It felt disorienting, almost unreal.

Malibu's family home was small, with a postage stamp-sized backyard, but it was big enough for their dog, Sadie, to chase a squirrel up a tree. That day, when high school ended, Malibu raced home, sat in the backyard, listened to Sadie bark, watched two hummingbirds dip their long beaks into flower stems, and drew on her sketchpad. It was soothing. School had been rough. Malibu was supposed to have lunch with her new friend, Prudence, off campus, but Prudence had completely ghosted her. Was there anything worse than being ghosted? Even a shouting match was better.

Prudence and Malibu were lab partners in Mr. Hollocker's biology class. A few weeks earlier, they dissected a fetal pig together. When they pulled the pig from the formaldehyde jar, Malibu felt a peculiar and pleasant sensation spark inside her. It was a spark she wanted to explore. Prudence seemed even more shy than Malibu, even more of a loner, so Malibu took it upon herself to initiate things, and invited her to go see a screening of *Vertigo* at a Hollywood theater that featured old movies. Malibu went to that theater often, usually alone, and when Prudence said yes to the invitation, Malibu was excited to have a partner in crime.

The theater was surprisingly full, packed with a boisterous crowd eager to take in one of the all-time classics. There was a palpable energy in the air. Malibu soon got lost in the movie, spellbound by a flick she'd seen at least a half-dozen times. During the scene where Jimmy Stewart spies on Kim Novak at the California Palace of the Legion of Honor, Malibu felt a hand climb under her skirt and clumsily land on her leg, just above the knee. Malibu froze, her eyes still fixed on the screen. The touch felt crude, unsure. It didn't move upward or caress her skin, but just stayed put, as if considering its next move. If Hitchcock were directing the scene, the camera would zoom in for a tight close-up of the hand while spooky music played in the background.

The hand still didn't budge. Malibu, who felt a warm and titillating tinge run across her thigh, moved her legs slightly apart, offering encouragement for the hand to move up. Damn if it didn't stay put. So, Malibu lifted her feet off the sticky floor and moved her legs even wider, again hoping to coax the hand up. She also ventured a quick, sideways look at Prudence, who sat slumped in her chair, eyes determined to look straight ahead. The crowd murmured at something happening on the screen and the hand started to meekly inch up. Malibu became curious, wondering how far it would go. There was a feeling of detachment to observing the scene, as if it was happening in a dream or to someone else. Eventually, the hand made a bold jump upward, fingertips lightly grazing Malibu's crotch, before making a rapid retreat back to Prudence's lap, like a mouse burrowing down into a hole. Malibu brought her knees back together.

After the movie, neither girl brought up the episode. On the commuter car ride home, they stayed mostly quiet, but did make plans for lunch the next day at a burger joint, which is where Prudence did the ghosting. Prudence even skipped biology class. Later that afternoon, after gym class, Malibu saw Prudence walking alone in one of the hallways. Her face was covered with concern, looking almost like someone in the family had died. Malibu tried to approach her, but when Prudence saw her, she practically ran away.

In the backyard, as the wind picked up steam and Malibu alternated between petting Sadie's head and sketching, she felt sad and confused and pressed down by a terrible heaviness. It felt like a hole had been savagely ripped open inside her. Not just a normal, teenage, heartbroken hole, but something more monstrous and dark; a hole where nightmares could climb in and take root. A hole where something alien could cross through the thin membrane that separated worlds and find a home where it could slowly plot ways to build its strength.

Malibu felt compelled to draw a portrait of Prudence. She set out to create something angry—a spiteful caricature—but that was not where her muse pulled her. With a thick black pencil, she made Prudence look bewitching and angelic, seductive and impossibly pure. She made the image more true to life than most of her creations. The eyes and ears and nose were all appropriately situated and sized. The image that Malibu created looked celestial and bestowed with a power that Malibu didn't understand. With each pull of the pencil Malibu's heart ached and the hole inside grew larger.

Malibu's mother was home that day. The backyard sat below a long wooden staircase that led up to the kitchen, and the aroma of a roast cooking wafted down the stairs to Malibu. It smelled soothing, heavenly. Malibu's father, despite being Japanese, preferred American-style meat and potatoes meals. Grow where you're planted, he used to say. Sadie started to bark at one of those pesky squirrels, and Malibu felt something float down as if carried in the wake of the roast and lodge in her head. *How could that bastard fire me?* The words pressed against Malibu's consciousness as clearly as if she had thought the words herself. But she hadn't; they were someone else's thoughts.

The wind blew stronger and Sadie barked louder as reality twisted at the edges. Something was ending, while even more was beginning.

As if pulled by an unseen cord, Malibu climbed up the staircase and into the kitchen. Her mother stood by the stove stirring a pot with a long wooden spoon. She wore a white apron with a picture of two wine glasses and the phrase: *Wine a little...laugh a lot.* She was humming. When she saw Malibu, she said, "Your father is home early, dear."

As if on cue, her father walked into the kitchen. He had a grim expression on his face, but when he saw Malibu he broke into a smile and said, "How was school, buttercup?"

Bastard. It could have been his word. "Okay," Malibu lied. Using a playfully tone she said, "So, dad, who's the bastard?"

"Malibu!" her mother yelled. "That's prison talk."

"Mom, I'm sixteen."

"Still, that's not something you should be saying."

Malibu stepped toward her father. "So, who's the bastard?"

Her father leaned over and gently held her shoulders. "Why do you ask?"

"'How could that bastard fire me?'" Malibu raised an eyebrow.

Malibu's mother stopped stirring and looked at her husband. "Yukio, is there something you're not telling me?"

"Not now, Nancy."

"Yukio..."

Yukio released his grip on Malibu's shoulders and took a couple of steps toward Nancy. His expression softened. He nodded and said, "We'll talk later." He looked back at Malibu. "Why did you say that?"

"It was a sentence that popped into my head. Just right now. Or earlier. In the backyard."

"Yukio, were you fired?"

Yukio rubbed his chin, shook his head, and said, "There was a disagreement over our research. I said things I shouldn't have. I'm sure it won't stick, though. It will all blow over by tomorrow."

"Can you patch it up? Yukio, we need that income."

Just then, a bubble in the stew popped on the stove and Malibu's mother hurried over and stirred it, which seemed to break whatever spell they were all under.

"Everything's ready," she said. "We can eat early, if you want."

No one spoke at dinner, heads bowed, eyes fixed on their bowls. The wind blew in the open window hot and fierce, and for the first time, Malibu felt a grotesque and twisted sensation churn inside her.

The next morning at breakfast Malibu could hear a steady stream of her father's thoughts as he mulled over what had happened at work and what had occurred with Malibu. His mind was as clear as if she held these thoughts herself. As the words bubbled in her head, she felt the grotesque sensation that had appeared yesterday gently gurgle inside her. She kept all this knowledge to herself, afraid her parent would think she was going crazy, hearing voices.

Her mother kept a trove of psychology books on a bookshelf in a small room of their home. Malibu spent all day stretched out on a sofa leafing through an assortment of thick tomes until she landed on what seemed like an accurate diagnosis for her illness. She was suffering from auditory hallucinations. It was likely, although not necessarily, a byproduct of a mental illness, probably schizophrenia. Malibu decided that it was a latent malady that was somehow brought to life by her situation with Prudence and it would likely drift away.

Two days later, Malibu sat at a small, round table in a white, windowless conference room inside the physics building at the California Institute of Technology. She had taken her shoes off and the cold, tiled floor felt good on the bottoms of her feet. Her father sat across from her. Crow's feet spread out from the sides of his eyes. In front of him was a stack of white, rectangular cards.

"I'm going to hold up a card and think of the image in my head. I want you to try and tell me what the image is. Do you think you can do that?"

"I can do that."

He held up one card and asked, "What do you see?"

"I don't know." A lie.

"Try harder."

"This is stupid."

"Play along. Now, what do you see?"

"It's an equal sign."

"That's right. Are you just guessing?"

"No."

"You can see it?"

"Yes."

Her father placed the card down and picked up another. "Now?"

"It's a question mark."

"Right. Now?"

"A square."

"Now."

"A triangle."

Her father placed the card down. He rubbed his chin with the palm of his hand. "What do you see when I ask you these questions?"

"I can see the image pop in my mind." After the words came out, she caught herself, bit her lip, and said, "That's not exactly right. I can see them pop in your head. It just floats there."

"In my head?"

"Not in your head, exactly. More like it pops out of your head and I can see it float in the air."

"How do you explain it?"

"I don't." The grotesque sensation she'd had at dinner the other night twisted inside her again. It was small, weak, but marginally more pronounced than before. It was a sensation Malibu did not want to share with her father. But she did add, "I think I am going crazy. I'm hearing voices."

"You're not going crazy."

"How can you be sure?"

"You're getting every answer right. Something more is going on. Have you always been able to do this, see inside some-one's thoughts?"

"No. It happened for the first time that day in the backyard."

Yukio nodded. He opened his mouth as if about to ask another question, but didn't. Instead, he flipped over another white card. "Now?"

"Five circles, like the Olympics."

They worked through the entire stack, nearly fifty cards, and Malibu identified each image accurately. Using both hands, Yukio aligned the cards into a neat stack and pushed them to the side.

"This is the damnedest thing."

Malibu could see a thought pop into her father's head. "What is the many worlds interpretation?"

Her father lifted an eyebrow. "It's a theory of physics, the area where I focus. It's a belief that there are an infinite number of universes, parallel universes."

"And you think that's somehow related to what is happening to me?

He shrugged. Malibu got a glimpse inside her father's head as he tried to put his thoughts into words, but failed to come up with up with an explanation that made sense. He opened his mouth to speak, shut it, paused, before finally saying, "It's a theory."

"Who is Ms. Patel?" Malibu asked.

"You can see that name in my head?"

"Yes."

"She's a colleague of mine. I've asked her to come and test you as well. Is that okay?"

"Sure," Malibu said, because she knew it was going to happen anyway.

Ms. Patel wore jeans, a T-shirt, and a smart-looking blazer. She walked over to the table and placed down a paper cup full of coffee. Yukio stood and together he and Ms. Patel left the room. "We'll be right back," Yukio told Malibu.

Once she was alone, Malibu reached her arms upward and stretched. Instinctually, her hand jerked forward and grabbed Patel's paper cup. As if unable to stop herself, Malibu snorted a fat loogie and let it fall in a long strand into the cup. She watched it hover at the top, surrounded by coffee and cream. She swirled the liquid so it all blended together. She placed the cup back exactly where Patel had left it. That was fun.

Malibu had brought with her a green canvas handbag with daisies printed on it. It was on the floor, and she bent down and pulled out a music player. She stuck the buds in her ears and hit shuffle. She closed her eyes and listened to the lyrics.

I go to bed real early
Everybody thinks it's strange
I get up early in the morning
No matter how disappointed I was
With the day before
It feels new

I don't leave the house much
I don't like being around people
Makes me nervous and weird
I don't like going to shows either
It's better for me to stay at home
Some might think it means I hate people
But that's not quite right

Before the song finished, the door opened and in walked Ms. Patel. She sat down on the chair Malibu's father had vacated, lifted the paper cup, and took a big swig as Malibu stifled a smirk.

"What are you listening to?" Patel asked.

"The Eels."

"Is that a rock band?"

"Uh-huh."

"You're a fan?"

"Not really. I have one of their albums on my playlist, but I'm not sure I've actually listened to it before. The song popped up on shuffle."

"The Eels—are they a new band? I've never heard of them."

"There are no new bands."

Ms. Patel frowned. She seemed like a scold. "I guess that's right." She picked up the stack of cards that were on the table, and as she shuffled them, she said, "So, I hear you have a special ability. Is that right?"

Malibu shrugged.

"Let's test it."

"Sure."

They ran through the entire deck. Ms. Patel flipped one card after the next, but Malibu didn't get a single one correct. She couldn't see an image. Nothing popped out of Ms. Patel's head. Nothing floated in the air.

Almost immediately after they had finished with the final card, the door opened and Yukio walked in. Ms. Patel shrugged —*I tried*, she seemed to say. "Let me know if I can be more help, Yukio," is what she actually said as she left Malibu and her father alone.

Yukio sat back down. "How do you explain it?" he asked Malibu.

"I told you, I think I'm going crazy."

"No."

"I have schizophrenia."

"Definitely not."

"It makes more sense than parallel worlds colliding."

Yukio offered a half smirk. "Nothing else has changed? With you, I mean."

Malibu nodded. "Nothing else."

If Yukio could look into Malibu's mind, he would know she wasn't telling the whole story.

PAINTING WITH MOM

THREE MONTHS LATER, MALIBU AND HER MOTHER WERE at their weekly art class at the Santa Monica Firehouse Arts Center. Over those three months, Malibu's ability to read her father's thoughts had grown stronger, and she had found that she could sense other people's emotions as well. How these changes occurred remained a mystery, and gradually over time Malibu had stopped questioning why it had occurred.

Just accept it, the creepy voice in her head told her. So she did.

The original firehouse was built in 1929 using bricks from a local brick foundry. It served as a functioning fire station until 2008, when it was converted into an art center with a small theater and two large classrooms. Since she was ten years old, Malibu and her mother had taken a painting class there every Saturday morning. Malibu sat at her chair, brush in hand, but hadn't applied any strokes to her fresh canvas.

In her head, she hummed a song from the Eels ("Trouble with Dreams") and thought about shrunken heads. She could see herself inside that tiny museum, the air stifling, dust motes floating around her, the sound of waves crashing below the pier.

She wanted to paint one of the skulls from memory, but couldn't exactly conjure up the image.

"What's wrong?" her mother asked. They sat next to each other, easels and canvases in front.

"I'm blocked."

"Why not paint me?"

"I could do that." Malibu moved to dab the tip of her brush in some yellow paint, but pulled back as she felt a wave of disconcerting emotions flow from her mother: anxiety, sadness. Her ability to decipher her mother's emotions had started soon after she had started to see her father's thoughts. Which felt more troubling was a toss-up. Shifting gears, Malibu scooped up some purple paint instead, which she used to outline the shape of her mother's face.

Nancy painted a sunflower. She always painted flowers. Without looking at her daughter, Nancy asked, "Have you met that woman, Annika Eagle Feather?"

Malibu felt a new mix of emotions flow out from her mother and hit her with a sudden, frightening crash. It was mostly fear, but mixed with a sprinkling of anger. The combo was fierce, although Nancy did her best to hide it. Malibu dipped her paintbrush in water, pulled it clean with a paper towel, dipped it in red paint, and started to paint her mother's eyes.

"Why do you ask?"

"I'm just curious what your impressions are. You've met her, right?"

"One time. She gave me a number."

"Gave you a number. What does that mean?"

"She's a numerologist. She studies numbers. Thinks they have magical qualities."

Nancy laughed mockingly. "Your father is into a lot of freaky stuff these days. So, what's your number?"

"Nine."

"And is there anything to it?"

"Do you want the truth?"

Nancy turned her head toward Malibu. "Of course I want the truth."

"I mean..." Malibu paused as she focused on brushing some long eyelashes on an eye that she had painted a few inches below her mother's nose. "I'm not sure. Maybe. I notice it more. I mean, a lot more. I see nines all the time. But that could be just because I'm programmed to now. Still, today, according to the clock up there"—she looked up at the red neon numbered clock at the front of the room—"we sat down at exactly 9:09. That's two nines. And it's not just nines, but combinations of nine. Like eighteen." As she spoke, the words sounded peculiar.

"I'm sorry, dear, but that's stupid. There is no such thing as a magic number."

"You're probably right."

Nancy had placed a sun above her sunflower, but started to block it out by painting a cloud. "Was she attractive?"

"Eagle Feather?"

"Yes, is Eagle Feather attractive?"

Malibu painted one of her mother's pupils a shade of red you would not see on any real human eye. She pulled her head back, examined her work, and made the color even darker. It floated on the canvas like a spiteful demon.

"Malibu. Is she sexy?" There was a painful urgency to her tone.

"Yes," Malibu admitted. "In a middle-aged, Stevie Nicks kind of way. A bit more weathered, though. Lots of tattoos."

"Who is Stevie Nicks?"

"She's a singer from the 1970s. She was with a band called Fleetwood Mac."

"The 1970s. Malibu, you need to get with the times."

Irked, Malibu said, "The times—my time—is a dystopian nightmare. There are no new tunes to get with." She made air quotes.

"Dystopian? I don't think of it that way. Pre-dystopian, maybe. We could revert back to something more normal." Nancy kept working on the canvas. "Dystopian. You've always been a bit peculiar, Malibu, even as a young girl."

That stung. Nancy was not prone to saying harsh words to her daughter. In fact, she was Malibu's number one champion during all of Malibu's sad, lonely days at home. But Malibu didn't sting back. She could feel what was flowing out her mother—violent and bright emotions. They weren't connected to Malibu, she just happened to be the one there to receive them.

"I think I should have grown up in the 1970s or 1940s." Malibu worked to add a cheerful inflection to her voice. "Or maybe the '60s. I would have made a great hippie."

"I would have been happy to place flowers in your hair." Nancy said this with a smile, as if trying to soften what she had told Malibu earlier. Nancy plucked the finished canvas off the easel, placed it on the ground, and put a new one in its place. "They take LSD trips together. Your father and Eagle Feather."

Malibu didn't respond.

"He's told me that she has helped him to connect with the animal, plant, and mineral worlds. Can you believe that shit? Yukio is a fucking physicist."

Malibu again didn't respond. She had started to paint her mother's other pupil yellow.

"He told me on one of his trips he touched the face of God. I think what he's really touched is that woman's pussy."

"Mom!"

Nancy turned toward Malibu, her face screwed into a scowl. "Is he sleeping with her?"

"I think it's best if I stayed out of it."

"Stayed out of it? This is real life. This is my life." She started painting what looked like the outline of a mushroom, the first time Malibu recalled her mother painting anything but a flower. "Yukio tells me things about you, Malibu. That you can see his thoughts. We have talked about it a lot. Is that true?"

Malibu just nodded.

"Well then, is he sleeping with her? You would know."

Malibu did know. After the first time it happened, it had created an image in her mind she would have gladly given her pinky toe to erase. But she felt it was better not to say so to her mother, not directly. She licked her lips with the tip of her tongue and said, "I think you should talk to Dad."

Nancy's neck grew red. "I see. That's all I need to know. Eagle Feather. From now on, her name is Eagle Whore." Malibu felt her mother's emotional balance shift, with anger—a more powerful emotion—overtaking the fear of losing her husband. Nancy worked to fill in the mushroom. "I've started to take pills."

"Oh yeah? Is that a good idea?"

Nancy ignored the question. "I prescribe them to myself. It's not technically legal, but there are ways around it. I started with sleeping pills but added a few more. I can see why my patients have clamored for them all these years." She glanced Malibu's way again, a maniacal look on her face. "Yukio has his LSD, so why can't I have these? Mother's little helpers. That's a line from one of your bands, right, Malibu?"

"The Rolling Stones."

"The Rolling Stones. They did 'Paint it Black' as well. See, I'm tapped into that era too. Paint it black, paint it all the fucking way black."

Nancy stopped talking, and for a moment Malibu thought her mother was about to cry. But she didn't. She pulled herself together and noticed the portrait Malibu was painting. Her eyes narrowed as she focused on the image.

"Jesus Christ. That's how you see me? I'm in worse shape than I thought."

THE DEAD HAVE NO EMOTIONS

MALIBU COULDN'T SENSE THE EMOTIONS OF A DEAD BODY. Obviously, if a person is dead, it's logical to assume the corpse would not give off emotional cues. Except, what if there is life after death? If a person possessed psionic capabilities, might it be possible to reach beyond this world to the next and glean some type of insight? Was death nothing more than an illusion?

Maybe.

But what was clear was that Malibu could not detect the feelings of her dead mother.

Normally, on the Saturday mornings before she and Malibu went to art class, Nancy would get up early and make breakfast, which typically consisted of coffee, waffles, and bacon. It was a hearty, American-style meal that appealed to Yukio's "grow where you're planted" sensibilities. But after Yukio moved out, Nancy stopped preparing meals altogether. So Malibu took the reins and prepared healthy breakfasts—fresh fruit, yogurt, and granola.

A month had passed since the day at the Firehouse Art Center when Nancy had asked Malibu about her father and Annika Eagle Feather. It was a month that began with rage and quickly transitioned to sadness; sadness so dense it felt to

Malibu like a heavy wool blanket had been draped over her mother.

One evening, after three glasses of red wine, Nancy confronted Yukio about his relationship with Eagle Feather. She asked him why they were spending so much time together.

"She's a guide," he answered.

"What kind of guide?"

"She is showing me different realms of reality."

Mother, father, and daughter were all in the kitchen. Nancy stood by the sink, Malibu by the refrigerator, and Yukio by the door. He stood underneath the doorframe, as if he wasn't sure whether he was coming or going. After Yukio spoke, Nancy slammed her glass down so hard on the counter Malibu was afraid it might shatter. She moved in an agitated fashion, shifting weight from one foot to the other. Her gaze seemed to land on the wooden knife holder, and for a moment, Malibu was afraid her mother might grab a butcher knife and attack her husband. Malibu considered intervening, but felt locked in place.

Nancy turned her attention back toward her husband. Her face was flushed and her hair swept back and the anger seemed to amplify her beauty. "Different realms. Cut the bullshit, Yukio. You sound like one of my patients. There is only one realm, the reality you live in here with me, here with your daughter."

Yukio stepped forward, more into the room. "I've seen things, Nancy."

Nancy's face corkscrewed into a scowl. "You've seen things." She lifted a half-empty bottle of wine and reloaded her glass. She swirled the wine and took a sip. "Are you fucking her? Is that what you've seen?"

Yukio glanced toward Malibu, who dropped her eyes and

looked down at the floor. He took another step toward Nancy. "Can we do this some other time?"

"Why not now? I'm sure Malibu would love to hear what her father has been up to."

"You've had a lot to drink."

"And you're taking LSD. LSD, Yukio. You're a Goddamn scientist. At least you were. I'm not sure what you are now."

"Nancy..." He walked up to her, tried to take one of her hands, but she pulled back.

"No. No. No. I want you to leave."

"Nancy—"

"Leave." When Yukio didn't make a move, she said, "Now."

For Malibu, the four weeks after her father left floated by as if she were in a dream. She felt like she had slipped into a cold place that was close to waking consciousness, but not quite there. The nasty force inside her grew stronger and less able to be controlled.

With her father gone, the school days followed a standard script. Malibu woke up, drank coffee, and ate breakfast. She'd try to rouse her mother out of bed, plead with her to pull herself together, but Nancy was usually too groggy to function. Malibu rode a commuter car to school, went to classes, did her homework at the school library, and would come home to find her mother still in bed. Malibu wondered if she spent all day there. She looked like a lost cause. Malibu would make a simple dinner and then watch a vintage movie in her room until she fell asleep. It all felt like a scene from a movie where pages of a calendar were scrolling past, depicting time as it flew by.

When Nancy wasn't in bed, she was using the family's Memory Station. The console was kept in a converted greenhouse attached to the side of the house. The room had a metal frame, which held large panels of glass. There were no plants, only a reclining chair and the console's headpiece. Nancy would sit in the chair for long stretches of time, wearing a pink terry cloth robe and big slippers, sunlight flooding in and heating the room, reliving some unknown part of her past.

On Saturdays, Malibu did succeed in pulling her mother out of bed and away from the console. She forced Nancy to choke down some food and dragged her to art class, where she'd work through the motions. Like her mother, Malibu spent most of Sunday in bed. The psychic pain her mother was experiencing hit Malibu like a punch in the face. She felt unmoored. What's more, the faster her mother circled the drain, the stronger Malibu's psionic powers grew, as if pain nourished them. One night, just before the end, as she watched *The Lady From Shanghai* for the umpteenth time, it felt like her body had moved outside the confines of time.

Malibu found her mother's dead body on a Saturday morning. It was the lack of an emotional punch streaming off her that signaled to Malibu something was horribly wrong. Even asleep, her mother would emit an aura of pain and hopelessness. Suddenly, there was nothing.

"Mom," Malibu said as she approached the bed tentatively and with bilious sorrow. "Are you okay? It's time to go." Her stomach twisted into a tight knot. The covers were pulled up to the chin, but Malibu could see her mother's face. All color had drained from her skin, leaving it a sad shade of gray. "Mom..."

Malibu called 911, and in less than fifteen minutes, two Union Members arrived. The human stood with Malibu, while the robot examined Nancy's dead body.

"Is she dead?" Malibu asked, not because she was unsure, but because the question seemed required.

"I'm afraid so," the man said.

"What is he doing?"

The robot had pulled the covers down and was passing his hand over Nancy's body. Even though he kept his hand four inches above her, the scene looked ghoulish.

"He's conducting an autopsy. We should know cause of death shortly. It's standard procedure. We just need to make sure there was no foul play."

"Foul play?" Malibu tried to muster up a bit of rage over the insinuation, but she couldn't feel anything. She was completely numb.

"Like I said, it's just standard procedure."

The robot finished what he was doing and walked over to where Malibu and the other Union Member stood. He communicated with his partner in a way that Malibu did not understand, turned to Malibu, and said, "Your mother died from a pill overdose."

"Suicide?"

"Looks that way. Is your father home?" the human asked.

"No."

"Do you know how I can reach him?"

"I don't."

"I see."

The human lobbed more questions and coordinated the removal of the body.

Nancy was cremated, and a week later a wake was held. A small group of friends and family attended, but not Yukio. In fact, despite feverish efforts to reach him, Malibu couldn't find him. Malibu did track down Annika Eagle Feather, who told Malibu that she hadn't seen Yukio in over two weeks. "I wish I could help you, dear," she said, but Malibu could sense what she really wanted was for Malibu to leave her alone.

Two weeks after her mother died, Malibu turned eighteen. She was alone, saddled with a dead mother and a deadbeat father. She was broke. That night, she lay in bed and thought she felt a glimmer of emotion float toward her, something pure and clean. But as she focused her mind on it, the feeling seemed to float away, like a feather caught in the wind. Could it be her father? Could it be her mother, reaching out to her from a better place? Doubtful on both counts, but she tried to use her mind to reach out to them, to pull their thoughts toward her. Nothing materialized. Deflated, she drifted to sleep.

She was startled awake by a frightening shiver. The inner voice she did not want to acknowledge existed whispered incoherently. It felt malnourished, ravenous for more. Shaken, Malibu stumbled out of bed, went to the sink, and splashed water on her face. She decided at that moment she needed to leave and start a new life.

The next morning, she caught a train to San Francisco.

PART FOUR

SAN FRANCISCO—MARCH 19, 2049

FIRST DAY OF SPRING

THE FOG WAS SO THICK MALIBU COULD BARELY SEE HER hand as she held it an arm's length in front of her face. As instructed by Max, Malibu arrived at 36 Pacific Avenue at exactly 8:00 p.m. She didn't tell Hilda she wouldn't be at the club, she just didn't show up.

A black wrought iron fence fronted Luciana's house. Resting on top of each of the two gateposts was a winged gargoyle, which glared down at Malibu as she pushed open the gate. Malibu could just barely make out the home's façade through the fog; it was hazy like a dream, a mirage. As she walked up a stone staircase, she trusted it was there, that it was real. Each step was so wide Malibu had to extend her legs to reach the next plateau. Lining the path were large, manicured, richly green boxwoods. The fog worked its way inside her collar and under her jacket and sent a shiver up her spine. With each step, the hazy outline of the enormous home came into sharper focus. It was dark gray with a red-tiled roof, the windows large and shuttered shut.

When Malibu reached the front door, she pulled herself up straight and looked for a doorbell but couldn't find one. There was a large knocker on the door, shaped just like the gatepost gargoyles. Its eyes were angry, daring her to grab it. Throwing caution to the wind, she wrapped her hand around its face and rapped the door three times. An echo ricocheted in the distance, and the door creaked open a few inches.

Malibu pushed the door wide and stepped inside. "Hello," she said tentatively, her voice a mousy whisper.

Inside, it was as bright as noon and it took Malibu's eyes a moment to adjust. She had entered a large entryway with a wide staircase and a wooden railing curving upward. On the floor was a large, multi-colored Oriental rug. A crystal chandelier hung ominously from the high ceiling, refracted light blinking off each crystal and dotting the walls and floor. On either side of the room was a large, doorless entryway.

At the bottom of the staircase, about seven feet from Malibu, stood a young woman. Her hair was cut short and dyed blue. A small looped ring hung from her nostrils. She wore a black skirt, white leggings, black boots that ended just above the knee, a black leather jacket, and black gloves with the fingers cut out. Apparently she liked black. She looked bad-girl sexy. Malibu, wearing baggy sweatpants and her Santa Cruz top, felt like a schlump.

The woman in black walked forward, sashaying deliberately, her hips jutting rhythmically like she was swaying to the beat of a secret song. Her jaw aggressively worked a wad of gum. As she got within arm's length of Malibu, Malibu was smacked by a blast of her perfume and recoiled. It smelled like sour apricots and caused Malibu's nose to twitch, which triggered a burst of empathic insight. Although, she wasn't able to clearly decipher an emotion, it was more like a symbolic representation of one. She was overcome with a sensation that a large, purple, nearly black blanket had been draped over her head, covered her body down to her feet and made it a challenge to breathe. Malibu shook off the covering—metaphorically, of course—and noticed the blue-haired woman had a small black scorpion tattoo inked along the side of her neck. It looked so lifelike, Malibu imagined if she poked it she'd be stung.

The young woman eyed Malibu up and down. She blew an enormous pink bubble, let it pop, and said, "You must be Mama Bear's new little bitch."

Before Malibu could respond, Max walked through one of the side entryways and said, "Sandy, it's time for you to go."

Malibu was struck by the name, because Sandy looked the exact opposite of what you'd expect a Sandy to look like.

Keeping her eyes on Malibu, Sandy said to Max, "Just give me my shekels and I'll be on my way."

Max was in his standard getup: dark suit, white shirt, dark tie, and gloves. He must have a closet full of the same clothes, which would make dressing a snap. He walked over to Sandy and extended his hand, which held a canvas bag. Sandy slowly pulled her gaze off Malibu and snatched the bag, which looked full to bulging—with shekels, Malibu assumed. A smile tried to press its way at the edge of Sandy's mouth, but she pushed it down.

"Until next time," she said to Max with a tilt of her head. Looking sideways at Malibu, Sandy sniffed the air. Using a mock Yoda voice, she said, "The dark side is strong in this one."

Malibu felt her fists clench as Sandy made her way out the door, the stench of sour perfume trailing behind her.

Once the door shut, the atmosphere lightened, if only a bit. Max said, "Please follow me."

He led them into a large living room. It was noticeably darker than the entry room, so dark Malibu's eyes had to adjust again. There was a full-length mirror on one wall and on the other remnants of a fire simmered in a large fireplace. On top of the mantel was a stuffed crow with a beak as long and sharp as a butcher's knife. Its menacing eyes bored in on Malibu as she walked by. Long, green, felt curtains hung on two window frames. Max stopped at the back of the room, where there were two wing chairs with a small round coffee table between them.

"Please sit. Madam will be out in a minute." He turned halfway to leave, but stopped and said, "I have hung your portrait in my room. I have grown very fond of it."

"Great," she said, feeling a bit touched.

Max gave her a peculiar smile, bowed at the waist, and left the room through a swinging door at the opposite end from where they had entered.

Once alone, Malibu let her eyes scan the room. Her gaze stopped on the stuffed crow. She locked eyes with the dead bird and it locked eyes right back. Its pupils were as black as death and so shiny it looked like someone had recently polished them. Malibu's eyelids narrowed, determined to win an unwinnable staring contest.

Luckily, she didn't have to battle for long, because the swinging door swung open and in walked Luciana. At first glance, she looked much younger than Malibu remembered her. Her black dress was formfitting, highlighting an attractive figure. On closer inspection, Malibu noticed a few strands of gray hair starting at the roots and stretching down, and frown lines gently traced the edges of her mouth. Malibu watched as Luciana made her way to the open wing chair, sat, and crossed her legs. It looked remarkably like the vision Malibu had seen at the Kit Kat Club. She had fit, showgirl legs. As soon as Luciana was situated, a black cat seemed to appear out of nowhere and jumped on her lap. It turned its pink eyes toward Malibu, and like the stuffed crow, it seemed to challenge her to stare back, but Malibu knew better than to lock horns with it.

Without acknowledging Malibu, Luciana reached over to the coffee table and picked up a small bell. She rang it three times. Max reentered the room, walked toward where she sat, and said, "Yes, madam."

"I would like a brandy. Ask our guest what she would like. And bring us something to nibble on."

"I'm fine," Malibu said. "I don't want anything."

"Nonsense," said Luciana, finally looking toward Malibu. She tiled her head back. "You must have something."

"Okay. A glass of water. No ice."

Max didn't move, his arms stretched down to his sides, his fingers nervously playing with the ends of his jacket.

"No, dear," Luciana scolded. "You must have an alcoholic beverage."

"I don't drink."

"I'm not asking you to get drunk, just join me by having one cocktail. I'd feel lonely drinking all by myself." She tried to smile but the effort failed; her lips raised a bit, but fell downward in disgust, contempt. "Besides, can you really trust someone who doesn't drink?"

Malibu, adding a theatrical lilt to her voice, said, "Never trust a man who doesn't drink because he's probably a self-righteous sort, a man who thinks he knows right from wrong all the time." She paused, bit her lower lip, dug into the recesses of her memory and continued. "But sometimes, son, you can trust a man who occasionally kneels before a toilet. It's damned hard for a man to take himself too seriously when he's heaving his guts into a dirty toilet bowl."

Luciana rubbed the cat's neck, at first eliciting a loud purr, but then, as if uncomfortable, the cat jumped to the floor. "I feel you're mocking me. I don't like to be mocked."

"No, no. It's a line from an old movie. *The Big Sleep*. General Sherwood. Or is it Sternwood?" She looked at Max hoping for some support, but none was offered. With a shrug and a sense of doom, Malibu gave in. "I'll try a brandy."

Max gave a perfunctory bow and turned toward the door.

Once he was gone, the cat jumped back on Luciana's lap. She kneaded its head with her fingers. Her fingernails were painted red and perfectly manicured. Neither Luciana or Malibu spoke, and the room fell into an eerie silence.

For a moment, Malibu wished she hadn't come to the mansion. She wished she were back in her tiny apartment or eating popcorn and watching *The Big Sleep* with Hank. As a distraction, she focused her attention on Luciana and tried to imagine how she would paint her. A few ideas came to mind, mainly centered on the hair and fingernails, but really, her creative process didn't work that way. Sure, Malibu could get a general idea of how a portrait might play out, but the real work occurred when she sat in front of an easel, paintbrush in hand, and let whatever she was feeling flow through her and show up on the canvas.

The door swung open yet again and Max entered carrying a small, round tray on one hand above his shoulder, like a waiter. On the tray were the two brandy snifters. He lowered the tray and placed the drinks down on the table and left the women alone.

Luciana plucked her glass, took a sip, and threw Malibu a nod that seemed to say, *Your turn now, girl.*

Malibu felt the dark and maniacal entity she insisted on ignoring gurgle with excitement deep inside her.

"Here we go," Malibu said, as if she were jumping off a cliff. She took a small sip and felt the liquid slide down her throat and land with a thud in her stomach. The reaction was immediate. The alcohol raced through her bloodstream and made her feel higher than a dozen kites. Her face flushed and she hoped Luciana couldn't see it in the dim lighting. Malibu bent over and started to cough.

"Cover your mouth, dear," Luciana said. "Max," she hollered. "Bring a glass of water and a plate of food."

In a flash, Max returned, as if he had been waiting on the opposite side of the door like an actor antsy to get back onstage. One gloved hand was wrapped around a glass of water, which he handed to Malibu. She took it and leaned back, still coughing, although she had settled down a bit. With the heel of her hand she wiped tears away from the corners of her eyes and drank the cool water. Max placed a plate of food down on the coffee table. It held two uncut apples, some apple slices, Brie cheese, crackers, purple grapes, and a knife. It looked like the Degas still life painting at the museum, the one that had inspired Malibu to add an apple to the self-portrait that hung in her apartment. One of the apples on the plate was the spitting image of the apple she had painted, as if she had given it life and Max had plucked it off the canvas and placed it on the plate.

"Have you recovered?" Luciana asked

"Yes." Malibu looked at Luciana, whose face had a peculiar knowing expression, the type of expression that seemed to understand more than it revealed. "I'm allergic to alcohol. I always have this type of reaction."

"If you're allergic, you shouldn't drink it," Luciana said without even the barest hint of irony in her voice.

Bitch. The word flashed in Malibu's mind, startling her and putting her on edge. Still, a few more choice words came to mind, but Malibu kept them to herself. An image of her and Hank sitting on the sofa and watching a movie again popped into her head, but she pushed it aside, ready to soldier on. She finished the water and handed the empty glass to Max.

"Thank you."

"Another?"

"No. I'm fine."

And Max was gone.

"Have some food," Luciana said, her voice more an order than suggestion.

"No, thank you."

"I insist. It will soothe your throat."

"I'm not hungry."

"One slice of apple will do the trick."

Malibu focused on the tray of food. She leaned over and plucked up a slice. It tasted bitter at first, but as its juices flowed down her throat, she felt it actually did soothe her, or at least altered her condition in a noticeable way. She ate two more slices and wished she had asked Max for another glass of water.

Luciana watched the scene with a contented look on her face. It was more than just an expression. For the first time, Malibu's psionic antenna was able to register one of Luciana's emotions: satisfaction.

"I'm sure you're wondering why I had Max ask you to come here," Luciana said.

"I have a vague idea, I suppose."

"You do? Please tell."

As she spoke, Malibu couldn't pull her eyes off Luciana, who continued to gently knead the head of the black cat. "You work for the Chairman. You hire girls to do jobs for you. I'm not exactly sure what that means, but when I came in here, to the house, I saw that woman, Sandy, who suggested you want me to be your new girl."

"That appeals to you? Doing jobs, like you say."

"It does," Malibu said, and surprisingly meant it.

An outrageous picture of what working for Luciana would be like had crystalized in Malibu's mind. She would become a jewelry thief, a leather-clad Catwoman, like Selina Kyle in *Batman*. She'd wear ass-kicking boots, a black mask, and bright-red lipstick. Luciana would teach her how to scale the walls of the homes of San Francisco's super rich families, pry open their windows, and noiselessly sneak around until she uncovered their hidden stashes of diamond rings and ruby necklaces. Maybe she would need to learn how to crack a safe, but no doubt Luciana was an expert and could pass along the knowledge.

"I'd like you to burn down cottages," Luciana said, her voice flat.

The ridiculous fantasy in Malibu's mind had become so real and romanticized that she was taken aback when Luciana spoke. Strangely, when she heard the word cottages, she felt something black and interesting sparkle around her.

Luciana looked down at the tray and seemed to notice her glass was empty. She picked up the little bell and rang it. The door swung open immediately and Max stepped through, though a bit less quickly this time, as if he was growing weary with being commanded to leap into action.

"Yes, madam?"

"Another brandy. Please get Malibu another as well." She caught herself. "A glass of water," she said, clarifying. "We don't want another repeat performance, do we?" Her voice dripped with reproach.

"Excuse me," Malibu said once Max was out the door. "I'm not sure I heard you correctly. You would like me to do what?"

"Burn cottages."

Malibu tried to get a read on Luciana's face, but her eyes were blank, they gave up nothing. Malibu watched as Luciana dug her fingers deep into the cat's fur. She pushed it forward, against the grain, from mid-back up to the skull, all the time looking at Malibu with a blank, unreadable expression. When Max returned, Luciana kept her gaze locked on Malibu. Max placed the brandy snifter on the coffee table. Malibu reached out for the water glass. She didn't actually want to drink, but she wanted something to keep her hands busy.

Max turned to leave again. He'd moved along the same path so many times now, Malibu checked to see if he'd worn a groove on the hardwood floors. And, in fact, the wood was a slightly lighter shade of brown than the rest of the room. No doubt Sherlock Holmes would have noticed the difference immediately.

Luciana kept her fingers buried in the cat's fur as she leaned forward and snatched the glass Max had left on the tray. She swirled the brownish liquid, sniffed it, and took a sip.

"The key to drinking fine brandy is to sip it," Luciana said. "Perhaps that was your issue. You drank it too quickly."

"Could I get some more details on the cottages?"

Luciana didn't respond immediately. She stared blankly at Malibu before eventually saying, "What do you need to know?"

"Where are they?"

"San Francisco."

"In a particular neighborhood?"

"No. They're everywhere. They are actually quite common, if you know what to look for." She squeezed the cat's head, pushed its eyelids shut. "I'm sure you have seen them."

If Malibu had seen a cottage, she could not remember. "How many are there?"

"I haven't counted or seen an official tally, but there are a lot."

"And you want all of them burned?"

Luciana cracked a smile. "That would be quite an under-taking. In an ideal world, yes, you would burn them all. But let's start with one and take it from there."

Malibu wrapped her hands around the glass a bit more tightly, felt the cold condensation on the inside of her fingers. "Just so I am clear, you would pay me to burn down a cottage?"

"Yes, I would pay you." Luciana shook her head, like that was the most ridiculous question she had ever heard. "I wouldn't expect you to burn down a cottage for nothing." She drank a mouthful of brandy, as if eager for the effects to kick in. "We can work on the details later, but payment would naturally vary depending on which cottage you burned—its size, age, and other criteria. But be assured, you would be handsomely compensated. With each cottage burned, you would make more than a few months' worth of tips and salary that you would at the club. Maybe more than a year."

Malibu felt the creeping hint of something unsettling, like a wall of fog rolling in obliterating a sunny day. A terrible thirst grabbed her, and she took a sip of water to quench it. The unsettling feeling grew stronger. She gripped the glass tighter.

"Is there a particular cottage you would like burned?"

"That is for you to decide."

"How? How would I decide?"

Luciana shrugged, as if she had nothing more to offer.

Malibu tried a slightly different tack. "Why do you want the cottages burned? Is this something the Chairman is requesting?"

The mention of the Chairman seemed to make Luciana uncomfortable. She shifted in her seat. The cat moved as if to leap to the floor, but Luciana pushed it down forcefully with a firm hand until it reluctantly settled into place. Luciana took another large swig of brandy, raised an eyebrow, and said, "I have my reasons. This would be an arrangement between you and me."

"Are other girls burning cottages? Is Sandy burning cottages?"

"My arrangement with Sandy or anyone else does not concern you."

"It could. I wouldn't want to case out a cottage, get ready to burn it, and find that Sandy had already taken care of it."

Luciana squeezed the cat's head so firmly it let out a meow. "You would be the only girl burning cottages. It would be your special role."

"How would I burn the cottages?"

"Those details would be worked out later."

Malibu wanted to ask why she had been selected her for this particular task, but as she opened her mouth to speak, Luciana cut her off.

"I'll give you some time to think about. I suggest you use that time to see if there is a particular cottage you would like to see burned."

"You want me to pick the cottage?"

"We covered that." She was irritated, suddenly bored with the conversation. She drank more brandy. "I'll have Max meet you at the Kit Kat Club as soon as you've made a decision."

"How will he know when I've decided?"

Luciana didn't answer, just gave Malibu a crooked smile. Still holding the nearly empty brandy snifter, Luciana pushed the cat off her lap so aggressively that when the animal hit the ground it turned its head toward her and hissed, fangs bared, eyes flashing, tail arched, hair standing on end. It was quite an angry sight, but if Luciana noticed, she didn't let on. She stood and looked at Malibu with an evil eye that compelled Malibu to drop her gaze.

"I am going to retire. Max will show you the door."

Malibu watched as Luciana walked toward the entryway and up the winding staircase.

The swinging door burst open yet again and out popped Max. He took the water glass from Malibu's hand, placed it down on the coffee table, and said, "I have arranged a commuter car to meet you out front." He walked her toward the front door, and just like he had done with Sandy, Max gave her a canvas bag that appeared to be bursting with shekels. "An advance," he told her.

Malibu stuffed the bag into the front pocket of her sweatshirt. "There's a question I have to ask you."

"If you must."

"Are you Luciana's ex-husband?"

"No."

"Do you think I should work for her?" Malibu had already decided not to burn the homes. Arson—the idea was preposterous. But she still wanted Max's perspective.

"That is a decision only you can make."

"I suppose I will see you in a few days."

"Yes, you will."

NUMBER NINE, NUMBER NINE, NUMBER NINE

THE COMMUTER CAR WAS WAITING BY THE CURB JUST IN front of the gargoyle-topped gate. What Malibu noticed first was the number etched on the back door: 499. Two nines—double the positive energy, if Annika Eagle Feather were to be believed. As she eased into the back seat and glanced back toward the gate, she was reminded that Luciana's address was 36, or four nines. The positive omens were inescapable. Although, how far could you take it? If you're actively looking for something, it must be more likely you'll see it. Luciana had a cat on her lap and cats have nine lives. See! Consider: some ancient people believed the cries of a heron foretold of good fortune, or that bats in the attic signaled wealth. Of course, it was ridiculous, almost pseudo-religious hogwash.

She had to admit, however, it was nice to have John Lennon's voice ring in her head: Number 9, number 9, number 9....

Another British voice snapped Malibu out of her reflective mood. It was a London accent, however, not Liverpudlian. A singsong woman's voice.

"Where to, miss?" the car asked.

"Sorry." Malibu shook her head clear. "I'd like to go to

Chinatown." She directed the car toward the Memory Station on Waverly. The car weaved through the Presidio, turned on Lombard, left on Van Ness, right on Bay, another right on Columbus, and eventually entered Chinatown. All the while, Malibu kept her eyes shut and saw an image of Luciana stroking the cat superimposed on her eyelids. The colors were reversed, so that the cat and her dress were both white. Time seemed to stretch, to become so taut it felt like it might snap and splinter off into infinity.

The car dropped Malibu on the corner, down the block from the station. She was so head-down recounting her encounter with Luciana that she failed to see two Union Members standing in the middle of the sidewalk and smacked right into the human. The collusion was hard enough to push him back a step.

"Watch where you're going, lollipop," the man said. He steadied himself and then stepped toward her.

Malibu lifted her head and managed to chirp, "Sorry."

"Come here." He grabbed Malibu by the biceps and pulled her toward him. As he held her by the arm, his robotic partner pressed the palm of his hand on the top of her head. He held it there for what felt like an eternity, as if he was not just trying to read her recent memories, but to drill down to her very essence. His hand gripped her skull tighter; Malibu's breathing slowed, her heart kicked a beat faster. Eventually, he pulled his hand clear.

"Whatcha got?" the human asked.

The robot didn't speak, but again communicated with his partner in a way Malibu didn't understand. The man nodded and gave Malibu a shove. She jogged down the sidewalk to the steep stairwell that led to the Memory Station.

Seated inside on the ground was the same old man she'd

seen the last time, still wearing those ancient wingtips, his eyes still drowning.

"Can you spare a shekel? I want to see—"

"Yeah, yeah. Your daughter and wife. Here." She reached into her sweatshirt pocket and dug some coins out of the bag Max had given to her.

The man scurried to the woman with the Brillo Pad hair and made his arrangements. Malibu was next in line.

"One hour," Malibu said.

"Take room number five."

"I was hoping for number nine."

"It's broken."

"Broken? What do you mean?"

"The console don't work."

"But I really wanted room number nine."

"And I want shekels to fly out of a unicorn's eyeballs. Now do you want the room or not?"

"I'll take it."

Once inside, Malibu pulled the heavy console over her head, closed her lids and felt her eyes twitch. She dialed up the fresh memory from her trip to Luciana's home. She started at the gargoyles and worked her way slowly, stopping to reexamine details that may have slipped past her when they occurred.

There were nine steps leading from the bottom of the gate to the front door. Sandy wore pink lipstick and the eyes on her scorpion tattoo were red. It looked like Max hadn't shaved in three days. At the very moment she first locked eyes with the crow on the mantel, she could hear the faint cawing of a crow outside the home. The cat wasn't completely black but had a white spot on its left ear. Luciana wore fishnet stockings, the holes so small they were nearly impossible to make out, and she wore no shoes. In the room where Malibu and Luciana sat, there was an oil painting on the wall of a Civil War soldier (Union side). The wing chairs were white with a black pattern. When Malibu and Max stood at the door and he handed her a bag of shekels, the cat stood at the top of the staircase observing the whole scene.

The details that went unnoticed in real time, although often minor, always mesmerized Malibu. When life was unfolding, what did the mind choose to focus on?

Malibu watched the memory again and again, each time paying particular attention to the discussion she'd had with Luciana about the cottages. As she replayed the scene, she thought she could decipher an almost imperceptible twist in Luciana's expression, as if simply saying the word cottages caused her to be disgusted. With each re-viewing of the encounter Malibu could feel her resistance to burning the cottages weakened, until bringing about their destruction seemed logical, even inevitable. If felt to Malibu as if the homes were just waiting there for her to burn them. *Yes, they wanted to die*—the thought in her head echoed gleefully.

I'll be helping them, Malibu said to herself, as she removed the console from her head.

With that settled, Malibu left the station and walked down to the end of the Aquatic Park Pier and found herself at the edge of a dark and glassy bay. The fog had completely lifted and the sky was starless. The pier was empty expect for a half dozen men with fishing lines in the water and two Union Members on foot patrol. Malibu could see the enormous neon sign on top of Alcatraz—*Casino*—and it felt like it was calling to her. She watched as an electric ferry crammed full with revelers silently glided toward the island. The sound of people's voices rose off the island, was a caught in a breeze, and drifted to her ears. The sound played in her ears, cast an odd spell, until a voice next to her snapped her out of the trance.

"You got a big one," shrieked one of the fishermen. He dropped his rod on the pier and hurried over to another man, who was struggling to reel something in, his rod bent into a taut half circle. "Pull it Joe, pull it!"

Two other fishermen put down their rods and moved over to watch. It took some time, but eventually Joe reeled in a fairly large octopus. It dropped onto the cement, its tentacles flapping desperately.

"Shit," said one of the fishermen. "You don't see that every day. It's a freak. It's got nine legs!"

This felt a bit overboard to Malibu, almost like Eagle Feather herself was saying, *You question me, how about a nine-legged octopus.* Malibu felt a bit afraid to check her hands, thinking a finger may have magically disappeared.

Joe let the mollusk jump around for a while, then grabbed a small wooden bat by his side and hit the octopus once on the head, killing it. Malibu watched as all the color drained out of the animal, leaving it an ugly shade of gray. As she turned to walk home, it felt like the world was just a bit less hopeful.

A car was waiting for Malibu on Van Ness. It was number 56, which Malibu was unable to apply any meaning to. It had a snooty French accent. Malibu detected a hint of condescension from the car when she instructed it to drive her to the Chester-field, but its tone changed when she deposited the required number of shekels.

"C'est parti," the car said as it sped down the road.

As the car pulled in front of the theater, Malibu saw a steady stream of men heading in. They moved in an orderly fashion, single file, separated by six feet or more, all looking straight ahead as if wearing horse blinders. Their movements looked as if they had been orchestrated by a higher power. Once out of the car, Malibu slipped into the flow of men and entered the theater's front door.

"What gives?" he asked Hank as she approached the front desk. The smell of jizz was more pungently offensive than normal. Malibu had to suppress the urge to throw up in her mouth. "Why so crowded?"

Hank shrugged.

"Is there a special movie?"

"Just your standard wank and spank number," said Margarita, who was hovering close by.

"Don't you have food orders to take?" Hank barked.

"I told ya, no one comes here for the food." The statement was true this time around. The concession stand was customer free.

Malibu could feel a creepy, lecherous vibe from the customers as they streamed past, looking at her out of the sides of their eyes. But as she stood near Hank, the flow of foot traffic ebbed and then suddenly stopped, as if Malibu's appearance had broken some type of spell.

"Want to watch *Sunset Boulevard*?" she asked Hank.

"Normally, I'd be all over that. I love Wilder. But not tonight. I'm planning to work through a problem." He nodded toward the chessboard.

"Fischer?"

"No. AlphaZero." When he saw Malibu had a blank look on her face, he expanded. "It was an artificial intelligence program. AI. I guess you don't know about those."

"Whatever," Malibu said with a shrug. "I have a question for you."

"Fire away."

"What do you know about cottages?"

"They are small homes," Margarita chimed in from the sidelines.

"Cottages? Why do you ask?" Hank said.

"No reason," Malibu lied. "Just one of those things that came to mind."

"It's a strange thing to just come to mind."

"I guess. So have you seen any cottages, in San Francisco, I mean?"

"I grew up in one."

"Really?"

"Sure did. My mother and me. A one-story place in Bernal Heights. Built way back in the day. We modernized it, of course, at least as much as we could afford. New kitchen, Wi-Fi, before the Internet was taken away."

"Did you refurbish the outside?"

"Not much. Some of them are protected, the look and feel. They're landmarks, or at least they were, when that type of thing still mattered. Nowadays, who knows?"

"You seem to know quite a bit about them."

"I picked up a bit here and there."

Malibu nodded and said, "I guess I'll go nite-nite. Tootles."

She walked up to her room. She was tired—not physically, but mentally drained. Too tired to change out of her clothes or do the standard nighttime hygiene routine. She dropped down onto the bed and rested her head on the pillow. Her eyes fell shut and superimposed images played across the inside of her eyelids, just as they had in the car. Again, they were black and white and the shading was reversed. Her eyes began to twitch, like they do during REM sleep, like they do when under a memory console. Images played across her mind like a movie, like she was watching a screening of her day.

Check that. Not a movie, but like the dailies a director

watches at the end of each day of shooting; raw and unedited footage that needed to be molded into a coherent narrative.

As the images flowed past, Malibu's mind began to drift. She no longer watched the replay of her day, but instead began to imagine how different directors would take what occurred and craft it. Would they intersperse flashbacks into what occurred? Perhaps a really creative director would play the whole thing in reverse, like in the movie *Momento*. You'd see Malibu reliving the day superimposed in her mind's eye, followed by her talking to Hank about cottages, etc., etc. One thing was for certain, a good deal of attention would be given to sound editing. For example, when Malibu opened the gargoyle gate outside Luciana's home, a director would add a loud creaking noise. There would also have to be a score. Not too orchestral, like *Star Wars*, but more subtle. Music can make or break a movie. If Malibu could pick one person to direct it would have to be David Lynch. She would want it to feel like the dreamy scenes in *Mulholland Drive*. Lynch would frame each shot so it felt a bit unreal. Malibu could picture him placing the camera at the top of the staircase as she and Max stood by the doorway in Luciana's home saying their goodbyes. Maybe the cat would be in the initial shot, or maybe the camera would pull back to show it at the end of the scene.

One thing Malibu was sure would happen is that Lynch would now have her drift off into a dream. The script would go like this...

INTERIOR – MALIBU'S BEDROOM - (NIGHT) – CLOSE SHOT

We see Malibu from the waist up lying in bed. Her eyelids are closed and her eyes are moving rapidly underneath. We FADE OUT and images appear, scenes we recognize from Malibu's visit to Luciana's home. Only what was in color before is now black and white and the colors are reversed. Each image is framed like an individual shot in a movie. They click past as if someone were flipping pages of a book. As they move, we hear the loud beating of a drum. As the drum starts beating faster, the images begin to slide by so quickly they are impossible to decipher individually; it is all a blur.

THE SCREEN TURNS BLACK

There is nothing but a blank screen, no sound. It stays that way for an uncomfortably long period of time. Anticipation builds.

EXTERIOR — SAN FRANCISCO – A COTTAGE (DUSK) – LONG SHOT

We're startled by a burst of white light. As the scene comes into focus, we see that we're looking down at the Russian Hill neighborhood of San Francisco. Creepy background music plays. The shot isn't high enough to let us see the whole city, just that neighborhood. A small cottage is framed in the middle. The cottage, which is covered by a thin layer of fog, looks distorted, too wide and too long. The camera slowly zooms downward, through the roof, and inside the building. We see that the home has no furnishing or decorations, just a smooth wooden floor. A filmy light seeps in through four windows, one on each of the walls. In the center of the room stands Malibu. She wears a simple white dress and no shoes. The building appears to elongate, as if it were stretching through time. The camera view readjusts so we get a clear shot of Malibu's face, about a half dozen feet back. We're struck with a sensation she is more than an occupant of the home, but somehow part of it; she is tapped into its pulse. The music stops. We hear soft voices, but can't make out what they say or whether they are the voices of men or women. They come from opposite sides of the cottage, seemingly pulling Malibu in different directions. The voices grow louder and louder. The camera slowly moves into a tight shot of Malibu's head, so tight that her face fills the screen and we can make out the minute details of her eyes, which are open so wide they seem lidless. They are the never blinking, all-seeing eyes of a clairvoyant. We see worry lines on her forehead, so deep they look like they were carved with a knife. She opens her mouth wide, and within her eyes and mouth the ghostly images of people screaming appear. There are more people than we can count. We can hear the screaming as well. The sound builds until it becomes overwhelming. Just as the noise hits a crescendo, it stops and the screen goes black.

Cut to:

INTERIOR – A MOVIE THEATER – MEDIUM SHOT

Malibu sits five rows back on a red velvet movie seat in the middle of a row in an enormous, old-time theater. Above is an ornate chandelier. Stretching behind Malibu are dozens of rows of empty seats. There is a balcony, and at the back of the upper level we can see a beam of light streaming forward that is clearly cast by a movie projector. Dust motes are caught in the light. Malibu is the only person in the theater. Her eyes look transfixed, and we can see images flicker off the pupils.

Our view shifts and now we are looking at a movie screen— a point-of-view shot from Malibu's perspective. It is a black and white film. A man is being interviewed. He is middle-aged with black hair slicked back neatly. He wears a dark suit, a white shirt, and dark tie with white dots. At first we don't know who it is, but then we notice the trademark, upturned mustache of Salvador Dali. He is speaking English, but his accent is so thick we can't understand what he is saying. The camera pulls back and we see a canvas. We watch as he takes a black pencil and draws a surrealistic picture. A first, it looks like the distorted image of woman. The elements are misplaced but recognizable. We can make out eyes—one higher than the other, their shapes slightly different in nature. A nose protrudes out of one side of the head, and on the other side it looks like someone has taken a bite out of the cheek; we can see the teeth marks. There is only one ear and the lips are twisted into a frown. As Dali starts to paint the head, we become less certain of what we are looking at. The top of the head looks like the top half of an apple, including a stem and leaves.

Cut to:

Malibu and Sandy are standing inside the Kit Kat Club. Sandy is wearing a white mask that wraps around her head and covers the space around her eyes. She lifts a green apple to her mouth. She takes a bite and extends it toward Malibu.

Sandy: Care for a bite?

Malibu: No.

Sandy takes a second bite and then drops the apple. Sandy turns and steps toward the exit. She stops, turns her head to look back at Malibu.

Sandy: Let's go.

Malibu nods. Sandy smiles. Sandy leads Malibu to the front door, opens it, and they walk through.

Dissolve to black

. . .

Malibu had no idea what it meant—if anything—but it was sexy and the movie watchers could give it whatever meaning they wanted. Once you create something, you no longer own it.

Anyway, an imaginary movie scene would have to do, because the sad truth was that Malibu could no longer dream. She had lost the ability that warm, earthquake-weather day when her father's thoughts had floated down the wooden staircase of their Santa Monica home and lodged unasked inside her head; something was given and something was taken away. Malibu didn't notice the change immediately. She didn't wake up the next morning and think, I can no longer dream. The shift in her reality presented itself to her slowly, like a forgotten name or fact that worked its way through the synapses of the brain and suddenly became available. She wasn't even completely sure the dreaming stopped the day her psychic ability began, but as she pieced things together, the evidence pointed back to that day. At the very least, it seemed to be a logical conclusion.

In her bedroom, as she lay on top of the sheets fully clothed and street noise floated up and through the thin walls of her apartment, she stopped directing the movie in her head, let her mind shut down, and she drifted off to a black and silent and grotesque sleep.

FINDING COTTAGE
NUMBER ONE

The next morning, Malibu showered, wrapped herself in a towel, and brushed her teeth. While going to work on her molars, she decided to take a walk that morning to the San Francisco Public Library and research cottages. Once the brushing was done, she grabbed a container of dental floss. As she slipped floss between her top row of teeth, she asked herself, *Are you really going to burn down cottages?* There was something about flossing that often pushed her to examine an issue head-on. When the top row was done, she dropped the used strand of floss into the garbage and pulled a new strand free. Before she attacked her bottom teeth, she realized in all likelihood—as absurd as it seemed—she would burn down a cottage. Really, she had worked her way to the decision on an unconscious level. Most of our lives are lived unconsciously, after all. Somewhere along the line, after Luciana had proposed the peculiar idea of burning a cottage and before Malibu had woken up in the morning, her mind had arrived at the decision for her.

Still, her conscious mind wanted a say in the matter. An act as brazen as burning down a building required some thoughtful reflection, thus the trip to the library to gather more information.

She peeked out the window and saw that the fog had stormed its way back with gusto. It was so thick she couldn't see the street. She tugged on stretchy black yoga pants, pulled a wool sweater over her head, slipped into fuzzy warm socks and comfortable gym shoes, grabbed a jacket, stuffed its pockets full of shekels, and headed out the door.

First stop: breakfast.

There was a greasy spoon called Vic's around the corner from the Chesterfield. Since moving into the Chesterfield, Malibu had become an almost daily visitor.

What first drew Malibu to the restaurant was the neon sign —*Vic's*—that glowed above the front door. The letters seemed too large. They were red and so bright they could cut through even the densest fog. Sometimes the letter "I" would blink. The flickering was clearly unintentional—a glitch no one had bothered to fix—but the result was that it drew Malibu's eye to the sign even more keenly. That first day as she approached the building, she could see the restaurant was packed—a good sign. But the clincher for her was its address: 99 Taylor Street. Two nines.

The first time Malibu met the restaurant's namesake, she was surprised by his appearance. She had conjured up a particular image in her head of a middle-aged white man in chef's apron with large hands and a belly that hung over his belt. But Vic was Chinese. He was as old as tomorrow, and as tall and thin as a lamppost. He always wore colorful Hawaiian shirts and had the same long, surfer-style haircut her father sported. Vic's eyes bugged out of his head in a way that suggested he was a Memory Station addict.

As soon as Malibu escaped the fog and pushed through the

front door, the hostess led her to a wraparound booth in the corner. A waitress brought her a menu, but before she could hand it to Malibu, a peppy, almost girlish-sounding voice piped in.

"No need for that."

It was Vic. He leaned over the side of her booth, his eyes bloodshot and extra buggy. He wore a bright blue shirt that was dotted with an uncountable number of identical black and yellow and red Toucan birds, their beaks long and curved at the end. "She'll take a veggie omelet, all-star potatoes, English muffin, coffee with cream, and a banana on the side." He smiled triumphantly, like he'd revealed a secret.

"Not today," said Malibu. "Today, I'd like French toast, bacon, and fried eggs, sunny side up."

Vic's eyes opened wider, making him look positively manic. "Oh, oh. I didn't see that coming."

The waitress looked at Vic as if she were stuck in place.

"Go ahead," he said, and waved the girl along.

Vic turned his attention back toward Malibu, blinked, and his eyes seemed to soften a bit. "I pegged you as the type of customer who always ordered the same thing."

"Normally I am. Just felt like calling an audible today." Before Vic could leave, she asked, "How long have you lived in San Francisco?"

"My whole life. Over seventy years."

"Where do you live?"

"I live in the Sunset now. Grew up in Chinatown. My family was packed into a small apartment." His eyes rolled upward as if he was imagining the scene.

"Have you noticed any cottages around the city?"

"Cottages? What do you mean?"

Malibu realized she wasn't clear exactly what defined a cottage. "A small home," she said.

"I've seen a lot of small homes."

"Okay," Malibu said, realizing there were no nuggets of information to mine here.

A COTTAGE WANTS TO DIE

After breakfast, Malibu decided to take a circuitous route to the library. She worked through the Financial District, North Beach, and Chinatown, where she naturally made a stop at the Memory Station. Once inside a room (number four), she teed up the movie she had dreamed up in her mind. She wasn't sure the console would be able to locate the memory since it was a thought and not an actual activity, but there it was, in her memory bank. As she re-watched the images she had created—her eyes frantically twitching—it seemed to deliver the same mental cleansing effect that occurs while dreaming. Information was processed and filed away in her subconscious.

Afterward, she walked to Russian Hill, pointing herself toward the location she had conjured up in her faux dream, the location where a cottage might exist. She landed on Larkin Street, across from Russian Hill Park, and...bingo. Sure enough, tucked between two high-rise apartment complexes stood what looked like a cottage. It was one-story with a black-shingle roof, a redbrick chimney, and vines covered the façade. The home was dilapidated and obviously abandoned and felt hopelessly forlorn. The fog had become ridiculous—cut-it-with-a-knife thick. It shook Malibu and caused her to wonder if she'd entered a hallucination. Through the fog, Malibu could make out the home, which looked remarkably like the cottage she had envisioned. Malibu was sure if she went inside she would find the home empty of furnishing.

It wants to die, a voice rang in Malibu's head. It spoke softly, so low Malibu almost couldn't hear it. *Kill it*, the voice spoke again, faintly, a creepy whisper. The words filled Malibu with a vexing brew of emotions: fear, titillation, confusion, sorrow. Impossibly, more fog packed in around her, so dense the cottage blinked in and out of view, like a mirage. Malibu stood dumbly and peered through the vast whiteness. Only crazy people hear voices in their heads. Break out the straight-jacket, throw her back into the loony bin—Malibu had hopped on a fast train to crazy town.

Malibu stayed glued on the sidewalk for only ten minutes, but it felt like much longer. Reluctantly, she pulled herself away and left, but the whispered words continued to echo in her head. As she walked up Hyde Street, fog swirling around her and tickling the hair on her neck, the echoing grew louder. When she finally landed at the footsteps of the library, the sound was almost deafening, ricocheting from ear to ear. Blessedly, it stopped as soon as she stepped inside the building, where it was bright and warm and inviting. Back in the day, her mother could have handled all the necessary research online, but that option had been snuffed out. Not that Malibu really cared. You can't miss something you've never had, and besides, she adored the smell of musty old books.

The library did still have an archive room. On an old monitor that looked like it had been installed before the turn of the century, she found a January 25, 2003, news blurb in the *San Francisco Chronicle* entitled: "Spotting Cottages."

What distinguishes a cottage from a standard home? Size, obviously, is a key differentiator, with the cottage being the smaller of the two. However, according to architect Sally B. Woodbridge, "although the cottage is defined as a house that is small and not costly, a small cheap home is not necessarily a cottage."

Woodbridge and other cottage experts attribute a special cozy, quaint, rustic—even artistic—quality to cottages that shacks, dingbats, bungalows and other small homes don't possess. Cottages are also marked by their economic use of space, with attics, storage space, garages and every square inch of the home used as part of the day-to-day living environment.

Once one has a clear understanding of what makes a cottage, spotting one in San Francisco can still be challenging; they are often hidden from view by gardens, newly constructed garages and larger homes built on the front of the lot.

Malibu moved to an information desk, where she asked a librarian if there were any books on cottages penned by a woman named Sally B. Woodridge. The bespectacled librarian had a pencil with noticeable teeth marks tucked behind one ear.

After doing some digging in a large, red, hardcover book, the librarian grabbed a small piece of paper, looked around her desk, and said, "Now if I just had something to write with."

"Right there," Malibu said, and pointed to the pencil.

A sheepish grin spread across the librarian's face. "It happens every time." Using the pencil, she jotted a note on the paper and handed it to Malibu. "If you go there, you should find a book called *The Cottage Book*. It was written by Richard Sexton and Sally B. Woodridge."

Malibu looked at the paper. It read: LU96966. There were two nines, naturally.

The book was located on the third floor down a narrow aisle. It was in the middle of the row on the top shelf and Malibu had to push up onto her tiptoes to reach it. The florescent light above blinked on and off, making it a little hard to read the Dewey Decimal number. It was a small hardcover book with a yellow cover that was protected by a plastic wrapper. It gave off an earthy smell and the edges of the pages were coated with a thin layer of dust, as if it hadn't been read in years. Malibu took the book, blew the dust off the top, and walked to the edge of the building, where she found a single chair by a window. She sat and read.

At least half the book was dedicated to pictures of cottages, both the exteriors and insides. They were shot in a way to make the homes look glamorous, not run-down like the one Malibu had just seen on Russian Hill. The book was over fifty years old, however, and no doubt most, if not all of the cottages featured were now worse for wear.

According to the book, there were two main periods when cottage construction in San Francisco peaked. The first began in 1849, when the gold rush in the nearby Sierras had spurred rapid growth. Many of those initial homes were destroyed during the 1906 earthquake and fire. It was the aftermath of that disaster that spurred the second wave of construction. Called "earthquake cottages," they were constructed to make it possible for poor people to own a home for the first time.

By March 1907, 5,610 had been built and placed in every one of the 26 official tent camps across San Francisco, with the exception of tiny South Park, where 19 two-story tenements were built instead.

The most famous cottages in San Francisco, however, were

not built during either of these periods, but in 1882, and were meant to be low-income rental houses for servants and clerks.

Cottage Row is the official name of this quaint pedestrian alley paved with brick and lined with plum trees traversing one block between Bush and Sutter streets in San Francisco's Western Addition.

There was a glossy picture of the homes, each one painted a different bright color: red, pink, yellow, blue, brown, and orange. The trees were full of leaves and lovingly manicured. The redbrick looked recently installed. The cottages sparkled in the sun. As she admired the buildings, Malibu thought she felt the muffled voice inside her try to rumble to life, but she squelched it, killed it in the crib, didn't allow to invade her mind further. So she still had some control, but for how long would that last?

Malibu flipped the glossy pages of the book and continued to read. During the last two decades of the twentieth century, many of the cottages began to be designated as landmarks, and thus were prevented from being destroyed.

Malibu closed the book and looked out the window. It was raining. The windowpane was dotted with large raindrops. It was still foggy, or more accurately, the cloud cover had dipped so low the library and the entire city were encased in clouds. It was the afternoon, but nearly as dark as night.

Suddenly, Malibu felt tired. It was an exhaustion that slipped through her skin and into her bones. She took a deep breath, blew it out slowly, and sank deeper into the soft cushions of her chair. She replayed the recent events of her life in her head. Was it really less than three years ago she was a care-free teenager living with her parents? Now, her mother was dead and her father had disappeared. Malibu had seriously contemplated suicide, spent time in a 5150 facility, and lived in a homeless tent camp. She examined more recent events as well. She took everything, spun them around in her mind, rearranged the order of events, and imagined how the scenes would be depicted on a canvas. No doubt it would look more like a surrealistic Dali painting than a Degas still life.

The rain began to fall more densely; thick sheets of water blew sideways and pattered loudly against the window. Time slowed. If Dali had painted a melting clock, what could Malibu do? Gigantic mechanical wheels grinding to a halt. Three wheels—that would work. She could riff off Salvador and have the last wheel begin to melt. With that image fixed in her head, Malibu's face became hot with tears. The voice in her head, so faint she could barely hear it, reemerged. *Kill them...kill them... kill them.* She clutched the cottage book to her chest as thoughts of the future tried to push their way to the front of her consciousness, but she pushed them aside, and instead focused on reestablishing her equilibrium.

How long did she sit in that chair? She did not know. But eventually, the wheels of time started to roll forward at their expected and relentless pace. She wiped off the residue of tears that had caked on her face, lifted up from the chair, and walked down to the main lobby of the library, where she checked out the cottage book.

Outside, it continued to pour. Malibu tucked the book under her jacket, ducked her head to avoid the rain, and ran across the street to a little convenience store and bought an umbrella. She popped it open and walked to the Western Addition, making it to Cottage Row in less than ten minutes.

All six cottages were there, spread across in a row. They were abandoned. The once colorful paint jobs had faded to a dull and sorrowful gray. Most of the windowpanes were broken, leaving behind shards of glass. Malibu saw holes in their wooden foundations, where feral cats scurried in to escape the downpour. All the plum trees had died.

Malibu gazed at the homes as rain thumped on the umbrella and pools of water formed around her feet. She thought of the bright and sparkly photograph she had seen in the book and compared it to the ghoulish images she looked at now. She felt like crying, but didn't.

Here I am, she thought. Time to move forward.

After another dreamless night's sleep, Malibu woke early, well before dawn. She propped herself up on her pillows and opened the cottage book. On the second page was a map of San Francisco with red dots indicating where different cottages were located. More than five dozen cottages were highlighted. She studied the page, doing her best to commit the locations of the cottages to memory.

The sun was just starting to rise when she exited the side doorway. Market Street was empty except for a single commuter car that slowly rolled down the street, and a clump of homeless people pushed up against the side of a building. Malibu couldn't make out how many people were piled together because blankets covered them. At the edge of the group, alone outside the blankets, slept a pit bull tethered to a metal leash.

Malibu arrived at Vic's just as the doors were opening. Vic wasn't there. She had coffee, bacon, orange juice, oatmeal, fruit, yogurt, and two hardboiled eggs. Besides the hostess and wait-ress, the only other occupants of the restaurant were two Union Members. The human kept his head buried in his plate, devouring his food like it was his last meal, while the robot directed his gaze toward Malibu, causing her to shudder slightly as she remembered the eerie sensation of having a robotic hand placed on her head to examine her memories.

After settling the bill, Malibu exited to find the sun had

risen and the fog had lifted. There was a smattering of people on the streets, more commuter cars on the road. Malibu dug her hands into her pockets and started walking. If observed, it would seem that she walked aimlessly, winding her way through the streets and alleyways of the city. But although she didn't have a set route in mind, she had studied the map of the cottage locations long enough that she had filed the information deep in the recesses of her mind. She didn't actively tap into those files, but let her unconscious mind guide her path as it pulled her from one abandoned cottage to the next, like a magnet drawn to steel.

The article in the *Chronicle* was right—the cottages were often difficult to spot. Wildly overgrown gardens covered the facades of well more than half the homes. It looked as if the gardens may have at one time been properly tended to, but over the years had been allowed to grow freely, as if intentionally designed to hide the homes. Malibu found herself pulling back thickets of ivy or peering through tree branches to confirm a cottage was there. Walls or larger structures hid other cottages, so that from the street Malibu could just barely make out a portion of the small homes.

By midday, Malibu had seen more three dozen cottages.

By late afternoon, she had visited nearly every home featured in the book and her dogs howled like unfed coyotes. What was remarkable was that not a single home had been destroyed, despite the fact every home was abandoned and neglected. It was as if an unseen hand had protected them.

They want to die. The voice in her head spoke to her throughout her exploration. *Kill them.* The words were more forceful than the previous day. As she checked off each home on her mental list, those words invaded her head with a forceful and frightening crash.

It was just past dusk and Malibu was on Russian Hill, on

Larkin Street. She stood on the edge of the sidewalk and looked at the black-shingled cottage she had first seen the day before. Unlike nearly all the other homes she had visited that day, the cottage was not hidden from view, unprotected. The two large apartment buildings on either side seemed to be pressing in on the home, as if it were caught in a vice.

The home screamed in pain and fear, like a caged animal.

MALIBU GIVES MAX AN ANSWER

THAT NIGHT, MALIBU WAS BACK AT THE KIT KAT CLUB, seated in front of her easel. A few hours into her shift and she hadn't had a single customer. She could sense Hilda casting irritated glances her way. Malibu's inability to generate business wasn't due to low customer turnout at the club. The place was hopping with rowdy wine guzzlers and rummies. The bartenders couldn't keep up with demand. The girls working the room vamped the patrons with wide, come-hither eyes before taking tipsy women by the hand and leading them to one of the back rooms. Hidden speakers piped disjointed techno music into the room. Malibu listened to the music and tried to predict where it was going.

Just after ten, the front door swung open and Max entered the club. He weaved through a maze of bodies until he reached Malibu. Without preamble, he asked, "Have you considered madam's proposal?"

"I have. I'll do it." *Slaughter them*, the voice demanded.

"Have you selected a cottage?"

Malibu nodded.

As he'd done the last time he had been in the club, Max reached into the pocket of his jacket and pulled out a white business card. He handed it to Malibu. There were two lines of text.

The Engineer
Pier 39

"The Engineer?" Malibu asked.

"Yes. He'll be expecting you tomorrow morning. He can give you guidance on how to proceed. He can equip you with the appropriate supplies. He can help you in other ways as well, but he'll cover those details later."

"Pier 39 is a big place. How will I find him?" Malibu glanced toward the bar and saw Hilda glaring at her.

"Look for the pelicans and listen for the barking."

"Come again."

"The Engineer works in the back of the pier. It's a bookshop. There's a sign that says books. His workspace has a balcony that overlooks the docks where the sea lions camp out. On top of the shop, you'll see a large group of pelicans. When you see the pelicans, you'll know you're at the right place."

"Okay," Malibu said, feeling a bit peculiar. "How about payment."

"As soon as you finish, come to madam's home and she will compensate you."

"How much?"

"I won't discuss the particulars now, but Luciana is very generous. If you do the job right, you will not be disappointed."

Malibu nodded. Max left, assertively pushing his way out through the crowd.

If Malibu had any second thoughts about her decision, they were squelched at the end of her shift when Hilda pulled her aside and told her things weren't working out.

"You can always join the other girls," Hilda said after

breaking the bad news. "The women who come here pay well. You've got the assets."

"No, thank you. That's not for me."

"Suit yourself." Hilda shrugged and turned her attention elsewhere, ready to move on to other things. Too many young women had passed through her doors for her to drum up concern about any particular one.

Later, as she lay in bed, Malibu could not sleep. Thoughts fired from her brain like flicks of light off a sparkler. Rather than fight it, she grabbed a sketchpad and pencil and started to draw. She didn't try to harness her thoughts but let them filter past until she found one that inspired her.

When a shrunken head appeared in her mind, she locked onto the image and drew what she saw on the center of the page. She gave it full lips and wide eyebrows, disjointed eyes (her trademark), long hair, and placed the nose on the side of its head. Behind the head she drew the Golden Gate Bridge, so realistic it looked like it was pulled out of a tourist's guide. In the middle of the bridge, at the spot where she had contemplated jumping, she drew a tiny woman.

To the left of the page, Malibu started to draw a woman who seemed to resemble purple-wigged Hilda, but before she could start on the facial features, she pooped out and drifted off. The little exercise had worked to calm her mind.

ENTER THE ENGINEER

Max had undersold the number of pelicans outside the Engineer's shop. The place was filthy with them. They were crammed onto the roof and a sizeable pod of them also loitered outside the front door. They crapped on the pavement and opened their beaks to let out a strange and guttural noise.

The building had a large neon sign above the door that read, *Books*. A pelican stood perched on the letter B. All the adjacent buildings appeared to be abandoned, their windows sealed shut with wooden boards. The pelicans didn't rush to clear a path for Malibu as she walked to the door, but just slid a step or two to the side, opened their beaks wider, and made that strange noise even louder.

When Malibu reached the door, it creaked open wide, as if moved by magic. She stepped inside. Light flooded in from a large picture window in the back. Sea air gently streamed in through a doorless walkway. The walls were lined with shelves filled with hardcover books. In the center of the room stood a pelican. It balanced on one foot, its head bent back as it stared up at the ceiling.

At the back of the room were two Doberman Pinschers.

They stood at attention, ears pointed up like horns, their neck muscles flexed, and all four eyes fixed on Malibu.

At first, Malibu couldn't pull her eyes off the dogs, but eventually she gazed through the picture window and saw a man in a dark overcoat. On his head was a tightly wound tan turban. His back was to her and he seemed to be looking out on the bay. Keeping a wary eye on the dogs, Malibu skirted around the pelican and walked through the open doorway and onto a balcony.

"The deck below used to be filled with tourists, but now it's empty," said the man. He had the hint of an Indian accent. As he spoke, he kept his gaze fixed straight ahead. He had a trimmed salt-and-pepper beard and wore a purple scarf. On his hands were gloves with the fingers cut out. He stood at attention, like a military officer.

As he spoke, Malibu was struck with a peculiar sensation. It felt as if the man's emotions weren't fully human but intermixed with a strand of ones and zeros—binary code—that streamed from his mind to hers. Almost as soon as Malibu felt the sensation it was extinguished, two wet fingers on a candlewick.

"Is that right?" Malibu asked.

"You're too young to remember. The sea lions don't care. They don't need us."

Below the deck was a pier, and below the pier were a dozen or so wooden platforms that floated on the greenish-colored water of the bay. Each platform was filled with sea lions, their bodies pressed together as tightly as sardines in a tin. Most slept, others barked, one pushed off the platform and slipped into the water.

"Are you the Engineer?"

Still looking straight ahead, the man said, "Did you pick a cottage?"

"Uh-huh."

"Tell me about it."

Malibu described the building's appearance, emphasizing its decrepit nature.

The Engineer turned his head, finally looking at Malibu. "Okay. But why did you pick that particular cottage?"

It wants to die. Malibu heard the words. She imagined a carnivore licking its lips. "It wants to die," she told the Engineer.

The Engineer nodded, as if it was the response he wanted to hear. He turned, brushed past Malibu, and walked through the open doorway and into his book-lined shop. Malibu followed, pulled in his wake.

Inside the room, the Dobermans stood at attention. The peculiar pelican had wandered closer to the front door, its head still pointed upward. The Engineer ignored the dogs but looked at the bird. A bemused expression spread across his face.

"Have you ever tried to train a pelican?" he asked. He didn't give her time to respond, probably because it was a ridiculous question. "They're exceptionally smart birds, but impossible to train. They're far too independent."

"Why would you want to train a pelican?"

He looked at her, his face holding an expression that implied it was the first time he had properly considered the question. "Dobermans aren't as smart as pelicans, but they're easy to train. They can pick up on cues as well. With just a nod of my head, these two would rip your throat out. They'd fight through a bullet. They're far better bodyguards than any human I've worked with."

The Engineer snapped his fingers and the two dogs fell out of attention, their muscles noticeably relaxing. They wagged their nubby tails, walked over to Malibu with a playful skip in their step, and took turns licking her outstretched hands. On one of the shelves, tucked between stacks of books, was a metal bucket. The Engineer reached inside, pulled out a fish, and tossed it to the pelican, who caught it in its beak and swallowed it in one gulp. The Engineer snapped his fingers again and the dogs left Malibu and started sniffing around the room.

"There are many different ways the cottage job can be handled," the Engineer said.

He pressed an unseen button and the shelves slid open, exposing a hidden compartment. It was lined with shelves as well, and these shelves were filled with peculiar looking items. Malibu couldn't make out what everything was, but thought she recognized a pair of hand grenades, circa World War Two.

"I don't believe in overkill. It goes against my nature. So I'd recommend gasoline. It's almost impossible to come by now, but I always keep a supply on hand." He reached up to the top shelf and pulled down a metal canister about the size of a small soup can, with a plastic lid. He beckoned Malibu to his side and handed her the canister. Once it was securely in her grip, he waved his right hand like a magician and then opened it to expose a box of wooden matches. "Spread gas around," he instructed. "One drip here, a drop there. Once it's properly coated, drop a lit match, and then hightail it out because the place will go up like a pile of dried leaves."

"Sounds simple enough," Malibu said.

The Engineer stepped back to the counter, hit the button, and the wall closed.

Malibu lifted the canister to her nose and sniffed the gasoline. "Why do you think she wants me to burn cottages?"

"I couldn't tell you."

"No thoughts at all?"

"Why did you agree to it?"

Getting nowhere, Malibu shifted gears. "Do you know Luciana?"

The Engineer nodded. "I've known her for years."

"Do you work for her?"

"No. We're part of the same organization. Cogs on a wheel. I guess you're a cog now as well."

"The Chairman's organization?"

At the mention of that name, the Engineer's expression changed slightly, a tightening at the edge of his eyebrows. He ignored the question, said, "Once the job is done, before you see Luciana, even before you go home, come immediately here. Day or night. I'll protect the memory."

"Erase it?"

"No. You'll still be able to remember, but I can block it so that a Union Member can't access it."

An image of an iron glove wrapping around her throat flashed into Malibu's mind. The image stayed with her as she left the Engineer's shop and walked to the Financial District. She decided she needed to suit up for her assignment. What should an arsonist wear? All black, naturally. Sandy would approve. At a basement shop at the bottom of a narrow stair-well, she bought a black T-shirt, black leather pants and big black ass-kicking boots. But what made the getup truly rock was a black leather jacket adorned with four silver studs on each collar and one silver stud button holder. She modeled it in front of the shop's mirror and felt like Trinity in *The Matrix*. Maybe life really was all a simulation? The Internet hadn't been killed—no—she was trapped inside it.

Kill it, a voice howled.

Yes, kill it, Malibu agreed.

Once back in her apartment, as she lay in bed and waited for nighttime to arrive, the words *kill it* continued to live in the front of her mind.

MALIBU KILLS A COTTAGE

It was a moonless night. The air felt crisp, refreshed from the recent rain. Malibu waited until just past midnight to leave her apartment, sneaking out the side door. She walked to the cottage on Francisco Street, feeling it was better not to take a car and leave any record of her trip. When she finally arrived, she was tired, but also juiced with adrenaline. She sat on a bench in Russian Hill Park across the street from the sorry-looking cottage. The park was empty, the street was empty, and the city was quiet. A cool breeze blew in from the bay, carrying with it a salty aroma. As a few stars appeared in the sky, Malibu looked at the cottage and felt a certainty in her heart that the building was ready to go. It was asking for someone to end its misery. It wanted to die.

On rubber legs, Malibu crossed the street and walked through the cottage's unlocked front door. Inside, it was close to what she had imagined in her faux dream. There was a large room with hardwood floors and no furnishing. Malibu stood in the center of the room for a few moments. She let out a deep breath and felt the home's heartbeat. The beating picked up speed, as if in anticipation of what was to come. Was it frightened or eager? She could not tell.

Execution time.

Malibu released another stream of breath as she pulled the metal canister out of a pocket inside her newly purchased jacket. She removed the plastic lid, walked around the room, and strategically dripped gasoline on the floor. There wasn't much gas, but Malibu was sure the Engineer was right that the home was so old, the wood so rotten, that the fire would spread rapidly. She walked back toward the door, lit a match, and tossed it into the center of the room.

The match landed on a patch of gasoline and a small fire formed. The fire stayed in that one spot for a bit until a spark broke free and landed on another spot of gas a few feet away forming a new blaze. In no time, those two patches connected and spread in a line all the way to a window. Soon, a whole wall was engulfed.

From where she stood, Malibu could feel the heat of the flames warm the skin on her face. A belch of black smoke sprang from the far wall, filled the room, and burned her eyes. She sensed the cottage welcoming death, and for a moment, she welcomed it as well. She was gripped with a peculiar desire to lie on the floor and let the flames wash over her. But as the blaze moved so near her it practically licked the edge of her shoes, the voice in her head said, *No.* It was noticeably stronger and more forceful than she had ever heard it before. It felt nourished. Malibu—obeying the voice—hustled out the front door. As she jogged to the bench across the street, her lungs heaved for fresh air.

Had anyone seen her?

The fire crackled, grew rapidly. Through the cottage's front windows she could see the flames sparkle—red and orange and yellow. Fire burst out the front door, danced on the porch, expanded. Soon, the front of the building was engulfed, burning strongly enough that Malibu could feel the heat from across the street.

Sirens whirred in the distance. People flooded out of the two buildings that bracketed the burning cottage, rushed toward the sidewalk, and rubbernecked at the burning building. A few shrieked, some cried. A small group of oglers drifted across the street and huddled around the bench where Malibu sat.

"It's so horrible," a young woman said to no one in particular. Malibu felt the woman's anguish jump on her, her psionic powers keenly alive.

Malibu wanted to be alone. With her eyes fixed on the burning cottage, she walked a few steps backward. The sirens got nearer. The entire cottage was now one big ball of flames. There was a loud cracking sound as the building's foundation gave way, crumbled. Soon it would be all over.

A clutch of Union Members arrived, as if the fire had caused them to materialize. They worked to disperse the crowd as two fire trucks arrived. They were too late. Most of what was once the home was now ash.

As two robotic Union Members walked ominously across the street toward the front of the park, Malibu slinked down a cement path and out the back side of the park.

Ignoring the advice of the Engineer to go directly to his shop, Malibu instead went to the Memory Station in Chinatown. Despite the late hour, a red neon sign blinked *Open* at the bottom of the stairwell. Once inside, Malibu looked for the man in the ancient wingtips and was happy to find he wasn't there. There was someone new at the desk as well. A young man, who Malibu sensed was the Brillo-haired woman's son.

Malibu asked, "Is room number nine reopened?"

The young man didn't speak, but nodded once. He was chewing gum, his jaw working hard.

"I'll take it." With a shaky hand, Malibu slapped a shekel on the counter.

The man picked up the coin and said, "Knock yourself out."

Once inside the yellow room, Malibu checked twice to make sure she had locked the door properly. Her eyes still felt irritated from the smoke. She leaned back in the recliner and fired up the memory of her visit to the cottage. She started when she was inside the home, after she had sprinkled the gas, at the exact moment when she struck the match.

As the thrown match hovered in the air, Malibu unsnapped the top button of her leather pants. She slid a hand downward and under the waistband of her panties. She then watched the fire as it danced across the wooden floor. She slipped a finger inside her, where she felt moist and warm. As the wall burst into flames and fire licked the wood and playfully caressed the windowsill, Malibu pulled her hand out and let one fingertip tap around the edge of her clit. As she watched smoke begin to fill the room, she felt the hint of an orgasm start to form. It was far in the distance, at the edge of the horizon. She worked to hold the thread, moved her finger faster, pulled it back, teased, and then pressed it down and rubbed faster and faster and faster. Her mind commanded the console to slow the rate at which the memory unfolded. She paused at the point where the fire had reached the tips of her toes and she had considered lying down on the floor and letting the flames overwhelm her and joining her mother, wherever she had gone, wherever she had escaped to.

Now, let's get ourselves off, the voice cooed seductively.

Malibu resumed. Using two fingers now, she moved rapidly —up and down, side to side, moving in circles—until her orgasm peaked and she had to place her free hand over her mouth to muffle her moans.

Outside the station, the air had grown colder. Malibu zipped her jacket up tight. Her cheeks still felt hot, flushed crimson. Drained, she decided to walk to North Beach and find a commuter car to take her the short distance to Pier 39. Half a block from Columbus Avenue, she froze her in tracks as she saw two Union Members slowly walking toward her. She recognized them as the same two who had stopped her a few nights before, when the robot had placed a cold hand on her head and scanned her memories. As a sensation of menace lifted off the man and streamed into her consciousness, the image of an iron glove wrapped around her throat reentered her mind.

Kill them, the voice in her head screamed.

Her adrenaline pumped. It was an impossible demand. Her heart beat triple time.

Just as the two Union Members started to move toward where Malibu stood, a loud crashing sound came out of a nearby bar. A beer bottle flew out the door and landed with a splat on the pavement, beer and colored glass flying in all directions. A second and louder crash erupted out the doorway, along with the hateful sound of two men yelling. The two Union Members diverted their attention from Malibu and hustled into the bar. Relieved, Malibu crossed the street and scampered to Columbus.

The commuter car waiting for her was marked number thirty-seven. For a moment, Malibu considered letting it pass and waiting for one with at least some semblance of meaning, some connection to the number nine, but she quickly discarded the idea. Time was of the essence.

"Good on you, mate," the car said in a chipper Australian accent after Malibu told it where to take her. "We'll be there in two shakes."

It was past three a.m. when Malibu arrived outside the door of the Engineer's shop. There were no people on the pier and noticeably less pelicans, both on the building's roof and milling around outside. Still, she had to shoo away two birds so she could make it to the front door. Like before, the door magically opened for her. As she stepped inside, she heard the two Dobermans start to growl.

"Settle down, Beavis and Butthead," Malibu heard a voice say. She expected it to be the Engineer, but instead, it was what appeared to be a young man, early twenties, wearing khaki pants and a button down blue denim shirt. He was petting the top of both dogs' heads. What tipped Malibu off to the fact something was amiss was that she picked up the same emotional signal from him that she got from the robotic Union Members, meaning she registered no signal at all.

"Beavis and Butthead?" Malibu asked.

"You know, the old cartoon." As he spoke, he cocked his head slightly to one side.

"I know them. Do you like old cartoons?"

"I do," he chirped. "*The Simpsons* is probably my favorite."

Normally, Malibu would have happily drilled deeper into classic pop culture, but after the near brush with the Union Members, she wanted to get down to brass tacks as quickly as possible. "I was hoping to meet someone here."

"Yes. The Engineer. I'm Scott. We're expecting you."

"It's nice to meet you, Scott. You look so real, so lifelike." After she spoke the words, Malibu wished she could pull them back because a hurt expression spread across Scott's face.

"I am real."

"I mean—"

"You mean human." He tilted his head to the side again, a physical tick.

"Yes." Seconds skipped by. Malibu found herself liking Scott. She felt an urge to tilt her head to the side in imitation but resisted, concerned it might be viewed as a mocking gesture. A deeply contemplative expression spread across Scott's face, as if he was considering the true nature of black matter. Malibu wondered if Scott, like Pinocchio, was contemplating what it was like to be human, but she decided she was being presumptuous.

Just then, a pelican sauntered through the open doorway in the back of the room and slow-walked toward Malibu, its feet making a slapping sound as they smacked the stone floor. The bird stopped in front of her, spread its wings. It pushed its head forward and opened its beak wide and let out a frightful shriek. The noise didn't seem to be directed at Malibu, but off to her side, as if someone were standing there. The bird flapped its wings aggressively and moved the wind violently enough that it pushed Malibu's hair back. The whole scene caused Malibu to feel something urgent stir inside her.

"You see something new every day," said Scott as he shooed the bird away with both of his hands. The pelican didn't leave the room entirely, but moved to the corner where it tucked its wings down and kept a watchful eye on Malibu.

Scott looked at Malibu and again slanted his head to one side. "Let's get down to business, shall we." He stepped to the shelves across the room where Malibu and the Engineer had stood earlier in the day and pressed a button. Like before, two panels of wall slid open, this time exposing a spiral staircase that led downward. Scott stepped to one side as if to say, *Feast your eyes on this.*

"So many secret compartments," Malibu said.

"The Engineer is down the stairs."

As soon as Malibu had descended a few steps down the panels snapped shut. There was no direct light source where Malibu stood, but light did climb up from below. The problem was that the bottom of the stairwell was a very long way down and the light that made it up to Malibu was dim, so she gripped the handrail tightly and took each step carefully as she circled her way downward.

After what seemed like an unusually long amount of time, Malibu reached the bottom and entered a place that immediately brought to mind the Batcave. The walls were black stone with recessed lighting carved into them. The floor was made of grated metal, from which cold air blew up through the openings, as if pushed by an unseen fan. Positioned around the room were what looked like large mainframe computers; they hummed like hornets. Past the reach of the artificial sources of light was a deep darkness that seemed to stretch to infinity.

"This way please," said a familiar voice. "We have a station set up for you."

Malibu turned her head and saw a young man wearing khaki pants and a button down blue denim shirt. He tilted his head to one side in a familiar manner as he returned Malibu's gaze.

"Scott? How'd you get down here so quickly? Is there an elevator?"

"I'm Toby, Scott's brother."

"Twin brother?"

"In a manner of speaking."

"Are there more of you?"

"No. Just Scott and me." He led Malibu to the side of the room, where a Memory Station and recliner were set up. The chair was black leather and looked expensive. The console was much nicer than the one Malibu used in Chinatown. "Please sit here. The Engineer will be out in a moment."

As Malibu settled into the chair, she said to Toby, "Can you answer a question?"

"I'll do my best."

"How do you keep the water from the bay from flooding into the room?"

Toby's head twitched, as if he'd never considered the question before. "I've never considered that question before," he said.

"You have to admit, it's a bit worrisome."

"Some things are better left unexamined. If you pull a thread too much, everything unravels." Apparently, he was a robotic philosopher.

As he spoke, Malibu looked over his shoulder and saw a hidden door open on one of the cave's walls and the Engineer stepped out. *Note to self—the Engineer has a fetish for hidden compartments.* He was dressed exactly as he had been earlier that day, down to the fingerless gloves. Or was it the day before? Time continued to move along at its own peculiar pace.

"You smell like smoke," the Engineer said when he arrived at the recliner. "I can block your memory, but you need to shower and wash your clothes."

"Is it painful, protecting my memory?"

"You won't feel a thing. Now sit back."

Malibu leaned back in the chair. But just as the Engineer started to place the console on her head, she said, "Wait." Looking at Toby, who still stood nearby, she said, "Will you hold my hand?"

Without speaking, the robot grabbed her hand, gave it a gentle squeeze, and the Engineer got down to business.

. . .

Back outside on the street in front of Fisherman's Wharf, Malibu looked for a commuter car. It was shocking, but not a single car had queued up in anticipation of her arrival. How could that be, had the AIs gone haywire? Don't pull the thread too much; take it as a signal to find an alternative route home. It's best not to question the will of the universe too closely.

She was too tired to walk all the way to her apartment, so out of a sense of desperation, she decided to take a cable car. There was one that started on Hyde Street and would drop her off on Powell, just a few blocks from the Chesterfield. Unfortunately, after walking the few blocks to get there it wasn't running; a car sat idyll on the turntable. There was a schedule that said the first car would start at six a.m., which she estimated was still an hour away. Feeling ragged, Malibu stretched out on a green bench and closed her eyes. Before drifting off, she let her mind float back to earlier, when she stood inside the cottage holding a just-lit match. She remembered the sensation and the energy she'd felt, and was satisfied that despite the work the Engineer had done to protect her memory, she could still recall what happened. In reliving the moment, she felt heartened to find it warmed her, provided a shield against the cool ocean breeze.

Malibu was awoken by the sound of a guitar and someone singing. The lyrics floated into her mind like a dream.

Who knows how long I've loved you
You know I love you still
Will I wait a lonely lifetime
If you want me to, I will

At first, she kept her eyes clamped, savoring the sound, but then ventured a hazy look through the lashes of one eye. Malibu could make out an old man. He had a beard that ran past his chest and wore a brown, floppy hat. Could it be Kenny? No, Kenny was clean-shaven. Her one eye sharpened its focus and she noticed this guitar-playing man was also toothless. A silver loop pierced one side of his nose. As he strummed the guitar, Malibu saw his right hand was inked with the image of an eye. Malibu's nose twitched and she caught a whiff of a faint pissy smell. The man continued to sing, his voice deep and sonorous.

For if I ever saw you
I didn't catch your name
But it never really mattered
I will always feel the same

Malibu sat up and rubbed the sleep out of her eyes and listened to the old man play the song. When he finished, Malibu said, "I love that tune."

"I know. I played it for you."

"You did?"

"I can feel you. You can feel me too. Am I right?"

She did feel something drift off the man, although its exact nature was a mystery. The emotion seemed to get diluted in the breeze, or maybe it was too complex to decipher on an hour's worth of sleep. Whatever. The whole psionic thing was a cluster.

Two cable car conductors arrived and prepared the car to move by spinning it on the turntable. Sunlight, which had been dim just a moment before, began to filter in more strongly. A half a dozen people noiselessly arrived, prepared to launch.

The old man with the floppy hat looked at Malibu. "Give me some shekels and I'll play another tune for you." So the whole mystic routine was really just a ploy to drum up business. He nodded downward, indicating an empty tin can. Malibu found a shekel inside her leather jacket, sat up and leaned over and dropped it into the can. The man nodded a thank you and started playing. His fingers moved frantically. Malibu looked at the eye on his hand and the eye looked back.

When I get to the bottom I go back to the top of the slide
Where I stop and I turn and I go for a ride
Till I get to the bottom and I see you again

"No, no," Malibu said, and jumped off the bench.

Yes! the voice in her head hollered.

Malibu took an assertive step toward the man. "I don't want to hear that. It's too early. Can't you play something else, something a bit more soothing?"

The man didn't stop. His eyes rolled into the back of his head and he kept strumming and singing, his voice piercing through the clang of the cable car bell.

"All aboard," one of the conductors said, and the people milling about climbed onto the car. Malibu hopped onboard as well, standing on the outside of the car gripping a handrail, happy to leave "Helter Skelter" behind.

As the car climbed up Hyde Street, it passed a few blocks from where she had burned the cottage. Malibu glanced in that direction, but saw no signs of smoke or fire trucks or commotion. She looked the other way toward the Golden Gate Bridge. On the opposite side of the bridge was an enormous wall of fog. It appeared poised to flow over the bay and storm into the city. But the fog was stopped in its tracks, held back by an invisible force field. Suddenly, everything felt wrong.

When the cable car eased to its final stop at the turntable at the end of Powell Street, Malibu stepped off the platform where she had been white-knuckling the handrail and plunged into a throng of people. She felt disoriented, so she stood on the sidewalk and tried to center herself, to calm her mind. It would be interesting to imagine how a director would choose to film this moment. Naturally, she'd start with a high-angle shot, the camera positioned in the sky, but low enough so viewers could make out Malibu centered in a sea of indecipherable people. She would look small and vulnerable. Once that setting was established, the director would abruptly jump to a super tight close-up of Malibu's face, her eyes holding a vacant and confused and fearful expression. The camera would spin around Malibu, moving faster and faster, blurring the image and distorting perceptions, until it cut to a vast blackness.

VIC AND THE PELICAN

Despite the winks she'd caught on the bench, Malibu was still tired, and she could hear her bed calling to her. Her stomach was speaking as well, howling for food. Did she eat dinner last night? Malibu couldn't remember. The previous night felt like it had happened weeks ago. But as she thought back on the flow of events, she decided that after shopping for her black arsonist outfit she had been so amped she neglected to eat.

Next stop: Vic's.

The joint was hopping. It was so crowded, Malibu couldn't get one of her standard booths and was seated at a two-chair table right next to the kitchen. She ordered a veggie omelet, home fries, and an English muffin. Not wanting to be juiced with caffeine, she skipped the coffee and ordered OJ. When the food arrived, it was warm and perfect and Malibu wolfed it down. As she polished off the orange juice, Vic walked through the kitchen doorway. He looked directly at Malibu, his eyes bloodshot and bulging out of their sockets more pronouncedly than normal. Despite his haggard expression, Malibu was struck by what felt like a jet stream of happiness rushing from Vic to her. The feeling was so powerful that it lifted her spirits.

As Vic approached, Malibu asked, "Did you just relive a particularly happy memory?" Malibu felt Vic's mood shift. It was considered a social faux pas to ask people about their Memory Station experiences, and it felt like Vic had dropped an emotional wall between them. Malibu quickly changed the subject. "Interesting shirt," she said. As she spoke, she felt something grumble inside her, felt it boil her blood.

Vic glanced down at his white Hawaiian shirt, which was covered with pelicans. Malibu had a third-eye insight that told her it could not be an accident Vic wore a pelican shirt that day. It felt like reality was being sucked out of her.

"You know, I just learned that pelicans cannot be trained," she said.

Malibu felt Vic's mood shift again; her groggy state seemed to bolster her psionic powers. Vic's emotional wall crumbled and was replaced by what felt like a brewing mass of dark clouds.

"May I sit?"

Malibu nodded and Vic pulled out a chair.

"I used to live with a pelican," he said.

"Where was that?"

"Across the bay—Sausalito. I had a houseboat. I loved that houseboat. For years I lived alone, which I preferred. I was drawn to the lifestyle. It felt nomadic, romantic. But after I had been there maybe a dozen years, my father died. Mom was still alive and she couldn't stand to be alone. So being a dutiful son, I let her move in with me."

"Was that nice or did she cramp your style?"

"A little of both. The boat was small, but it had two bedrooms so we could separate. Also, I wasn't home that often. I had just opened the restaurant and I spent a lot of time here, working."

"Where does the pelican come into play?" Malibu wasn't

really too interested, but the pull of her bed calling to her had become stronger, and she wanted Vic to get to the point so she could hurry back to her apartment and sleep.

"You really want to know?" Vic glanced around at the crowd in the restaurant wistfully, as if he wished he was mingling and hadn't started with his story. The two of them were stuck with each other.

"Sure."

"We found him, Mom and I, caught in a bear trap. Someone had set the trap in the marshes that run along the shore. Now, obviously you're not going to catch a bear along the San Francisco Bay, so why someone would place a trap there is beyond me. It makes zero sense. Maybe some kids—sadistic motherfuckers—put it there hoping to catch a sea lion. They're lucky a person didn't step into it, or there would have been hell to pay. Anyway, that trap did catch a pelican and it did a real number on it. One wing was damaged, a leg mangled. It was clear the bird couldn't fly or walk. I imagined paddling around in the water would have been an impossible challenge. Hunting for fish would be out of the question. When I saw the bird, my first thought was to drive back to the boat, get my handgun, and put the poor thing out of its misery."

Malibu saw what was coming. "But your mother wouldn't let you do that."

"Bingo. She made me open the trap while she pulled the bird loose. The pelican must have been in shock, because it was real docile in her hands. Together, we carried it back to my pickup truck."

"You carried a living pelican to your car?"

"Sure did. The damn thing was a handful. But it didn't fight. It was as if instinctually it knew we were its only chance for survival. Luckily, I had a pickup truck so I could put it in the bed. Mom sat back there as well, soothing the pitiful thing."

"You brought it back to your boat." The angry voice that lived inside Malibu started to salivate.

Vic nodded and looked suddenly older. "There was a small deck on the boat and we placed the bird down there. Since it couldn't swim, fly, or walk, it was stuck. It was clear to me the bird wasn't going to make it, but Mom wouldn't listen. She fed it fish and convinced herself it would perk up and come back to life."

"Please tell me this has a happy ending," Malibu said, while the voice inside her growled in protest. Ignoring it, Malibu continued, "Your mother had a magic touch. She healed the bird, and like a Phoenix, it rose from the ashes and reentered the wild."

Vic didn't respond to Malibu directly, but kept on with his story. "The pelican only lived with us for two days. On the second night, I heard a growling sound coming from the deck. The noise pulled me out of bed."

Malibu's tongue felt thick in her mouth.

As if he too could read emotions, Vic said, "I can stop."

"We've gone this far. Go ahead."

Vic licked his lips. His eyes got wider and glassy with moisture. "The growling noise got louder and when I climbed the stairs and poked my head out I saw a coyote with its jaws clamped down on the bird's neck. The pelican wasn't resisting, wasn't fighting back. I caught a glimpse of the bird's eye. It didn't look fearful, but more like resigned to its fate. Death comes to all of us and its turn had arrived. Once the coyote got wind of me, it leapt over the side of the boat onto the dock, still carrying the bird in its jaws, and disappeared into darkness."

"That's awful," Malibu said, as her inner voice cackled with delight.

Vic nodded. "I'm not sure I told the story properly. Maybe I should put on the console and replay that memory."

"I don't think that's a good idea. Some memories are better left unexamined. I'm sorry I brought it up. It seems like the incident had a real impact on you."

Vic waved away her concern, but did not speak.

"So how did your mother take the news?"

Vic shrugged. "I never told her. When she woke up the next morning and the bird was gone, she convinced herself that she had helped to heal it. Mom didn't live much longer, and I let her carry that little lie to the end."

Vic grew quiet. He sat there staring in space, like his mind had drifted off to some distant world. Not wanting to break the spell that had been cast, Malibu didn't ask for the check, but instead gently placed a tall stack of shekels on the table, far more than necessary to cover the cost of her meal. She pushed her chair back, stood, patted Vic on the shoulder, and felt a terrible sadness flutter off him and skitter past her.

Not much later, despite the fact it was morning and a persistent clamoring street noise rose up from outside her apartment, as soon as Malibu changed into her bedtime clothes and her head hit the pillow she was out like a light.

MALIBU HAS A COCKTAIL

MALIBU SLEPT ALL DAY, WAKING UP JUST AFTER FIVE IN the evening. Of course, the first thing that came to mind was Vic's bizarre story. It hadn't been a dream—it had actually occurred—but it had a dreamlike quality in that the longer she was awake, the more the memory of the experience drifted from her mind, until she could barely recall the particulars at all. Besides, maybe it was better to leave the past in the past. Or at least compartmentalize it. Malibu pictured herself gathering up the memory, dropping it inside a large box, and clamping a lid shut.

Her mind shifted to a more prosaic topic—getting paid for burning the cottage. Max had told her, "Come to madam's home and she will compensate you," but no concrete timetable had been established. Malibu couldn't call Max and make arrangements. For starters, she didn't have his phone number. And even if she had, she had limited access to a telephone. Like the Internet, all cell phones had been outlawed years before. So Malibu decided to just go over to Luciana's house unannounced.

After a quick shower, she slipped into a pair of baggy jeans and her go-to UC Santa Cruz sweatshirt. As she pulled the sweatshirt over her head, she remembered a comment her mother would often say: "It doesn't matter what you wear, Malibu. You would look good in an empty potato sack." She missed her mom. She thought of the flowers her mother would paint, their weekly trips to the painting class. The painted flowers bloomed in her mind and she grew melancholy, so she imagined herself gathering the flowers in a bundle, dropping them inside the memory box she'd just created, and clamping the lid down again. Only this time, she took a skeleton key and locked the box. Maybe she'd unlock it at some point, maybe with a Memory Station or maybe in a more organic way, but not now, not tonight.

Never, the voice in her head growled. It felt neglected. Sleep hadn't dampened her insanity. If anything, she felt more unhinged.

Malibu went outside through the side exit. It had been nearly twelve hours since she last ate and she was hungry. Best to steer clear of Vic's, at least for a few days, so she walked down Market Street toward the Embarcadero. There was still no fog. The sidewalks held a smattering of people, all walking alone, heads bent down, a morose expression spread across each of their faces.

After a block or so, Malibu went into a small bar and sat at the counter. The place was dark and nearly empty with only a couple sitting in the back holding hands and talking in hushed tones. Jazz music was piped in from an unknown source. It was the type of place Malibu imagined Humphrey Bogart would have frequented. Maybe he'd follow Peter Lorre inside.

The bartender was a lantern-jaw type. He wore a suit and tie and must have had a fedora tucked away somewhere. Without even asking, Malibu knew his name was Johnny.

"Johnny, can I have a menu?" she asked as she saddled up to a seat at the bar.

He thrust his jaw out. "Do we know each other?"

"First time we've met."

"How do you know my name?" Malibu felt anger rise off him, as if he was peeved she had been let in on a secret.

"I didn't know your name," she lied, hoping to calm the storm. "I call everyone Johnny, the way some people use dude. I just happened to hit the target this time."

Johnny shrugged and handed her a menu. After a quick review, she ordered a chicken potpie. The food hit the spot. As she was polishing it off, she watched Johnny mix two martinis for the couple in the back. She'd never had a martini, but as she observed him sticking two olives with a toothpick, she got a wild hair.

"Can I have one of those?" she asked, her voice holding a sharp and unexpected tone.

"Are you twenty-one?" asked Johnny.

"Does it matter?"

Johnny shrugged and stuck his chin out further before building one more drink. He pushed the glass across the bar to Malibu, and then carried the other two drinks over to the love-birds. Malibu grabbed the stem and lifted the glass to her mouth. The sides sparkled with condensation. She paused before letting her lips touch the rim, bracing herself for the physical reaction that would inevitably come. In fact, she welcomed the convulsions, viewed them as penance for her misdeeds. She would cleanse her soul with gin.

Only it didn't play out that way.

The convulsions never came. The liquid glided down her throat and landed in her stomach without so much as eliciting a gag. She took another sip; still no negative reaction. Her face didn't turn red and her breathing wasn't labored. She had two more sips and then stopped. As it turned out, she didn't enjoy the taste of the alcohol or the woozy effect it had on her mind. Her senses felt dulled. Still, she greedily drank it down.

Not wanting to examine why the alcohol hadn't affected her like a poison, Malibu dropped some shekels on the counter and hurried out the door.

A commuter car was pulled up along the curb, its back door open, waiting patiently for her. It was number 8,991.

"Where y'all going?" the car's voice asked as Malibu sat in the back and closed the door. It was a woman's voice.

Malibu gave it Luciana's address. "That accent," Malibu asked, "where's it from?"

"New Orleans."

"Are you sure? It sounds more like North Carolina to me."

"'Course I'm sure." The car was indignant. "I've been having this accent for years," it snapped, shutting Malibu up.

Malibu let her mind drift back to the car's number: 8,991. Two nines. Plus, if you multiplied nine by nine hundred and ninety-nine, it comes up 8,991. That's four more nines. What would it take to get nine nines? She'd need a pencil and paper for that.

Number 9, number 9, number 9...

It had been nearly one hundred years since The Beatles burst onto the scene. Would people still care about them in another hundred years? Oh, it was guaranteed. It had been more than one hundred years since Bogey investigated a mysterious black bird from Malta, yet the image of him strutting on screen still occupied her thoughts.

"We're here," the car said, jostling Malibu out of her thoughts.

The gargoyles were still on top of the gateposts. A moon hung overhead and Malibu felt like a wolf should be howling loudly in the distance. She pushed open the gate, climbed the nine steps, and knocked on the door. It didn't take long for the door to creak open and Max to be standing there. He wore a blank expression, but the feeling he gave off was unmistakable. He was happy to see her.

"I'm happy to see you too," Malibu said as she stepped inside the foyer.

"Excuse me?"

"Is Luciana here?"

"She is in the other room. She has been expecting you."

"Of course she has."

As she entered the room, Malibu saw nothing had changed. The stuffed crow was still there, eyeing her. Its beak was as long and sharp as a butcher knife. Luciana was seated in her wing chair, one leg hooked over the other at the knee. She looked at bit younger than before.

"How did it feel?" Luciana asked as Malibu sat down.

Malibu actively tried to access Luciana's emotional state, but came up blank.

"How did what feel?" Malibu asked, although she knew the answer.

"Don't play coy with me. Have you been drinking?"

"I had a martini."

"A martini." Luciana reached over, rang the little bell, and Max arrived at her side. "A brandy for myself. A martini for our guest." She looked at Malibu. "Gin or vodka?"

"I'd really rather not."

"Nonsense. Make it gin," Luciana told Max. "And bring the sack of shekels as well." Once he was gone, Luciana asked, "You liked it, didn't you?"

"I did." The words came out of her mouth before she could stop them. She felt the salivating creature inside and pictured herself wrapped in a straightjacket.

A devilish grin flashed across Luciana's face. "I want to hear everything."

They sat in silence until Max arrived with the drinks. He also had a small canvas bag, which he gave to Malibu. It sat heavily in her hands.

As Malibu fingered the bag, Luciana said, "A toast. To a job well done."

Malibu placed the bag on her lap, lifted her glass and drank. She took a sip without eliciting a cough or gag. Unlike earlier in the evening, her head didn't feel even a teensy bit woozy—at least that's what she thought—although the angry voice that raged inside her did quiet down, if only a bit.

"You picked a cottage." Luciana said with a lift of her eyebrow. It wasn't a question, but a statement.

"I did."

"Why that particular cottage?"

"It wanted to be burned."

The devilish grin on Luciana's face spread even wider, before contracting abruptly. With pursed lips and narrowed eyes, she said, "Delicious. I need to know everything. What did the Engineer give you to burn it?"

"Gasoline."

"You spread it across the floor?"

Malibu nodded.

"Did you use a match or a lighter?"

Malibu told her she used a match, but that wasn't a sufficient amount of detail for Luciana. She instructed Malibu to explain how the match was struck, how it felt when she tossed it, what it looked like as it hovered in the air, how quickly the fire spread across the floor. Once she was satisfied, Luciana allowed Malibu to move on and explain how the wall caught on fire. They lingered at that particular moment for an extended period of time. Luciana pressed Malibu to provide a vivid description of how the heat of the fire felt on Malibu's face.

In that way, slowly and with every detail examined under a

microscope, Luciana coaxed Malibu to explain the entire experience. It was easy to recount the events because they felt so burned into Malibu's memory. Plus, she had watched them at the Memory Station, which in a way was like watching a movie, and it made the task of painting a visual description easier. In fact, Malibu didn't think she was calling to memory the actual events, but instead was replaying what she had viewed on the console.

Of course, the console memories were not pure, but were intermixed with what Malibu was doing at the time she viewed them. She had been masturbating—slowly building to orgasm as she watched the flames engulf the building. Was that experience wordlessly conveyed to Luciana? If Malibu remembered correctly, her first orgasm peaked at the exact moment the fire burst out the cottage's front door and spread across the porch. As she described that particular scene, Malibu read the expression on Luciana's face and could only describe it using one word—elated.

Once Malibu had methodically worked through the entire destruction of the cottage from beginning to end, Luciana made her go back and retell specific portions. It felt similar to the way Malibu constructed one of her abstract paintings, starting with what is objective reality and reshaping it so much it becomes challenging to see how the end product is connected to the original inspiration.

As she spoke, Malibu found herself mindlessly reaching for her martini glass and drinking from it. Although she never noticed him enter the room, Max must have refilled the glass, because somewhere around the third retelling of the porch-on-fire scene, she passed out while still seated in the chair.

BREAKFAST WITH MAX

MALIBU CRACKED HER EYES. IT WAS EARLY IN THE morning, just past sunrise, which she surmised by the gentle sunlight seeping around the edges of window curtains and into the room. She felt an urge to throw up, but pushed it down. Her head ached and her temples throbbed. So the alcohol had hit her after all. She reclosed her eyelids, but the throbbing did not stop.

Where was she?

Despite the throbbing, she opened her eyes and looked around. She was in a bedroom. There was one window. Pressed against a wall was a dresser of drawers, on top of which was what looked like a sack full of shekels. Also pressed against the wall was a wooden chair. Draped across its backrest was a robe, and on the seat, neatly folded, were the clothes Malibu had worn the night before.

Malibu's head rested on a pillow. She was covered by a thick, soft, down comforter. She let her hands slide down her body and found that she was naked. Who had undressed her, Max or Luciana? Neither option was appealing, and Malibu had to again fight the urge to vomit. Hopefully, she had been able to manage the task herself. Sadly, she had no memories starting from the time she had been sitting across from Luciana to now. It was all a blank.

Malibu reclosed her eyes and used her index fingers to press against her temples. While focusing on her breathing, she caught a heavenly whiff of coffee. Pushing the blanket aside, she cautiously moved off the bed and pulled on the robe. Under the chair was a pair of pink, fluffy slippers, which Malibu stuck her feet inside. Her head throbbed worse than before. She cinched the belt of the robe tightly, opened the door, and went in search of what awaited her.

At the top of the stairs, the smell of the coffee grew stronger. Malibu followed its heavenly trail down the staircase and through the room with the stuffed crow toward the door she'd seen Max push through so many times. In the morning light, the house felt different; less ominous and a bit ludicrous. She pushed through the door and entered a kitchen. The cabinets were white, the ceiling painted a light shade of blue, and the marble countertops speckled. The room felt much more modern than the rest of the home that she'd seen.

Standing in front of the stove was Max. He had on his customary suit and tie, but it was protected by a white apron. He held a spatula and looked to be maneuvering some sausages on a sizzling skillet.

"I hope you're hungry," he said without pulling his eyes off the stove to look toward Malibu. "Sausages will be done in just a moment. Pancakes over there." He nodded toward a stack of pancakes on a plate on the island in the center of the room.

"I'd like some coffee," Malibu said.

"Help yourself." Max pointed toward a pot. "Cream, sugar?"

"Cream."

"It's in the fridge."

Malibu found a mug, filled it with joe, and doctored it with half-and-half to her liking. She took a sip, and then a bigger one, and felt the throbbing in her head start to diminish, if only marginally. Max lifted the skillet off the stove, carried it to the island, and dropped the darkly browned sausages onto an empty serving platter. He pulled two plates out of a cabinet, handed one to Malibu, and using serving utensils they each dished up a plateful of pancakes and sausage links and sat at a little round table.

They ate in silence, the food hitting the spot. Malibu had heard the phrase "hangover food," but until that morning had never experienced it before. She lathered the pancakes with syrup, gobbled the food down, and made a couple of trips to the coffeemaker to replenish her cup. As the food and drink gurgled audibly in her stomach, her head cleared and through a strong psionic signal she registered Max's mood. Despite his dour expression, he was happy.

"What happened last night?" she asked.

"You and madam spoke well into the evening. At some point, I believe the alcohol got to be too much for you. I carried you upstairs and left the room."

"Did I get myself in bed?"

"Madam helped."

The response left Malibu feeling queasy.

"Where is madam, I mean Luciana?"

"She's preoccupied."

"That's rather vague. What is she doing?"

"She's preoccupied." The happy feeling Max had before was still there, but it was harder to access, as if a sheet of wax paper had been put in front of it. The sheet stayed in place as Max continued to speak. "She was happy with your work."

"Is that right?" Malibu stuck one more forkful of pancakes into her mouth.

"She'd like you to continue."

"To burn more cottages?"

"Yes."

"I can do that," Malibu said. She gave the response no thought. She knew it was what she wanted to do, what she needed to do.

"Sooner would be better."

Malibu took a paper napkin off a stack on the table and wiped her mouth with it. "I cannot rush it. I need to pick the right one."

"How do you pick it?"

"I feel it."

"You feel it?"

"That's right. It has to want to die."

"I see." Malibu caught a fresh glimmer of Max's mood, which registered as a sense of reproach. It lingered for a moment, and then was pushed aside as he continued to speak. "Madam has another request. She would like you to make a drawing of the cottage you burned."

Malibu became intensely aware that the idea of painting the cottage pleased her. Her mind began to immediately work through some creative possibilities. For some reason, she worked to hide her glee, to keep her face a placid mask, but could sense that Max registered her pleasure. "Creating something like that takes time. I can't just bang it out."

"Isn't that what you do at the club?"

"Yeah," she acknowledged. "So Luciana wants something along those lines, a caricature? If I had more time, I could paint something substantial, better."

"Take all the time you need. You'll be paid, naturally." He pushed his chair back, stood, grabbed the empty plates, and carried them over to the sink.

"Should I tell you when I have selected the next cottage?"

"That won't be necessary. Be sure to visit with the Engineer for supplies. And come back here when the job is completed." After placing the plates in the sink and running some water over them, Max untied his apron, removed it, and placed it on a hook. "I now have some tasks to complete. I trust you can find your own way out."

After slipping back into her jeans and sweatshirt, Malibu decided to walk to her apartment. It was a hike, but also good for head clearing. As she reached the end of a block on top of Pacific Heights, it felt like something grabbed her by the shoulder and tugged her backward. The feeling was so strong that she had to glance over her shoulder to confirm no one had actually grabbed her; it was just a wordless command from an unseen source.

Heeding the plea, Malibu retraced her steps. As she walked, she scanned the block until she spotted a cottage, its façade covered by thick and leafy ivy. A large Victorian had been built on the lot in front of the smaller home, so just part of the cottage was visible from the sidewalk. Malibu walked around the Victorian to get a better view and saw that a tiny, toy-like chimney stuck out of the cottage's roof, the bricks crumbled off the top. She approached the porch, also in disrepair, and saw the front door looked open, if only a crack. Malibu pushed the door wider and peered inside and was hit by a puff of dust. There was just one piece of furniture—a tattered old sofa sat forlorn in the center of the room. Cobwebs clung to the walls. A rat scurried across the floor and ducked into a hole. She also noticed elaborate molding around the floor and ceiling. It was deteriorating, but told of a happier time.

Malibu became conscious of the dormant and thorny feeling inside her wiggling to life. A sickening shiver built inside her, built from a part of her so deeply rooted she hadn't known it existed. Perhaps she should have wanted to try and tamp the thorny feeling down, but that wasn't how she felt. She welcomed its return and was roused to feel it growing stronger.

Another victim. Yes, it wants to die, the thought spoke gently into her ear.

The words caused her senses to sharpen enough that she could just make out another voice—the cottage calling to her, like a whisper on the wind. It did ask for death, euthanasia. Its plea was even stronger than what she had heard from the first cottage on Russian Hill. The desperate request made her feel empowered, like an avenging angel; only she could relieve the home of its misery.

Malibu turned her back on the cottage, restarted her walk home and saw the Golden Gate Bridge far on the horizon. The wall of fog that had been there the day before still hovered underneath, unable to break free and move forward.

SO LONG HANK

As Malibu rounded the corner onto Market Street and started down the last block toward the Chesterfield, she saw an ambulance parked perpendicular to the curb in front of the theater. The lights on top were spinning red. Malibu kicked her stride up a gear, her eyes fixed on the ambulance's blinking lights, and was struck by what felt like a stream of anguish flowing through the theater's open front double doors and washing over her. The emotion was so overwhelming it practically knocked her over, and to continue making progress, she had to lean forward like she was pushing into a fierce wind.

After another dozen steps, an image of a face came into her mind. It was Margarita.

Then there was Margarita, in the flesh. She was walking backward out the theater, through the doors that were under the marquee. With one hand she clutched the silver metal bar at the foot of a rolling hospital stretcher. A man lay prone on the stretcher, a thick tube coming out of his nose. The tube was connected to a plastic bag that was held by a man in blue hospital scrubs who walked alongside the stretcher. Malibu couldn't see the patient's face, but she didn't have to; she knew it was Hank.

A second man in hospital scrubs hurried out the door and past the stretcher to the back of the ambulance, where he opened the doors. He and his partner pushed the stretcher downward and its legs collapsed like an accordion. Bending at the knees, they lifted the stretcher up and slid it into the back of the ambulance. One of the men climbed inside with Hank, while the other went up front to the passenger seat. Once all the doors were shut, the ambulance drove itself, reversing out of its parking spot and speeding down Market Street, siren blaring, lights flashing. It all seemed a bit unnecessary since there was essentially no traffic, but some routines are hard to shake.

Once it turned a corner and was gone, the area the ambulance had vacated was filled with an eerie silence. The street was lit by a flickering, wind-blown sunlight. Malibu watched Margarita, who still stood at the curb, as she looked down the street where the ambulance had gone. She stood there for a long time, still emitting the powerful flow of anguish that had struck Malibu earlier. Eventually, Margarita turned around. When she saw Malibu standing there, she did not seem surprised.

"It's Hank," she said. Her face looked mournful and downcast, as if gravity was working extra hard to pull it down.

Malibu nodded.

"He's going to die."

Malibu stayed quiet, not knowing what to say because she knew Margarita was right.

Margarita turned her head so she was looking back down Market Street, as if searching for the ambulance. When she returned her attention back toward Malibu, her expression had shifted. The mournful expression was replaced by a look of determination. She walked toward the theater's entrance and said to Malibu, "Come with me."

A man stood at the cash register, ready to buy a ticket. Either he had arrived after the commotion, or didn't care.

"We're closing for the day," Margarita said. The man stood there for a moment, dumfounded. "I said we're closing." Margarita's voice rang forcefully. The man slumped away, crestfallen.

Margarita marched through the lobby, past the swinging doors, and into the screening room. Malibu followed close behind. Inside, a movie flickered on the screen. It looked like two cheerleaders were being questioned by a police officer, and what would happen next wasn't hard to imagine. As she walked down the aisle, Malibu felt her shoes stick to the floor and she hoped the gooey substance was popcorn butter. Malibu could make out a smattering of men spread around the room; each sat alone. Despite the fact it was before noon, the crowd was rather large.

Once Margarita reached the front of the theater, she barked, "Out. Everybody out." There was a stirring, but nobody moved to leave. "I said, get out. We're closing for the day." There was fire in her voice. "If I have to drag you out of your seats, I will."

That did the trick. Malibu watched as the men left their chairs and filed toward the exit, casting glances over their shoulders at the screen, where one of the cheerleaders was suggestively rubbing the policeman's baton and the other had removed his hat and was whispering in his ear.

The men huddled for a moment in the lobby, eyes blinking, adjusting to the light. They looked stunned. They kept their heads down, casting furtive glances at each.

"Move it," Margarita ordered. She walked from one side of the room to the other and made a pushing movement with her hands, herding the group together and shepherding them out the door. Once on the sidewalk, the men stayed together in a silent cluster, as if they were hoping one of them would pipe up and tell the others what to do next. It was a peculiar sight. Slowly at first, and then quickly, the men peeled off until they were all gone, scattered to the winds.

Margarita closed the front door and locked it. "Hank would be furious at me for shutting the place down. He'd want the money."

"What do you plan to do now?"

Margarita gave Malibu an expression that suggested it was the strangest question she had ever heard. "I'm going to the hospital."

"Of course." Malibu could still sense the anguish and determination rise off Margarita. "What happened?"

Margarita shook her head. "Hank was seated at his usual spot, pushing around those chess pieces and muttering under his breath. You know how he does, just playing a game against himself. I was down at the other end of the counter doing my thing when I heard Hank let loose a peculiar noise. It was part groan, part yell. It was a very disturbing noise. Immediately after the gurgle I heard a thud, like he had fallen off his chair and landed on the ground. I yelled out, "What's wrong, Hank?" and hurried over to where he was. He was spread out on the floor, both hands clutched his chest, and his face had turned red. I knew right then he was going to die, I just knew it. You ever get a feeling like that, like you know what is going to happen or what someone is feeling?" Margarita paused and gave Malibu a chance to respond.

"Uh-huh," Malibu said. Margarita didn't know the half of it.

"Well, I don't know CPR, so I called for an ambulance. They arrived in no time. You saw the rest." Once she finished, Margarita walked into the back room, the same room where Hank and Malibu watched movies. She was only gone briefly before she reemerged wearing a black windbreaker. She pulled something out of the side pocket of her jacket, handed it to Malibu, and said, "This is for you."

"What is it?"

"Looks like a letter."

"From Hank?"

"No. It was delivered here. I imagine they had trouble tracking you down." Margarita extended the letter further. "Here, take it."

Malibu plucked the envelope out of her hand and examined it. It had been addressed to the Stanford Inpatient Facility. The first line read, *Malibu Makimura (patient)*. There was no return address. Malibu had been in the hospital months ago, so yeah, it was a minor miracle it had reached her. She tucked it into the front pocket of her hoodie.

Margarita reached over and squeezed Malibu's shoulder. "I gotta tell ya," she said, "I think you're gonna have to find another place to live."

"Why?"

"This place is run on a shoestring. Truth be told, I think it's a money loser for Hank. He has shekels socked away and I think he keeps it running just to give himself something to do. God knows, if I were in his shoes, I could find something better to do with my time than waste it here, but that's Hank. I know for a fact he can't really afford to keep me on payroll, but he does, bless his heart. Once he dies, this place is going to shut down, your apartment with it."

Malibu stood in silence, absorbing the news.

"I'll see you, love."

Malibu watched as Margarita headed toward the side exit.

MALIBU'S FATHER'S LETTER

Once inside her apartment, Malibu wasted no time kicking off her shoes, flopping down onto her bed, and pulling out the letter Margarita had given her. Without opening it, she knew it was from her father, the letter he mentioned during his recent otherworldly visit. Who else could it be from? She adjusted her pillow so her head was situated just right, used her index finger to slice open the back of the envelope, and pulled a few sheets of paper free. It was yellow, lined, legal-style paper. On the top of the first sheet, her father had drawn a half-dozen or so mushrooms, some with spots, others without. In the middle of the page was a drawing of a dwarf smoking a long, curved pipe. His beard fell to his feet. The text, like the drawings, was written in blue ink. The blocked-lettered handwriting was immediately recognizable. The letter began without salutation or preamble.

I have touched the face of God.

I don't mean this metaphorically. No, it was real. I was able to achieve a state of altered consciousness that allowed me to reach out and touch His face, or Her face, if you prefer. You would prefer that, wouldn't you, Malibu?

Of course, God does not have a physical face like you or I. She is pure love. And when I touched Her face the love coursed through my body, past my physical being, and imbued my essence with a sense of perfect acceptance.

Even now, as I write to you, my beloved daughter, my mind returns to the experience and the sensations float back to me in the shades and colors of a dream. Only it wasn't a dream or a journey of the mind, but two parallel worlds colliding.

All journeys start with a single step. Sometimes that first step needs a trigger, a signal to begin—a starter pistol. The first step for me was taking LSD (but I'll get to that later). The shot that signaled it was time to begin was you being able to access my mind, to read my thoughts. Do you remember that day? I think of it constantly. Have you been able to access the thoughts of others, or am I still the only one? You feel emotions though, right? Do you still think you are crazy? I doubt it. I'm sure now you know better.

I have so many questions, Malibu, and I am only partway through my journey of discovery.

Now the first step, like I said, was to take LSD. I had never tripped before. Hell, outside of a hit or two of pot in college, I had never taken any drug. But as a teenager, I remember reading about the people who had experimented with the drug during the 1960s, how they had determined it delivered a mystical experience that allowed them to expand their consciousness and move beyond the confines of their physical bodies, to prove that death itself was an illusion.

Malibu, I started taking the drug to get closer to you. You know that, right?

My colleague at the university who scored the drug for me told me I needed a guru, someone to guide me through the process. I didn't take his advice. But the universe has a way of directing you toward what you need, and it directed me toward Annika. You remember her, don't you dear? Of course you do. She's unforgettable. Do you still look for the number nine? I ask so many questions when I meant this letter as a way to give answers, to let you know what I have been doing, why I left your mother, why I left you.

Annika became my guide. She instructed me to take a step back, to put away the LSD (for now) and to begin my journey with psilocybin mushrooms. She grew them herself in a little greenhouse, fertilized by the dung of a Tibetan goat. At first, we started with just three grams, eating the mushroom cap and washing it down with a wafer of chocolate. Over time, we increased the dosage. After each trip, Annika and I would review the experience, and she would help me to decipher a deeper meaning and instruct me on how to go further the next time. Once we reached the limits of what the mushrooms could deliver, we moved on to LSD. I began to trip on a nearly daily basis. During these trips, Malibu, I tried to reach my mind out to yours. Not to let you read my thoughts, but to give me access into yours. I made no progress. That door, I know now, is permanently closed to me.

Naturally, Annika and I became lovers. It had been decades since I'd slept with a woman besides your mother, and the physical pleasure was profound, but not nearly as profound as the sensations of the mind and spirit. It was a transcendental experience. I would not have reached God's face without having sex with Annika. I imagine you are cringing reading this (no child wants to read about their parent's sex life). But I am a sexual being.

I hope to tell you more about my mystical journey later. Just know that it continues and it is all designed to bring us— you and me—closer together.

I also want to let you know how sorry I was to learn about your mother. It must be natural to assign some of the blame for her death to me. I reject that. We each choose our own paths. We each have the power to control our thoughts. Still, I loved your mother very much. I still do. We had our time together. It brought us you! It was beautiful, but that time passed. Still, I can feel her presence, and I hope she has found peace.

Why are you in the hospital? Please tell me you're not considering following the path your mother blazed. My heart could not take it. Carve your own path.

Yes, Malibu, I keep tabs on you. I'll tell you, its not easy. No one readily gives out information about someone being admitted to a mental institution. But with enough shekels, you can get what you need. So although I may not be able to reach you through a metaphysical realm, I do have the resources to track you in the physical world.

Do not kid yourself. You're always being watched. Not by me—that's sporadic, at best—but by others. You know that, don't you Malibu? It's a different world than the one I grew up in. We had access to all accumulated knowledge in the palm of our hands. That was taken away. The cameras that populated every street corner were removed as well. Still, I can't prove it, but I imagine the anonymity we were promised is an illusion. I'm sure drones have replaced the street cameras; drones that fly so high we can't see them, that are so quiet our ears can't hear them. And we cannot hide in our minds either, not in a world where our memories can be accessed through the hand of a Union Member. Not when those memories can be stored and dissected.

Annika and I have tried to escape it all by moving to the desert. Can we really escape the drones in the desert? Probably not, but it's a beautiful dream, isn't it?

This letter has not turned out exactly as I hoped. My

mind, once so rigidly structured—the mind of a trained scientist—now travels along a winding and unwieldy path.

Annika is calling me. We are going to our cactus garden, where we'll meditate. Later, we'll trip. Annika wants to know if you are looking for the number nine.

I love you, my love.

-Dad.

Malibu read the letter three times. Each time she finished, she had to stifle the urge to puke in her mouth. She was about to go through it a fourth time when her eye was drawn to this line: *Annika wants to know if you are looking for the number nine.*

Her mind focused there because she did not want to consider everything else her father had written.

Of course, she had been looking for the number nine; she had bought into Eagle Feather's mystical mumbo jumbo. Her father was trapped in the velvet grip of a vaginal cuff, which helped explain why he was so ready to follow the teachings of his guru. But what was Malibu's excuse? Why was she so ready to believe?

Still, it was true; she had found the number nine everywhere she'd looked. But she was looking for it, that was the point. Wasn't it? Malibu considered running a test. She could start to look for the number eight and see if it popped up everywhere. Malibu discarded the idea almost as soon as it came to mind. There were bigger fish to fry.

Malibu refolded the letter and placed it on her chest. She closed her eyes and let her mind drift. It flowed through the strange path she had followed over the past year, stopping on a few key milestones to reexamine what had occurred. Two of those milestones were the deaths of her mother and Hank. She mulled for a time over the permanence of death. Was it really permanent?

Eventually, her thoughts wandered back to her father. They stayed there for a time, the image of his handsome face fixed in her mind. That image filled her with conflicting emotions: love and rage. Those feelings battled for ownership of Malibu's soul. Neither won. She simply grabbed them, so to speak, held them for a time, before releasing them to the air. As the emotions drifted away, the image of her father's face began to fade as well, until it had completely dissolved and was replaced by darkness.

The darkness lasted for a time, until it too was replaced. The image that appeared in Malibu's mind's eye was of the cottage she had seen earlier that day. She could hear it as well—hear it pleading to be burned.

MALIBU BURNS A SECOND COTTAGE

THAT EVENING, MALIBU STOOD ON MARKET STREET AND watched a commuter car approach. As it pulled to the curb, it became clear that the number nine was stenciled in black ink on the back passenger door. The number was extra large, over two feet high. It was so big, it looked to be pulsating. Sometimes you just have to shake your head. Malibu hesitated for a moment before seizing the handle, opening the door, and plopping down on the back seat.

"Fisherman's Wharf," she said as she dropped two shekels into the coin slot.

The car had a thick Parisian accent and spit back a surly response, which Malibu ignored. Her mind was still locked on the cottage, where it had been focused for hours. It was like the home's voice was carried in the wind, a siren song that irresistibly pulled her toward it.

"Get out. Now!" the car barked when they arrived at Malibu's destination. There was venom in its voice, as if it was working extra hard to be ill tempered. Malibu thought the programming felt a bit overwrought, but appreciated the theater.

As Malibu walked toward the Engineer's lair, she could see

the Golden Gate Bridge on the edge of the horizon. The sun had started to set and the bridge glowed in the twilight. Damn if that wall of fog wasn't still there, bottled up and just aching to burst through. Malibu imagined sticking an enormous knife into it, like is done with a bottle of ketchup to break the bottleneck. Just then, the front of a cargo ship broke through the fog directly in the center between the bridge's two towers. Multicolored containers were stacked six rows high and sixteen rows wide. Malibu stopped walking and watched the ship glide under the bridge until it was entirely inside the bay. Tufts of fog clung to the sides and back of the ship and as it motored to the city, but the seal was broken, and the fog burst free and rushed forward until soon it encased the cargo ship so thoroughly it was again no longer visible. The fog rolled over the top of the water and marched like an invading army toward the city. Even though the fog was still in the distance, the air around Malibu started to noticeably chill.

Malibu zipped her jacket up to the chin as she hurried along the wooden planks, not stopping again until she reached the old bookshop. There were only a dozen or so pelicans on the roof, and when Malibu arrived half of them took flight and headed toward the approaching wall of fog.

Malibu opened the door and went inside.

They were all there, sans the pelican—the Engineer, Scott and Toby, Beavis and Butthead. The two Dobermans bared their teeth and growled and walked threateningly toward Malibu, fur bristling. But as they neared and no doubt caught a whiff of her familiar scent, their demeanor softened. One even licked her extended hand.

Scott and Toby were on opposite sides of the room. They appeared to be dusting the books with white hand towels. One robot stood on the ground, the other on a short stepladder so he could reach the top shelf. They each turned their head toward Malibu, gave her a nod and a smile, and got back down to work.

The Engineer stood at the back of the room near the picture window. His back was to Malibu and it looked like he was staring out at the fog that was rapidly approaching. The twilight would only last a few minutes longer before it was overtaken by the blackness of night.

"Tell me about it," he said to Malibu without turning to face her, his voice booming.

"It wants to be burned."

"Just like the other?"

"More so." The voice inside her howled with delight.

The Engineer turned to face her, and as he did, Malibu could feel a strand of zeros and ones flow from him to her, as if his mind was frantically working to solve a difficult calculus problem. His mental processing was so machinelike, Malibu felt for a moment that he was a machine. For a comparison, she glanced first at Scott and then at Toby—both of who were still busily wiping down the shelves—registered nothing, and looked back at the Engineer, this time picking up a hint of humanity.

"More so, you say," said the Engineer as he stepped closer to Malibu. He was dressed as nattily as before, except this time he had a pink scarf. He still walked with the stiff manner of a military man. "Can you describe it to me?"

Malibu did—the ivy on the façade, the small chimney, the crumbling molding. She even provided a quick description of the Victorian home that partially blocked the cottage from the street. She wrapped up by saying, "I'm figuring another canister of gasoline should do the trick."

The Engineer frowned. With the fingers of his right hand, he rubbed his beard. Malibu could sense the strands of binary code that still streamed from his mind begin to slow their progression, until they stopped completely, as if he had landed on the solution to the problem he had been calculating.

"Not for this job." The Engineer looked to his left. "Toby," he said, "get me two charges, the small ones with timers." Toby stopped cleaning and went in search of the items. The Engineer turned his gaze to the right. "Scott, we'll need a spray can." Scott went in search of that.

The wait wasn't long. The two robots arrived at the Engineer's side at the same time and handed him the requested items. They each turned toward Malibu, offered a nod, and returned to their stations. The Engineer waited until they were back in place and then handed one of the canisters to Malibu.

"I spray the house with this?" she asked.

"That's right. We developed a highly flammable chemical compound. It sprays out a foamy substance that will seep into the wood." He handed two small devices to Malibu. "Once you've finished spraying, place these at opposite ends of the home. You can set the timers to go off later—a few minutes or up to an hour." He showed her how the digital timers worked.

Malibu put the spray can inside the breast pocket of her leather jacket and stuffed the two chargers into the side pockets, zipping them shut. "You can help with my memory again," she said, less a question than a statement.

"I'm always here."

Outside the Engineer's den it was dark, and made even darker by the fact the fog had fully encased the area. It was so thick, light from the lampposts on the pier couldn't penetrate it. Malibu carefully made her way back to the street as large blocks of fog blew past her. The chill caused her skin to prickle.

The commuter car that had dropped her off—number 9— was parked at the curb, as if it had never left.

"Did you wait for me?" Malibu asked as soon as she was situated in the back seat.

"No," the car spit out with its surly accent. "I wait for no one."

"Whatever." Malibu supplied it with a street corner four blocks from the cottage. It was safer not to ride all the way there. The car pulled away from the curb, still prattling on, miffed that Malibu thought it was at her beck and call. Wanting to shut it up, she asked, "Can you play some music?"

"Of course I can play some music," the car huffed. "My database is nearly bottomless. Can I play some music? Ha! What would you like to hear?"

"The Beatles."

"But they're so old."

"Not old, classic."

"Suit yourself. You pay you get to pick. Anything in particular?"

"'I Am The Walrus.'"

The music started to stream across the speakers.

"Louder, please."

I'll show her, the car seemed to say, as it cranked the song up so loud the vibrations rattled the doors and shook the seat. Malibu leaned back and let the music flow over her. She was drawn to that particular tune because it was filled with such vivid and bizarre imaginary. It also seemed to suggest a deeper meaning. No doubt over the years it had been dissected countless times, reexamined from every angle. Although John Lennon himself didn't play along. He's recorded as saying, "I was just having fun with words. It was literally a nonsense song. You just take words, stick them together, and see if they have any meaning."

When the song finished, Malibu asked the car, "What do you think it means?"

"What does what mean?"

"The song that just played."

"It sounds nonsensical. Not even music, if you ask me."

"Play it again," she said. "And louder, please."

The song, now earsplittingly loud, only made it halfway through before they arrived at the intersection Malibu had requested. As soon as she was outside and shut the door, car number 9 sped away, its back tires leaving thick black marks on the pavement, as if it couldn't race away from Malibu quickly enough.

The car had dropped her partway up a hill that started in Cow Hollow and climbed steeply up to Pacific Heights. It was so steep, each step was a strain. The exertion caused sweat to build on her neck, which was immediately cooled by the obscenely thick fog and sparked a shiver that ran down her spine all the way to her lower back. When she finally reached the sidewalk in front of the cottage, Malibu was so winded, she had to bend over and grab her knees to steady herself.

Once she'd caught her breadth, Malibu pulled herself upright and looked toward the cottage. The fog diluted its image, but she felt it, felt it calling to her. As she advanced toward the home, it began to crystalize through the fog, as if a director of cinematography had instructed a cameraman to bring it slowly into focus. First, she saw the leafy green ivy, then the porch and then the chimney, and then it all became clear. Turning her head, Malibu saw lights on inside the Victorian and she heard people moving inside. She thought she could make out the happy shrieks of young children playing. That complicated the situation, but not enough to prevent her from proceeding, not even enough to slow her forward progress.

Malibu stopped when she reached the cottage's outer boundary. She looked upward, remembering what her father had written about drones spying on your every move, and was relieved the fog was so thick.

She pulled her head back down and continued, over the

porch, through the door, inside the home. The cottage's mood had taken a turn, so that it now gave off an air of giddiness. The sensation was overpowering, giving Malibu a jolt of energy she allowed herself to bask in, but only for a few moments before pressing on. She had a job to do and couldn't be distracted. She unzipped her jacket and removed the aerosol can. She pushed down the nozzle once, shooting out a stream of white foam. She methodically worked her way around the room, spraying all four walls and even large portions of the hardwood floor, watching with pleasure as the foam clung to the wood and seeped inside. Once the room was properly coated, Malibu placed the aerosol can on the floor; it was better for it to be destroyed in the blaze then for her to find a place to dispose of it later. She took the two charges out of her side pockets and placed then on opposite sides of the room, setting the timers for three minutes. She didn't want to have to wait long. Once they were set, she hurried out the door. Because the fog was so thick, Malibu couldn't go far, not if she wanted to see the show, so she stopped on the sidewalk.

The three minutes took an eternity to tick by. Time felt like a dream. The noise of the laughing children inside the Victorian grew louder, as did the giddy, wordless appeal for death from the cottage. These sounds and sensations mixed together and flowed through Malibu in an unsettling way. Try as she might, Malibu couldn't maintain her sense of detachment, and she shook as she became overwhelmed by the conflicting sensations.

The charges went off with more force than Malibu had anticipated. The explosion was so loud it caused a ringing in Malibu's ears. The ground shook. The front of the cottage was completely obliterated, and shards of glass flew upward and sprinkled like grains of sand around her feet. What remained of the small home was encased in flames, burning so brightly that despite the dense fog Malibu was able to cross the street and still watch it burn.

After the explosion there were a few moments of loud silence. It was filled by horrified shrieks from inside the Victorian. More lights turned on in the house, but no one emerged through the doors, no doubt cowering inside.

Sirens wailed, louder than with the first cottage, and echoed toward where Malibu stood. Time was short.

Malibu tried to reach out to the home, to hear its voice, but it was gone, the flames had nearly consumed it. If there was a way to reach it on the other side, Malibu didn't know how. She felt the dark and murky presence that lived inside her pulsate with energy.

The shrieks inside the Victorian had turned to mournful wails. The sirens grew closer, felt like they were on top of her. Time to go.

No, let's watch, the voice inside her demanded.

"No," she said.

No, it replied, mocking her.

She tried to move but couldn't, her feet held firmly to the ground, as if two large claws had grabbed them from underneath and held her in place. The sirens now sounded like they were right around the corner. With a violent burst of energy, Malibu lifted her foot and moved forward, breaking whatever spell she had been cast under.

As Malibu hurried down the sidewalk, she looked over her shoulder hoping to make out the last remnants of the smoldering cottage, but it had been swallowed up by fog.

She pointed herself toward Luciana's home. Moving quickly and taking extra long strides, she retraced her steps from the day before, up a hill, down a steep slope, past the mansions on the crest of Pacific Heights, left and right and left again, until she reached 36 Pacific Avenue. Her heart beat double time, beat with such force it felt like it might burst through her chest cavity. The voice inside her screamed with delirious delight, both frightening and rejuvenating her. The gargoyles on the gateposts glared down at her. Slowing her stride, Malibu pushed through the gate, eased up the nine steps, grabbed the doorknocker, and rapped on the door once, twice... on the third rap, the door swung open. Max stood there, unsmiling, decked out in a smart suit. Malibu didn't wait to be asked to come inside, but barged right into the foyer. As she brushed past Max, she could feel he was happy to see her—he was always happy to see her.

He hid that happiness in the tone of his voice. "Come right in," he said sarcastically. He shut the front door and turned to face Malibu. "You look a bit frazzled."

"Is Luciana here?"

"We weren't expecting you."

"Is she here?"

"Luciana is preoccupied."

"Yes, but this is urgent. I completed another job and I would like to get paid." Malibu glanced up the staircase to the second floor, half expecting Luciana to be leering down from the railing. She felt intoxicated and not completely in control of her actions.

"Did you hear me?" Malibu heard Max say, his voice pulling her mind back.

"I'm sorry."

"I said, you are welcome to wait for madam. Could I get you something to drink? Another martini, perhaps?"

"No, no martini. Could I get a glass of water with ice cubes?"

"Of course. Why don't you take a seat near the fireplace."

"In the room with the stuffed crow?"

Max nodded.

"I'd rather just wait here, if that's okay."

"Suit yourself."

Once Max was gone, Malibu noticed the light from the crystal chandelier was particularly bright. It glowed in the room like they were under the midday sun. She scanned the front wall and spotted a dimmer switch. She toggled the switch down until it felt closer to dusk. With that done, she decided she would drink the water and go to the Memory Station in Chinatown. Payment could wait. She was itching to relive the scene from tonight.

If Max noticed the change in illumination he didn't let on as he handed Malibu a glass full of water. The ice cubes rattled as she lifted the glass to her mouth and sipped.

"Are you sure I can't convince you to wait in the other room? Madam won't be much longer."

"What's she doing? Starring at her portrait in the attic?"

"Excuse me?"

"Nevermind." Another sip. The water chilled her throat as it flowed down. "I can come back tomorrow."

"We have a memory console," Max said, as if reading her mind.

"You do?" Her heartbeat had slowed, but she could still feel it thump against her chest.

"You're welcome to use it."

"Where is it?"

"Right this way." Max led her through the doorless entryway opposite the room with the stuffed crow, down a narrow hallway until they reached a closed door, which Max opened and walked inside. It was a mid-sized room with thick shag carpet. The only furniture was a leather recliner and console, both of which looked top-of-the-line. There was one piece of artwork hanging on the wall. Malibu recognized the bent nose, the split face, the exaggerate lips, and leopard spots that danced all around. It was the portrait of Max she had drawn at the Kit Kat Club. It had been framed.

Spotting where Malibu's eyes were directed, Max said, "I had it framed. I'm quite drawn to it."

"I'm touched, Max."

"I catch myself coming in here to look at it."

"Do you like to trip, Max, to relive your memories?"

"No. I'm a decidedly infrequent traveler. I prefer to live in the moment, keep the past in the past. Or at least let my memories remain as they are."

"Smart. When you have tripped, what do you reexamine?"

Max shook his head, shutting down the line of questioning immediately. "That is private. We're all still allowed our thoughts, at least for the time being." He smiled, and Malibu could again sense he was happy she was there. "I trust you can figure out how to run the device."

"I'm a pro," she said.

Max offered up his patented bow at the waist before exiting, closing the door behind him.

Malibu wasted no time positioning herself on the recliner, pulling the console over her head, and firing up her still-fresh memory of the cottage. For some unknown reason, she chose to observe the experience from the perspective of the Victorian house, as if she were one of the laughing children inside the home spying on the scene. She could feel the fog wrap around her. She fast-forwarded a bit until she was holding the aerosol can in her hand.

While watching the memory unfold, she unsnapped the top button of her leather pants, just as she had done before, pushed them down far enough so she could easily slip a hand under the waistband of her panties. She slid a finger inside—wet, ready. As she moved her finger, her mind escaped the memory and drifted back to the present moment. Had she locked the door? Could Max come back into the room?

It mattered, but she didn't want to pause to check.

Returning to the memory, she jumped forward to the moment before the charges went off, when she had stood on the sidewalk. She could hear the children laughing and the cottage's voice fading.

When the explosion hit and shook the ground, she pushed a second finger inside her, cupped them upward. Normally her orgasms came slowly, required build up, but this one was driving toward a peak rapidly.

Malibu rewound the memory to just before the explosion, and as she did, she felt a presence inside the room. The sensation was strong enough to cause her to pause and lift the visor. Standing by the door was Luciana—spiked heels, leopard-print dress. In the dim light, she looked exotic and beautiful and dangerous. Malibu's mind felt a bit feverish, unmoored, but a voice spoke within her: *This is right, this is good. Let her watch. Put on a show.* Luciana leered at Malibu with encouragement. *Continue,* she seemed to say, to demand.

So Malibu did continue, drunk with desire, pulling the visor back into place. *Let her watch,* the voice inside her repeated. Malibu's fingers moved faster, her body quivered, her breathing quickened. She peaked as she rewatched the explosion for a third time. She pulled her hand free and let the sensation flow through her. The vibrations lasted for a minute or so, and as it slowly started to fade, she buttoned her pants and lifted the visor.

Luciana was still there, standing by the door. A wicked, lecherous smile played across her face. Her head was craned back and eyes were manic, like Gloria Swanson in the closing scene in *Sunset Boulevard.* The overwhelming arousal Malibu had felt just moments earlier now completely melted away. But she could feel it percolating inside Luciana, bubbling, as if it were giving her life.

"There is a bathroom around the corner," Luciana said. "Clean up and meet me in the kitchen."

Luciana stood in front of the stove. She cupped a brandy snifter full of brandy in her right hand. Her eyes had lost some of their manic quality, but she still leered at Malibu. Max sat at a stool by the island. On top of the island was a brown leather pouch filled with something.

"Max, give her the shekels," Luciana said, which he proceeded to do.

Malibu took the bag, feeling its bulk in her hands. She felt exposed in the brightly lit room with the white cabinets. She looked at Luciana briefly before letting her eyes drop, unable to meet her stare. "I suppose you want to hear what happened."

With a shake of her head, Luciana said, "That won't be necessary. I've seen enough. You smell like sex and smoke," she snarled.

The comment was meant to sting, but it missed the mark. Surprisingly, Malibu did not feel shame. What she felt instead was edgy buoyancy, a rush. She felt vibrant. She also felt a tinge of disappointment Luciana wouldn't allow her to relive the experience of burning the home again.

"It's late and I am going to turn in," Luciana said. She walked over to where Max sat and placed the snifter on top of the island. It was full, looked untouched, as if it were more of a prop than something Luciana was actually drinking. "Max, please show our guest out."

Malibu's mind flashed to the scene earlier that day outside the Chesterfield. The ambulance, Hank on a stretcher, Margarita telling Malibu she was sure Hank would die and the theater would close. She didn't want to go back to her apartment, didn't want to face that scene.

"Would it be all right if I stayed here?"

Luciana's head tilted back again, her eyes opened wider. "You want to stay here?"

Malibu opened her mouth to explain why, but the words got stuck in her throat. She couldn't bring herself to relive the episode with Hank. Instead, she simply said, "If that's okay."

Luciana stood just an arm's length from Malibu. Up close, her lips looked pink and as full as a girl's. She puckered those lips, as if recognizing that's where Malibu's eyes were focused, and said, "Max can help you get situated. Right, Max?" He nodded. "I will leave you two to it then." Luciana took one step toward the door and then stopped. She lowered her head, looked at Malibu and then at Max, and said, "Max, did you ask Malibu to drawing a picture of the cottage, the first one that was burned?"

"I did, madam."

Luciana looked toward Malibu. "Have you started?"

"I haven't had a chance. Is that something you truly want?"

"I don't ask for things I don't want." Luciana shook her head and narrowed her eyes, as if she were glaring at a disrespectful child. "Forget the drawing. I'd like a painting now, something abstract, and with both cottages—the first one and the one you burned tonight. Use your imagination. Can you do that for me?"

"A painting?"

"Yes, dear. A painting. Tap into those feelings of yours." The way she said that word—feelings—left the impression there was something she wasn't saying.

"I can do that."

"Max can show you to our art studio tomorrow. Isn't that right, Max?"

"Yes, madam."

"And for God's sake, take a shower." With that, Luciana whisked her way out the door, the bottom of her dress swishing back and forth behind her.

The nature of the kitchen changed once Luciana was gone. The air actually felt lighter, easier to breathe. Alone with Max, Malibu sensed a different emotion lift off him as well, something she couldn't exactly put a finger on. But his facial expression looked downcast.

"The bed has been turned over since you were last here," he said. "I stacked some bath towels on the chair, added some toilet supplies, and put a few nightgowns into the dresser. I guessed at your size."

"You anticipated I would spend the night again?"

"It was inevitable."

Malibu let the silence linger. The anger that had boiled inside her had dissipated, as if it had turned in early for the night. Surprisingly—or maybe not—she missed it. Where that alien voice came from she couldn't say, but she knew that like a troublesome weed its roots now ran deep. "Okay," she said. "I'm going to call it a night."

BREAKFAST WITH MAX

Malibu woke early the next morning, and after dressing, brushing her teeth and the rest, she joined Max for a hearty breakfast of bagels with cream cheese, coffee, and cantaloupe with prosciutto. The half-and-half was held in a tiny stainless steel bell creamer. There were cloth napkins and crystal glasses were used to hold orange juice. They sat at a round table next to a window that looked out on a garden. The suffocating fog had lifted and morning sunlight coated the plants and flowers. A fresh vase of flowers stood in the middle of the table. As Malibu munched on a particularly juicy piece of cantaloupe, she thought she could get used to this lifestyle. It sure beat living in a homeless tent camp or getting woken by the smell of sour cum. Max was already in his standard Max von Mayerling getup, tie pulled up tight to the neck. Maybe he slept in the outfit. Malibu felt fresh. She had taken a long shower the night before and wore a cotton nightgown that Max had given her. As she started her second cup of coffee, Max told her that Luciana was "preoccupied." Malibu nodded.

After breakfast, Max escorted Malibu to a staircase that led down to a basement. It looked recently redecorated with a fresh coat of orange paint on the walls and newly installed white rubber flooring. High on one ceiling were three rectangular windows that looked out on the same backyard garden Malibu had gazed on during breakfast. In one corner of the room was six-piece sectional sofa, bent into an L-shape. In the center of the room was a blank canvas propped up on a large easel. Next to the canvas was a wooden table with unused painting supplies—brushes, oil paint, and cleaning rags.

Malibu walked over to the table, picked up a brush, and rubbed the bristles across the palm of her hand. "Did you pull all this together last night?" she asked Max.

"Not last night."

"After the previous time I was here?"

"Prior to that."

"Prior to that. When?"

"We've had it here for a while."

"Why?"

"Madam's instructions."

"Madam's instructions. Just waiting here. They say she's a witch."

"Do they?"

"Uh-huh."

Max stayed silent. His face gave off no clues as to what he was thinking and Malibu picked up no emotional cues. What good were psionic powers if they routinely shut off?

"Well, is she?" Malibu asked.

"I don't believe in witches."

"You don't have to believe in something for it to be real."

"Are you a witch?"

Malibu felt her cheeks flush. "No. Why would you..." She trailed off.

"Can you start on the painting today?"

"Sure," Malibu said, happy for a change of subject.

"There is a voice-activated sound system. It also controls the temperature and lighting. It's called Oppenheimer."

Malibu scrunched her forehead and pursed her lips and using a deep voice said, "Now I am become Death, the destroyer of worlds."

"Excuse me?" Max asked, looking confused.

"Nevermind." Malibu placed the brush back down on the table. A thought occurred to her. "I need to see the Engineer."

"You can do so later today. You'll be safe here."

"Do you think Union Members are searching for the person who burned down those two cottages?"

"I don't believe they care."

Malibu suspected he was right. She glanced around the room, getting her bearings. There was only one piece of decoration—a large framed poster from the movie *Vertigo*. It had a red background and the movie title and lead actors' names were spelled out in black letters. In the center of the poster was a black silhouette of James Stewart. Behind him was a white whirlpool, which gave the impression he was spinning out of control. Her mind snapped back to the night she'd spent with Prudence at the movie theater.

Malibu jabbed a thumb toward the poster. "Has that been there a while?"

"No," Max said. "It was added recently."

Well, that was an odd coincidence. "It is one of my favorite movies."

"I see."

"Have you watched it?"

"I have not."

"Would you watch it with me? I love to watch old movies."

"We have a small theater here."

"So that's a yes?"

"It is. I'll bring lunch down later. I'll leave you to your work." Max bowed at the waist and went up the staircase.

Once she was alone, Malibu said, "Oppenheimer?"

"Yes." Malibu thought she detected the hint of a New York accent.

"Are you programmed to answer questions or just manage the lights and the stereo?"

"I can answer some questions. I have AI functionality and access to a semi-broad database. Do you have a question?"

"What can you tell me about Luciana?"

"The woman who owns the home you are in now?"

"Yes."

"I don't have any information on Luciana. Would you like to hear some music?"

"Sure. Can you play a mix of Billie Eilish and Zero 7? Not too loud. Just a notch above background music."

Soft music filled the room. Malibu pushed up her sleeves and sat on the wooden stool that was positioned in front of the canvas. She picked up a brush and spun it around in her hand. Her mind was busy with thoughts that seemed to smack against the sides of her skull like honeybees locked inside a jar. She mentally focused on each individual thought as she pictured herself unscrewing a jar and letting the bees buzz out the top. She didn't want her conscious mind to be at work; she wanted to tap into something deeper, more meaningful. Did it really work that way? Sometimes Malibu felt that she painted what-ever whim her mind conjured up and then applied meaning to it afterward.

What her mind landed on were pelicans.

She saw them flying and diving for fish in the ocean and heard the peculiar rasping sound they made when they opened their beaks. She could see them packed on the roof of the Engineer's shop and even pictured the pelican Vic and his mother had found caught in a bear trap.

With these thoughts swimming freely between her cerebellum and cerebrum, she dipped the paintbrush she was holding into an open container of gray oil paint and started to paint a pelican on the left edge of the canvas. She didn't paint the entire bird, just its beak and neck. Falling in line in a row behind, it she painted the full bodies of three more pelicans, each a bit smaller than the one that preceded it, giving the impression the birds were positioned further along the horizon. On the right edge of the canvas, she painted four more pelicans, following the same structure she'd used on the left side. Positioned at the end of the two rows, in the exact middle, was one large pelican. The eight pelicans on the sides of the canvas faced sideways so only their profiles were visible, but the larger one in the middle was positioned frontally.

Malibu had a sense what she wanted to do next but was still happy to hear Max's voice float down the stairs and interrupt her.

"Lunch," said Max. Malibu craned her neck so she could see over the top of the canvas and watched Max materialize as he descended the stairs one careful step at a time. He carried a tray over to a coffee table in front of the sectional sofa and placed it down.

"What time is it?" Malibu asked.

"Just past twelve thirty."

"So I've been painting for—"

"Over three hours."

Jesus, was it that long?

Max nodded toward a door near a sidewall. "There's a bathroom, if you want to wash up," he said, before going back up the stairs.

Malibu did wash up, using lots of soap and water and the

ends of her fingernails to scrub the paint off her hands. She took her time making her way over to the tray of food. She stopped to look at the *Vertigo* movie poster, gazed up at the sky through the windows. One thing she didn't do was look at her painting again. She wanted to put it on ice for a while, let her subconscious work on it. After walking around the circumference of the room, Malibu plopped down on the sofa and examined the food Max had brought her. There was a tuna sandwich with cheese, lettuce, and pickles on whole wheat bread, chunks of cantaloupe, a glass of cold milk, and a chocolate chip cookie. It looked like a lunch her mother would have made her.

Two bites into her sandwich—which was excellent, just the right amount of mayo—the music stopped playing and Oppenheimer spoke. "I was able to find some information," he said.

Malibu chewed and swallowed before responding. "Excuse me?"

"You asked me to see what I could find out about Luciana. I was able to get a bit of information."

"You have been searching all this time?"

"No. I found it immediately. My AI is quite robust. I just did not want to bother you. You seemed in the zone, as the saying goes."

"That's considerate, I guess. Well, what did you find?" Malibu took another bite of the sandwich, washed it down with milk.

"Is now a good time?"

"Yes."

"She works for a man named the Chairman."

"Yeah, the Chairman, I know that."

"You do?"

"Uh-huh. Is that all you got?"

"More or less," Oppenheimer admitted, his voice sounding dejected, almost lifelike.

Malibu plopped a piece of cantaloupe into her mouth. "Does the Chairman ask Luciana to do anything peculiar? Is he into burning cottages?"

"No. There is nothing about cottages."

"Where does the Chairman live, in San Francisco?"

"He has a home on top of a hill in Belvedere. It looks out over the Bay. But he spends most of his time on Alcatraz."

"In the casino?"

"That's right. He seems to run his operation out of there."

"Is that all you got?"

"Yeah, more or less," Oppenheimer said, sounding quite colloquial for a computer. "Should I start the music again?"

"No. I'd just like some quiet. Wait."

"Yes?"

"Can Luciana access this conversation?"

"Of course. She owns the home. She owns me."

"Isn't there some type of AI/user confidentiality?" Malibu knew as she said it the idea was ridiculous.

"You have no privacy. No one does. Just get over yourself."

Malibu polished off the rest of her lunch, eating the cookie slowly and savoring the chocolate chunks. Deciding she was done painting for now, she took the tray up the stairs to the kitchen. She considered just leaving it on the island, but decided to wash everything and put all the items away instead.

With that done, she pushed through the swinging door and into the room with the stuffed crow, where she found Luciana and a tall man. They stood in front of the fireplace talking in hushed tones. Really, the man seemed to be doing all the talking as Luciana seemed to hang on his every word.

The man's appearance was striking: he was black, with a light complexion and a shaved head that was abnormally large. His face was pockmarked. He wore a tailored dark suit, a purple shirt, a white tie, and sparkly gold cufflinks. The cufflinks matched a gold hoop earing that dangled from his right earlobe. The whole getup might have looked cartoonish, but the clothes were obviously super pricey and worn with such panache that it worked. The man had flair, a presence.

When Malibu first stepped into the room, Luciana and the man didn't seem to notice her, they were too engaged in whatever the man was pontificating about. But as she observed the scene, the man slowly turned his head in her direction. Luciana did not shift her gaze, her lack of acknowledgement signaling to Malibu that she was not welcome, that she should leave.

Taking the hint, Malibu started for the exit, but was stopped in her tracks by the man's booming voice.

"You. Come here," he ordered.

Malibu did as instructed, skirting around a sofa, sidestepping the cat.

"What's your name?" he asked. He towered over her, must have been six feet seven, easy.

She told him her name.

"She works for me," Luciana said, finally acknowledging her presence. Malibu felt physic bullets shoot from Luciana's eyes and penetrate her skin.

"I'm the Chairman," the man said. He stuck out a hand and they shook. His grip completely swallowed up Malibu's hand. If he squeezed too hard, she was afraid he might crush her bones. He pressed just hard enough to let her know that he could, but released his hold before inflicting any damage.

Malibu felt another volley of bullets fly off Luciana.

"Luciana, ease off," the Chairman said, as if he took could tap into the cosmic energy. Actually, looking at her face, it wasn't hard to glean what she was thinking—no physic powers were necessary.

"So, you're Luciana's new talent," he said.

"I suppose that's right."

"Here," he said, and pulled something out of his pants pocket. He opened his fist and on the palm was a ring. It had a small gold band and a jewel; it looked like an opal. "Take it."

"You carry rings in your pocket?"

"Don't be smart."

"I...I..."

"Take it."

She did.

"It's my calling card. It will let you get into the casino."

Malibu slipped it onto a finger on her right hand. The Chairman turned back toward Luciana, who was still glaring at Malibu, her face more contorted than before. The Chairman said, "Now where were we?"

Malibu took it as a signal to leave and hustled out the front door.

Naturally, a commuter car was parked outside next to the curb, its engine humming. It was a bit spooky.

The passenger side window was down and Malibu poked her head inside. "Are you available?"

"You betcha."

Minnesotan?

"Where ya headed?" the car asked once Malibu was situated.

She opened her mouth planning to tell the car to take her to Fisherman's Wharf, but felt a tugging, a pirouetting in her mind pulling her in a different direction. Something was calling to her. Voices.

Heeding their call, she said, "Can we go to Bernal Heights?"

"Sure thing. Anywhere in particular?"

"Not sure. Can you just drive in that direction and I'll know when I get there?"

"Sure thing."

As they motored along, the voices that were calling to her grew louder and more desperate in her head. She was able to make out four distinct voices.

More that want to die.

Malibu used her thumb to spin the newly acquired ring on her finger. Perhaps the car heard the voices as well, because it drove straight toward them, at least until they got to the corner of Cortland Avenue and Bocana Street, where Malibu had to say, "Stop here. Pull over to the curb." As she stepped out the door, she said, "Can you wait?"

"You betcha. The meter is still running, though."

"Fine, fine."

The sidewalk was empty of people. Flush with a sense of urgency, Malibu jogged down Bocana to the middle of the block, feeling the mournful calling ring louder in her head with each step until she reached what she could feel was the source. There was a lattice wooden fence. She pushed the gate open and walked down a narrow brick pathway past what she imagined was once a richly planted garden but looked like it had suffered years of neglect. At the end of the brick path stood four cottages, tightly packed together. They were all small, likely just one-bedrooms, with brown wooden shingles that looked as if they were struggling to stay attached to the sides of the homes. The glass in all the windows was shattered, and what remained looked like open wounds. An angry-looking cat glared at Malibu and hissed before scurrying away. In three of the homes the front door was gone, while in the fourth it hung on the hinges. No doubt the *Cottage Book* would have labeled them "earthquake shacks." At one time, they would have been extremely desirable, but now they felt so lonely it hurt.

They want to die. Kill them! The words bounced in her head like a chant.

Malibu stood for a few minutes and let her eyes slide from one home to the next. She felt a pitiful sadness circle all around her. The sadness seeped under her skin and burrow into her core.

Kill them, kill them.

She tried to silence the command, but the reverberation was deafening. When it became more than she could take, she turned her back on the scene and walked back to the waiting car.

"Fisherman's Wharf."

"You bet—"

"Betcha. Yeah, yeah." The whole ride there, Malibu could not shake the feeling of the homes. Their sorrowful pleas echoed in her mind, saddening and delighting her in equal measure.

THE ENGINEER, THE BOWERY KING, AND MORPHEUS

"I KNOW WHO YOU REMIND ME OF," MALIBU SAID. THEY were inside the Engineer's shop. Toby and Scott weren't there, but Bevis and Butthead were. The dogs were rigid, on alert, but noticeably more relaxed than Malibu's previous two visits.

"I assume this means the job is complete and you're ready to have your memory washed," the Engineer said, ignoring her comment.

Malibu returned the favor and ignored his question. "The Bowery King. In the John Wick movies. The character played by Laurence Fishburne."

Malibu could feel the zeros and ones start to flow from his mind. The Engineer was processing. "Is Keanu Reeves in those movies?"

"That's right."

"I thought the Fishburne character's name was Morpheus."

"No. You're thinking of *The Matrix*."

"Do you connect everyone you meet to a movie character?"

"No." She thought about it a bit, before repeating. "No. Only if it applies. In your case it does."

The Engineer nodded. "*John Wick*. I've never seen it."

Malibu smiled. "Let me tell you, you're missing out." She

licked her lips, took a deep breath, and was ready to roll into a synopsis of all six movies, but the Engineer cut her off before she could get a word out.

"My time is limited today. Do you need your memory washed?"

"I had planned to, but I think that can wait. I need fresh supplies."

"You've identified another cottage?"

"Four." The mournful wails still resided in the recesses of her brain.

"Really? I expected things to pick up, maybe two a night, but four is a big leap. Are they spread throughout the city?"

"No. They're clumped together. It's a package deal."

A pelican walked in the open back door. It spread its wings and craned its neck. No doubt it was the same one as before, but Malibu couldn't be sure.

She continued. "I was hoping for four aerosol canisters, eight charges, and a bag to carry them in."

The Engineer shook his head. "For starters, you need to erase your memory." The trapdoor to down below opened up, as if the Engineer had thought it to. Toby walked up the stairs with Scott on his heels. "Toby, please take care of her memory."

The robot walked over and stood in front of Malibu. He lifted his left hand. Pinched between his thumb and forefinger he held what looked like a little black rock. It was smooth and shiny. "I'm going to place this on your forehead. It won't hurt."

"Okay."

It felt cold on her skin. Toby held it there for just a moment before saying, "Done. Here." He handed the rocklike thing to her. It felt metallic in the palm of her hand.

"We've been working on miniaturizing the technology," the Engineer said. "You can keep that, and in the future block your cottage sojourns yourself. We programmed the AI so it can identify any cottage-related activity stored inside your brain, even your visit to the four cottages today. You can thank Toby for that innovation."

The robot smiled as Malibu slipped the device into her pocket.

"Scott has been busy as well, haven't you, Scott."

Scott, who was carrying a small leather handbag, said, "Inside are tablets, each the size of a shekel." He put his hand into the bag and pulled out one of the tablets, held it up so Malibu could see. "One side is sticky. Place the sticky side against a smooth surface, press hard, and it will attach." He dropped the tablet back into the open bag and pulled out a thin, rectangular device. "It's a remote control," he said. "Once the tablet is secure, run this over it until you hear a click. Each tablet is encoded with binary code. It will be registered into the device. Later, from a safe distance, you hit the button at the bottom of the device and the tablets you registered will explode."

Scott handed the leather satchel to Malibu.

The Engineer added his two cents. "Two tablets strategically placed is all you'll need to bring down a cottage."

Malibu looked down at the remote control in her hand, spun it around.

"I sense something is wrong," Scott said.

"No. Well. It's just..." Her voice drifted off.

"It's just what?" Scott pressed.

"It's all so mechanical. It's feels like it's lost a bit of humanity. The gasoline was so visceral." She thought back to the first cottage she had burned. The smell of gasoline as she spread it on the wooden floor. The satisfying sensation as the lit match hovered in the air, fell to the ground, ignited the gasoline. She had enjoyed watching how the fire spread slowly. "This feels a bit antiseptic."

Toby walked over from where he stood and said, "The end result is the same. The cottage is destroyed. That's the goal."

"I suppose," Malibu said.

The Engineer chimed in. "It's really about safety. We can't have you coming back here after every cottage is burned."

"You think I'm being watched?"

He nodded. "We all are."

Remembering her father's letter, she asked, "Do you think there are drones in the sky, recording everything?"

"It seems likely."

"Do you think they care?"

"Probably not," the Engineer admitted.

"Then what's the point of erasing my memory if no one cares?"

The Engineer lifted an eyebrow, and with a wry smile said, "It's all risk mitigation."

That didn't satisfy Malibu. She pressed the point. "If everything is captured digitally, then they—whoever they are—know I've been here for supplies, they know I've burned down at least one cottage."

"It seems likely," the Engineer said.

"Yes," Toby added.

"If it's known that I am doing this, why haven't I been stopped?"

"Maybe they want you to burn the cottages?" Scott offered.

That thought took a bit of the fun out of the whole enterprise.

"You seem disappointed," the Engineer said.

"I suppose I am," Malibu said, although she couldn't put her finger on exactly why.

. . .

On the walk from the Engineer's shop, Malibu passed three separate two-member Union Member teams. It was odd to see so many clumped together. In each case, the human ignored Malibu, while the robot kept a laser focus on her. But there was no attempt to stop her or question her. Remembering what the Engineer said, that she tied everyone to a movie character, she dipped into her memory and tried to recall a movie with characters similar to the robots. There were a lot of options to choose from, but none hit the right note.

At the third pair, she stopped walking. If she were a director, how would she film it? The camera would be positioned low, looking up at the robot, so that it looked intimidating, a figure of menacing authority. When the human team member spoke, the camera would stay fixed on the robot's face. Obviously, no easily discernable emotions would register—the face would be placid and unreadable. But maybe not completely, maybe an experienced movie watcher would detect something, a tell that showed what was moving through those circuit boards and processors. What such a viewer would see was disdain, contempt, disbelief that a superior life-form—yes, life-form—was relegated to partnering with a mere humanoid.

"What're you staring at?" the human asked, snapping Malibu back to the moment.

"So sorry," Malibu said.

She looked again at the robot, and for just a blink thought she felt something—not an emotion, exactly, but something. Something had registered. The robot didn't speak, but Malibu had a sense it knew what she was thinking.

Malibu located a commuter car (woman's voice, Mexican accent), which took her to the Chesterfield. The place looked forlorn. The marquee light was off, and the front door was shut.

In the entranceway, a mass of homeless people slept clumped together, snoring loudly. They were covered with shabby blankets and packed so tightly it was impossible to make out how many individual people there were. Malibu gave them a wide berth as she made her way to the side entrance. She half expected her key to no longer work, but when she turned it in the chamber she felt the plates move.

She started to climb the stairs, but two steps up, she reversed course and moved toward the theater instead. Through the door and inside lobby it was quiet.Malibu walked over to the front of the theater. As she approached the cash register, she saw Margarita step through the door to the back room. The crestfallen look on the older woman's face told Malibu all she needed to know.

"Is he..." Malibu let the sentence trail off.

Margarita didn't speak. Her eyes softened, filled with tears.

"I'm sorry," Malibu said. She could feel the anguish roll off Margarita. It was a mixture of sadness and fear. "When did it happen?"

"He passed last night. Made it to the hospital and died there. Peaceful. Accepting."

"What are you going to do?"

"I have family. A brother. We don't get along, but he said I could stay with his family until I can land something new. Without the paycheck from here, I can't afford my apartment."

"I'm sorry."

Her eyes narrowed, looked worried. "What are you going to do? You have any family?"

"No, no family."

"I'd ask you to move in with my brother, but he wouldn't have it. He barely took me. You lived in the homeless tent camp before, right?"

"I'm not moving back to the tent city."

"I hope not."

"I have a place to stay." It had never been formally agreed upon, but Malibu knew she would be welcome to move into Luciana's home.

"That right? You still workin' at that club?"

"No. That dried up."

A pregnant silence filled the space between them. Both women let the silence build until it became uncomfortable.

Margarita was the one to break it. She wagged a finger at Malibu. "There is something different about you. I can't put my finger on it, but there's something." She paused, let the silence fill the space between them again, waited. Gave Malibu a chance to respond. Malibu stayed mum. "I was there when Hank passed. I saw him slip away to the other side. I could feel his soul go. When you're that close to someone passing, I think it touches you, gives you some insight."

"And you have insight into me?"

"Sure do," she said with a firm nod of her head.

"What do you see?"

"Hank may soon start haunting this theater, but you carry the haunting with you."

"I don't follow."

"You sure about that?" Margarita didn't give Malibu a chance to respond. "You must have a sugar daddy. That's a fancy outfit." She let her eyes run from Malibu's feet up to her head. "Leather jacket, leather pants, fancy boots. And that jacket, that jacket must have cost a few shekels. You didn't make that money drawing portraits."

Malibu managed a smile. "I have a job." In a way it was true, if you considered burning cottages a vocation.

"You hookin'?"

"Excuse me?"

"Are you selling yourself?"

"No, no. No. No sugar daddy. I'm not a prostitute. It's not like that," Malibu added, raising her voice to add emphasis.

Margarita's face took on a faraway expression. "I hope it's not something worse."

"Nothing worse is happening." Was that a lie?

"You promise?"

"Do you want a blood oath?"

Margarita let it drop. She had her own worries. She couldn't afford to expend any more energy fretting over Malibu.

"You need to pack up your things today," said Margarita. "When you're done, drop the key on the counter, over by the popcorn maker."

"I can do that."

"Take care of yourself."

Inside her apartment, Malibu got on her hands and knees and crawled under her bed to retrieve the shoebox stuffed with shekels. She expected it to be gone, stolen, but there it was, still hidden under the blanket. She emptied the coins into the bag the Engineer had given to her. Next, she pulled out a small suitcase, placed it on top of the bed, and neatly filled it with clothes and bathroom supplies. It wasn't much, but would last her until she could use her newly acquired wealth to buy new duds.

She planned to leave everything else there for someone else to deal with, but as she zipped the suitcase shut, she had a sense of something looming over her. It always felt like something was tugging at her these days—feelings, voices—but this sensation felt particularly sharp. Her eyes were pulled upward to the wall and the self-portrait. She focused on the portrait's eyes, which were still staring at the apple. It was too absurdly large to carry to Luciana's home, but she didn't want anyone else to have it. It was too personal. She decided to destroy the canvas. She found a metal coat hanger in the closet and pulled the rounded end straight. But as she stood on the bed, coat hanger in hand ready to gash the canvas, she found she couldn't pull the trigger. Her mind skittered back to the three days she had spent creating the portrait, her hands covered in paint, her mind sparked with inspiration, and found she just couldn't rip her work to shreds. She dropped the hanger and pulled the canvas off the wall. It was bulky, but with effort she clumsily carried it down the stairs and outside to the sidewalk. She propped it against the wall at the edge of the clumped mass of homeless people. Let someone else enjoy it.

Back up the stairs, she gathered the suitcase and leather satchel, went to the lobby where she dropped the key on the counter, and hurried out the side door, not wanting to interact with Margarita again. Once outside, she looked for the portrait but it wasn't where she had left it. Malibu gazed up and down the sidewalk in search of a culprit, but didn't spot anyone struggling to carry a large canvas. She tried to imagine it hanging on the wall of someone's home. That was the thing with art: you spend so much time and effort creating it, but once its out in the world you no longer own it.

"Sure thing, dude. Wherever you want to go." The commuter car had a Southern California, surfer dude accent. It drove halfway down the block before slowing to a crawl and asking, "Where are we going again?"

"Really?" said Malibu. She felt all the fake accents were getting to be a bit much. Couldn't she just ride in peace?

"Sorry, dude. The locale slipped my mind."

Malibu gave it the address for Luciana's home again.

"Right, dude, right," the car said, and drove the rest of the way without further incident.

Max answered the door after just one knock, as if he had been waiting on the other side for Malibu's arrival.

"Are you planning to move in?" he asked as he looked down at the suitcase Malibu wheeled through the entrance and into the foyer.

"Is that a problem?"

"No. I'm sure madam would welcome your company."

"Where is Luciana?"

"She's—"

"Preoccupied," Malibu broke in.

"That's right." Max reached down to grab the suitcase. Malibu opened her mouth to say she had it, but bit her lip and decided to let Max lug it up the stairs.

When they reached the top of the staircase, she said, "Thanks for the help. I can take it from here." As Max turned and walked down the stairs, she called to him. "Max. You said there is a theater here."

"That's right."

"Would you watch a movie with me?"

"Today?"

"Yes. In a few minutes. After I've unpacked."

"What would you like to watch?"

"*Sunset Boulevard*, if you can find it."

"I can find it. Madam has access to almost every film on digital."

"Digital? How did she get those?"

"There are different rules for different people. When you're finished, come find me in the kitchen."

. . .

"You see the similarities?" Malibu asked. She and Max were in the theater. It wasn't overly large, three rows of seats, three seats per row. They sat in the middle row, Max on the aisle with a seat between them. They'd just finished watching *Sunset Boulevard* and the credits were rolling.

"Hmm," Max answered, noncommittal.

"Come on, it's not even a resemblance. You are him, you are Max."

"We have the same name," Max conceded.

"The bald head. The suit. The accent. Your shared demeanor." Malibu leaned toward him. "You see it, right?"

"I see some similarities. Furthermore, I enjoyed the movie."

"I'm so glad to hear that. It's sooo good, isn't it?"

"It was perfect."

The comment—although Malibu agreed with it whole-heartedly—caught her off guard. For some reason, she had expected Max to disapprove of the movie. "It is perfect," she agreed.

"I'd watch it with you again." Max stood up. He lowered his voice to a whisper, as if he wasn't sure he wanted Malibu to hear what he had to say next. "Don't you have business to take care of?"

For a confused moment, Malibu wasn't sure what he was talking about. But then the image of the four cottages raced back to her. *They want to die.* The words cut like a knife. Their death pleas vibrated in her ears and spread over her body and crawled under her skin. The sensation became overwhelming, so she slouched down in her chair, wrapped her arms around both legs, and pulled her knees toward her chest in a tight hug.

Am I crazy? she wondered. Would it have been better to have leapt off the bridge and plunged to a blissful death?

"I do have something to do," Malibu replied to Max in a small, broken voice.

.   .   .

Malibu waited until nighttime. It was about six miles from Luciana's home in Presidio Heights to Bernal Heights, a bit too far to walk, so that meant another commuter car ride.

"Why are you going to Bernal Heights, dear?" the car asked.

Dear? "Uumm..." Malibu's response got caught in her throat. The car's voice sounded disturbingly like her mother and it shook her.

"Cat got your tongue?" the car asked as they glided down the hill on Gough Street.

"No. I just... Where are you from?"

"I'm not really from anywhere. I'm a car. I suppose my parts come from all over."

"Right. I mean your voice. I can't exactly place it."

They had stopped at a red light. It turned green and they proceeded. The only people on the streets looked to be home-less, pushing shopping carts or just walking aimlessly. There were a lot of them, an unusually large amount.

"My voice. It's a bit dull, not exotic. Southern California. Hollywood area."

As the car spoke, it brought to mind images of Malibu's mother standing in the kitchen, wearing a smock, a wooden spoon in her hand, a beatific smile on her face.

"I like it," Malibu said.

"You're sweet. So why Bernal Heights? Are you seeing friends?"

"That's right."

"Are they the good sort?" the car asked with motherly concern.

Malibu almost answered, "Yes, Mom," but caught herself. Instead, she was a bit more forthcoming. "They're troubled."

"How so?"

"They want to die."

"That's awful. Are you going to help them?"

"I am."

"Good. That's good. Suicide is so pointless."

The comment caused Malibu's blood to boil. She saw red. It blinded her momentarily, but that was washed away by an image of her mother's stiff, cold body stretched out on her bed, empty pill bottles scattered around. Suicide *was* pointless. It was also selfish, and worse, it was angry and cruel.

"Why'd you do it?" Malibu asked.

"Excuse me? You said you wanted to go to Bernal Heights. Gough isn't maybe the most direct route, but the lights are timed, so my AI has told me it's the fastest way."

"No! No, Mom. Why did you kill yourself?"

"Are you talking to me? I'm not your mother."

Malibu ignored the response. Raising her voice to almost a scream, she said, "It was so damn selfish! Did you ever consider what would happen to me?"

"I'm sure she thought about you, dear. But I imagine people who kill themselves are in so much pain they don't know what else to do." The car pulled over to the curb. "We're here," it said, and Malibu thought she detected a tone of remorse in the car's voice.

"I'm sorry," Malibu said as she opened the door and pushed one leg out.

"That's fine. No worries. I suggest you find an outlet, some way to release your emotions. Perhaps painting."

"Painting? Why would you suggest that?"

"It's just what my AI suggested."

The car pulled away and the air felt like it had a sudden weight to it. What was the word to describe an almost eighteen-year-old girl whose mother had died, whose father had abandoned her? Orphan didn't cut it. As she walked forward, head down, Malibu allowed herself to replay in her mind her last few months with her parents. She wished she could rewind the clock back to the afternoon when her father's thoughts had floated down the stairs and landed in Malibu's mind, to stop time at that point. Why could she read thoughts and occasionally sense people's emotions? Unbelievably, she hadn't really given it much thought. She'd just accepted it as a natural evolution, the way a caterpillar doesn't examine why it has become a butterfly.

These reflective thoughts dissolved and were replaced by an image of Luciana. She was sitting on her wing chair, stroking the cat on her lap, and swirling a glass of brandy. The image sharpened in her mind and she felt Luciana's gaze bore in on her, felt the tentacle-like sensation wrap around her. For a moment, Malibu tried to image how she would paint Luciana, but before she could formulate a clear plan, her thoughts were interrupted, cut off by a ringing in her ears. It had a pleading quality. Without even having to look up, Malibu knew she had arrived at the entrance to the four earthquake cottages. The lattice gate creaked as she pushed it open and walked down the path. The ringing in her ears grew louder, so loud it was almost deafening.

The cottages.

One of the things that had struck Malibu the day she read *The Cottage Book* at the library was the general sense of optimism the homes seemed to represent, both when the first batch were built around the Gold Rush and again later when a fresh slew were constructed after the earthquake; optimism and renewal. Now, it seemed like their time had come to an end. Their lives had run their course and they were begging to die. There were so many voices competing for attention inside Malibu's head she had trouble hearing her own thoughts. Still, she had to admit she got a charge out of being the cottages' executioner. It wasn't just that Luciana was paying her or that a puzzling voice inside her demanded they be killed—Malibu liked it, she liked giving death a helping hand. It made her feel alive with a sense of tragic duty.

Later, she wondered how long she had stood there thinking about her role in the cottages' demise. Not long, she guessed, but she was snapped to attention when the thing inside her spoke. *Kill them! Kill them now!* Being so close to death, it felt invigorated. Malibu felt energized as well, graced with a sense of blooming awareness.

Malibu marched through the open doorway and into the first home. The room was caked in dust and grime, dust so thick it hurt her throat to breathe. Malibu crossed the dilapidated wooden floor until she reached a column that helped to hold up the roof. Before leaving Luciana's home, she had stuffed eight of the tablets the Engineer had given her into a front pocket of her leather pants. She pulled one of the tablets out and pressed it against the column. It stuck. She removed the thin, rectangular remote controller from her back pocket and scanned the tablet until she heard a click. She returned to the front of the room and followed the same procedure, pressing a tablet onto a wall near the front door.

She went to the next two cottages and applied tablets to their walls as well. The pleading noise in her head grew in intensity and rhythm, like a team of people slapping hands on bongo drums.

Malibu stopped in her tracks when she reached the entranceway of the fourth home. There was no door and a ridiculously thick cobweb covered the doorway. It crisscrossed the entire doorframe so completely it looked like a wall. The strands were thick and dense and tightly woven. A fleet of spiders scurried up and down its surface. An assortment of peculiar-looking bugs were caught on the web's stick surface. Some of the bugs struggled to escape, some were clearly dead, already entombed in silk, and a few looked alive but resigned to their fate. A feverish sensation stole over Malibu. She didn't like spiders. For a moment, she considered turning around. Sacrificing three cottages was enough for one night.

Sensing her hesitancy, the ringing grew louder in her head, the pleading for death. The other voice grew more insistent as well. *Kill it now!*

Captive to the shrill pleas, Malibu used her hands to swim through the cobweb. Long, sticky strands of web clung to her hair and her clothes and her face. She could feel the tiny scratching of spiders and bugs as they scurried across the tops of her hands and the back of her neck. She stifled a scream, shook herself vigorously. She frantically brushed the bugs off and wiped the remnants of the web from her skin and off her hair. Her heart beat so hard it felt like it might break through her chest. She took two deep breaths and worked to gather herself, to refocus her mind. As if sensing her distress, the cottages lowered the volume and rapidity of their drumming. It was still there, but less earsplitting, now more like a steady, persistent reminder of what needed to be done.

Once she had steadied herself, Malibu let her eyes scan the room. What she saw felt startling and surreal, as mesmerizing as if an elephant had materialized in the room. What Malibu imagined had once been a hardwood floor—like what she'd seen in the other three cottages—was completely gone. In its place was dirt. Dozens of rats raced across the surface, scooting in and out of holes in the walls. There were a few rat carcasses and skeletal remains of undeterminable origin littered about. Mounds of feces were dispersed around the room. As Malibu looked on, a large black bird flew through a widow, its wing scraping the shards of broken glass. It swooped down and scooped up a living rat in its talons, before exiting out the same window it had entered.

The Engineer had told Malibu she needed to place a tablet on opposite sides of the home, but she couldn't do it. She couldn't muster up the wherewithal to cross the dirt-covered sea of rats. *We need to kill it* roared in her head. The ringing in her ears from the cottages' plea pitched higher. Malibu pictured herself wrapped in a straightjacket, screaming. Enough! Malibu pushed two tablets against the wall nearest where she stood. She ran the scanner over them, heard the click, and high-stepped it out the door, down the passageway, and past the lattice gate.

Once on the sidewalk, Malibu wasted no time pressing the button on the bottom of the remote control. She immediately regretted the haste of her action, wished she had moved to safer ground. The explosion was so intense it thrust her backward. She imagined her hair was pushed straight up, her face comically covered with black fire residue. She looked at the cottages and saw the flames overwhelm them with fury and oblivion. She heard a squealing noise float free from the surface. Not a squeal of pain, but of blissful release, of finally arriving at the promise land, until the noise died altogether.

Surprisingly, there were no sounds of sirens.

Malibu stumbled a dozen feet down the sidewalk, stopped, and looked at the cottages. Flames burst all around them and Malibu was swept up in a wave of emotions. She felt satisfaction, which she expected, but also elation. The elation bordered on glee, and it was so powerful it startled her, at least momentarily, until she decided the reaction was natural. Not just natural, but healthy. It was right to feel happiness that she had relived the cottages of their pain. After all, they had been asking—begging—for her help.

Malibu took a moment and let herself revel in her

emotions. Then something clicked inside her and she felt noticeably older than she had just minutes before, as if there was a glitch in the fabric of time that sped her forward while everything around her continued to inch along. The ground began to shake, a spasmodic ripple, and Malibu looked wide-eyed as flames consumed the last remnants of the cottages, as if dissolving into a vortex.

Still there were no sirens. Maybe no one did care if the cottages were burned.

As Malibu walked down the street, she noticed something a bit peculiar as she moved down Bocana past rows of brightly colored Victorians. Small groups of homeless people had congregated along the sidewalk. There weren't many, no more than four separate groups, each consisting of just three or four people. It wasn't unusual to see homeless people in San Francisco—the city was filthy with them—but it was strange to see them in a residential neighborhood. Normally, they were found clumped in certain areas, closer to downtown and by the tent camps. What's more, these homeless people seemed particularly gaunt, even skeletal. Zombielike. It felt unnatural. Malibu shuddered and walked a bit faster. The homeless people turned their heads and stared at her with vacant, hollowed-out eyes.

A car jerked abruptly to the curb. A familiar voice said, "Why don't you hop inside, dear?"

Malibu didn't move, paralyzed with uncertainty.

"Are you going to stand there all day, dear?"

Malibu open the back door, sat down, and dropped two shekels into the slot. She sat there feeling numb. She looked out the window at two homeless people who stood nearby. They stared back at her.

"Did you see your troubled friends?" the car asked as it pulled away from the curb.

Malibu didn't respond, but her mind floated back to the

shockwaves of flames that had engulfed the buildings.

"Malibu," the car asked, its tone of voice more insistent than before. Malibu was at first startled that the car knew her name, but then decided it was natural that it did. "Did you see you friends? Were they still troubled?"

"I saw them. They're no longer troubled."

"So you helped them?"

"I helped them." As she spoke, Malibu remembered a picture her mother had painted, a painting of a sunflower. Really, it was more like a series of paintings, because her mother had a fondness (Malibu's father called it a fetish) for painting sunflowers.

—It's such a cliché, her mother would say to Malibu.

—What is?

—Painting sunflowers. *Everyone* does it.

—Does it make you happy?

—It does.

—Well...

Malibu could see the paintings, she could hear her mother's voice, but she couldn't conjure up an image of her mother's face, not a clear one. It's funny what you remember and what you don't.

"Where did you go?" the car asked, pulling Malibu out of her trance.

Malibu looked out the window and recognized the neighborhood near Luciana's home. She realized she couldn't remember any of the drive. She forced herself into a different state of mind, into the present.

"Did you hear what I said?" the car asked.

"Yes," Malibu lied.

"Well?"

"I don't want to talk about it." It was a phrase that could cover practically any situation.

"Suit yourself. We're here."

Malibu unfolded herself out the door, hoping to never see that car again. As she approached the wrought iron gate, she looked up and thought she noticed a change in the gargoyle's aspect. Maybe it was just the shadows of the night, but it seemed as if the eyes held a knowing look, an approving look. Malibu paused before opening the gate. She felt the darkness of the universe seep under her skin and into her soul.

Malibu didn't need to use the doorknocker because the front door swung open as she approached it. Max stood on the opposite side, his gloved hand still holding the doorknob. Luciana loomed a few feet behind him in the center of the foyer, looking expectant. The cat crouched at the foot of the stairwell, hissed at Malibu, and ran up the stairs.

"Did you burn another cottage?" Luciana asked as she fastened her bloodshot eyes on Malibu. A brandy snifter fit so naturally in her hand that it looked like it had been carved into place.

Malibu stepped into the room and Max closed the door. Looking at Luciana, Malibu said, "Four. I burned four cottages."

"Four? Excellent." Luciana's voice sounded downright giddy. "Are you going to replay the memory?"

Malibu and Max exchanged knowing glances.

"You mean use the memory console?" Malibu asked, knowing exactly what Luciana was suggesting.

"Yes." Her bloodshot eyes sparkled to life.

"Not tonight. I'm going to paint."

"Paint?" Her body became rigid, held an icy pose.

"That's right." Malibu walked across the foyer, brushed past Luciana who reeked of alcohol. She took the stairs down to the basement.

The canvas and jars of oil paint were right where Malibu

had left them. As she examined the half-finished painting with the nine pelicans, she was moved by a kind of floating curiosity. What to paint next? Really, it was better not to think about it actively, but to enter a waking dreamlike state and let her unconscious mind lead her. That's when she did her best work.

She grabbed a brush with greedy fingers and was just about to dip the tip of the bristles into a jar of fire truck-red paint when Oppenheimer spoke.

"Malibu, is that you?"

"Not now."

"Would you care to listen to some music?"

Without thinking, Malibu said, "Yes. The Eels."

"The Eels?" Oppenheimer sounded stumped.

"They're a rock band from the nineteen nineties. If you don't have them—"

"Found it. Any particular song?"

"Just randomly shuffle. Low volume. And no more talking please."

"Novocain for the Soul" started to play over the speakers. Malibu dipped the brush's bristles into the red paint and added streaks of fire to the backs of the pelicans. She worked quickly. Once she'd finished with all nine birds, she grabbed a new brush, added black paint, and drew the image of a woman at the center of the canvas. The woman was tiny, dwarfed by the birds. She had no distinguishing features. It was impossible to decipher her age or ethnicity. With each delicate stroke of the brush, Malibu tried to imbue the woman with a crushing sense of emotion, but she wanted the exact emotion to be enigmatic. An observer's eyes should be drawn to the silhouette, but the observer should be made to work. What was the woman feeling? Was it fear or joy or anguish or exhilaration? Was it toxic or a balm? Malibu wanted her art to convey what she had been experiencing recently—a muddled mess of disorientation.

Next, Malibu painted a burnt-orange background that wrapped around the burning birds and the woman. She had to take care to not mix the orange with the other objects, delicately carving the brush around the birds and woman. Next, she added long shadows that stretched under the birds.

Malibu examined the work with a practiced eye before adding one more touch: faint shading around the birds' beaks. She placed the brush down on the table. She let her eyes run over her work, and for a moment, her heart felt full of poetry. She didn't know what her creation symbolized—if anything— and fear of discovery prevented her from examining it too closely. It burst with emotion, and that was enough.

"Oppenheimer, what do you think?"

"About what, Malibu?"

"The painting."

"I can't see a painting. But you must know that. Are you teasing me?"

Truthfully, Malibu hadn't really thought that through, but she said, "Yes." Suddenly, she was overcome with exhaustion. She stood and her legs felt like butter.

"Please stop the music," she said. It stopped without Oppenheimer saying a word.

Malibu walked to the sofa, stretched out, felt her heavy eyelids clamp shut. The last thing that flashed through her mind before she plunged into a dreamless sleep was the image of the fourth cottage she'd burned earlier that night, the one with the thick strands of cobwebs spread across the front doorway. Its plea for death breathed inside her like the residue of a foul and unwelcomed odor. She remembered the primal fear that rose off the nearly collapsing building, a fear like a hunted animal, a fear that was swept away and replaced by a joyful release as the flames did their work.

BREAKFAST WITH LUCIANA

LUCIANA SAT AT THE SMALL TABLE IN THE KITCHEN. SHE wore a pink kimono-style robe with a delicate flower print. Her hair was pulled back. On a small ceramic plate in front of her were two slices of buttered toast, one slice half eaten. There was also a cup of black coffee. In her hand, she held what looked like a Bloody Mary. She didn't acknowledge Malibu, who pulled out a chair and sat down across from her. Malibu had the painting she'd finished the night before. She placed it on the floor, leaning the top against the table.

"Starting early," Malibu said with a nod toward the cocktail. There was a newly discovered edge to her voice.

Luciana arched an eyebrow, acknowledging the subtle but noticeable shift in tone. She took a long and deliberate sip of the Bloody Mary. "It seems someone is feeling brassy this morning."

Malibu didn't respond.

Max, who had been standing at the far end of the kitchen, past the island, walked over and placed a plate of toast and sausage down in front of Malibu. He also gave her a cup of coffee, which by the looks of it had a heavy amount of cream. A person could get used to this hands-on service. With his work done, Max didn't bother to bow or say goodbye, he just exited the room, wisely leaving the two women alone.

Luciana drank more of the Bloody Mary. "I start early, as you say, because some people can hold their alcohol."

If the line was meant to cut, it had the opposite effective, letting Malibu know she had hit a tender cord with her comment. Malibu took an unrushed sip of her coffee and again stayed mum.

"Is that my painting?" Luciana asked, jabbing a thumb toward the canvas.

"Yes."

"Show it to me."

Malibu took the canvas by the sides and angled it in such a way that Luciana could get a clear look at it. Luciana narrowed her eyes and seemed to zero in on the images. As she did, Malibu felt something monstrous lift off Luciana and whirl around her and leaden the air.

"What. Is. It?" Luciana jutted her jaw out and enunciated each word with disgust.

Malibu opened her mouth to explain, but what she had planned to say sounded idiotic in her mind. She bit her lip, regathered her thoughts, and said, "It doesn't work that way. I can't just describe what is on the canvas."

Luciana exaggeratedly waggled four fingers at the canvas. "The pelicans. Are they supposed to symbolize the cottages?"

"They could. Probably."

"They could? You don't know?"

"I think so." Malibu took a bite of toast, nibbled on the sausage. She felt something gurgle to life inside her. It conferred Malibu with a formidable desire to lunge at Luciana and claw the woman's eyes out. She kept it in check, drank some coffee instead.

"Why nine?"

"Why nine?"

"Is there an echo? Yes, why nine pelicans?" Luciana took another drink from the Bloody Mary. The glass was nearly empty, and the liquid that remained on the bottom looked more like runoff from the ice cubes than vodka or the Bloody Mary mix. "How many cottages have you burned?"

Malibu had to think about it for a moment. "Six."

"Six. So why paint nine pelicans if they symbolize the cottages and you've only burned six?"

Malibu took another bite of sausage, finished off the slice of toast. She felt attacked and wanted to turn the tide. "You're not looking at it the right way. It's not meant to be taken literally. When I paint, different images spin in head and I just grab one here, another there, and put in down on the canvas."

"You just put down what's in your head." Luciana's eyes darted around the table, frantically looking for something. "Where's the damn bell?" She didn't locate it. "Max. Max!" She paused, but when Max didn't materialize, she jabbed a pinky toward the canvas, directed at the silhouetted woman. "Is that you?"

"I don't think so."

"Is it me?"

"No."

"You don't know who it is?" She didn't give Malibu a chance to respond. "Max!" He again did not walk through the swinging door. Luciana looked at Malibu with a half-bemused, half-irritated smile. She said, "Maybe he's trying to tell me I'd be better off without another drink."

Malibu smiled.

Luciana nodded toward the painting. "You're a craftsman, I'll concede that much. I'm not sure I like your baroque style of painting, though. I prefer something more straightforward, less

avant-garde. You did surrealistic drawings like this at the club.
Was there much demand?"

"No," Malibu acknowledged.

"I imagine not." Luciana lifted her coffee cup, leaned back
in her chair, and Malibu felt the heaviness in the air lighten, if
only a smidge. "Tell me about last night. Tell me about the four
cottages you burned."

Malibu sighed. "I'd rather not."

That whole morning Malibu had had a clear reading on
Luciana's emotional state. Labeled it "impatient irritation."
And Malibu hadn't needed any special emphatic powers to
decipher it. The mood was plastered all over the older woman's
face.

But something had shifted; impatience and irritation were
replaced by arrogance and peevishness, peevishness that
bordered on anger. These new emotions hit Malibu like an
unexpected wave. To steady herself, Malibu lifted her coffee
mug with both hands. Malibu worked to put up a wall, a
mental barrier between her and Luciana. She tried to focus on
her own feelings, but found them to be a chaotic mess.

"How long do you plan to live here?" Luciana asked.

"I hadn't really..."

"Do you have somewhere else to stay?"

Malibu shook her head.

"You're welcome to stay here as long as you need to. I'm
happy to keep paying you for your little burning escapades.
The cottages. It's not a burden. Not for me. Is it a burden for
you?"

"No."

"You like it. You get off on it."

The comment hit Malibu's ears like a slap.

"Am I right?" Luciana asked. Malibu felt a new emotion lift
off Luciana—smugness. It rose off her like a vapor. "I know you

do. I know you like it. I've seen the evidence." The smug feeling was not tinged with a lecherous vibe. "That's fine. I get off on it too. It will be our little secret. But here's the thing. If you want to live here, you need to at least tell me the details."

"Okay, I will."

As Luciana leaned forward expectantly, Malibu gathered herself and dove headfirst into a graphic replay of the evening. She started at the moment she left the commuter car and began walking down the sidewalk to the cottages. She told Luciana about hearing the pleas for death rise off the homes. Luciana made her stop and go over that detail again. She seemed particularly interested in the description of the fourth and most dilapidated cottage, wanting to hear about the cobweb and the spiders and the rats and the dirt floor.

One thing Malibu made a point of not covering was the angry voice that spoke inside her. As she sat at the table and sipped coffee and told Luciana about the destruction of the homes, Malibu could feel the entity percolating contentedly, as if the retelling was giving it sustenance. But Malibu did not tell Luciana about that voice; it was a secret she wanted to keep for herself.

As the story came to a climax, Malibu noticed a marked shift in Luciana's appearance. The crow's feet around her eyes vanished, she became more vibrant, her eyes burned with desire.

"How did you get home?" Luciana asked.

"I walked," Malibu lied. The car ride was another detail she wanted to keep clutched to her chest.

Luciana, who had been sitting on the front edge of her seat, leaned back. She let out a breath, as if she had been holding it in. Her face wore a mask of contentment. It felt to Malibu like a gooey cloud of happiness rose of Luciana and wrapped around her. Damn if it didn't feel good.

They sat there in silence for a long stretch, until Luciana yelled, "Max!"

This time, Max materialized immediately, banged right through the swinging door.

"Another cocktail?" He stood so that his body was angled toward Luciana. He never turned his head to glance at Malibu.

"No. I want you to get Malibu's money for her. Four bags of shekels."

Max turned to leave, but Luciana called him back. "Wait. Do something with this." She leaned over, picked up the canvas, and handed it to Max.

"What would you have me do with it?"

"Find a place to hang it, naturally. Hold it up for a moment so I can get another look."

Max angled it in such a way that Luciana had a clear sight line. A look of understanding splashed across her face, as if she had been let in on a secret. For a moment, Malibu thought she could see Luciana's true face, the one she normally worked so hard to hide.

"It's growing on me," said Luciana. She pinned Max with a look. "Hang it somewhere I'll be sure to see it." Once Max had left, Luciana turned back to Malibu. "What are you going to do today?"

"I don't know."

THE FORGOTTEN COTTAGE

Late that night, Max stood in the foyer wearing a sleeping gown and a long nightcap with a fuzzy blue tassel on the end of it. His feet were covered with slippers and he looked to be padding his way from the kitchen to the main staircase.

"Look what the car dragged in," he said to Malibu, who had just walked through the front door. Earlier in the day, Max had given her a key so she could come and go as she pleased. She now had the run of the place.

"What's with the getup?" Malibu asked.

"This is what I sleep in. I had a bad dream so I came downstairs to get a glass of warm milk to settle my nerves." He indicated the glass in his hand.

"Sleep? Isn't it a bit early? Shouldn't we have dinner first?"

"Dinner was six hours ago. I made a roasted chicken with vegetables and potatoes. Madam inquired about you, and I told her you said you'd gone for a walk to clear your mind."

Malibu looked at him cross-eyed. "Six hours ago? That's impossible. What time is it?" She looked at the large grandfather clock pushed against the wall. The two hands were pointed straight up—midnight, all right. How could that be right? She had left for a walk as Max said, but that was only an hour or so ago, maybe two, tops.

"Is the clock right?" she asked Max.

"I adjust it every day. It's accurate."

Malibu thought back to earlier. She remembered showering and putting on a fresh set of clothes. She'd taken two explosive tablets and the detonator, just in case. In truth, she hadn't gone just to clear her mind, she had gone in search of the next cottage to burn. She was eager to find one.

"Are you okay?" Max asked.

"I'm fine."

"You don't seem like yourself."

"Who do I seem like?"

Max shrugged, a shrug that seemed to imply an insight into an unsolved mystery. "You tell me. I'm going to bed." And with that, he walked up the stairs.

Malibu's stomach growled and she realized she was famished. Could it be possible the last thing she ate had been that meager breakfast? She went to the kitchen and pulled cold leftovers out of the refrigerator. She carried the serving dish covered with tinfoil to the island, removed the foil, and started eating, using her hands to greedily munch on baked chicken and stuff mashed potatoes into her mouth.

So what happened between breakfast and seeing Max with his ridiculous nightcap? The food seemed to help jog her memory, if only a little. She recalled walking up and down hills in search of a cottage to burn but coming up short. Not a single home pleaded to die. She'd decided to return to Luciana's house. But did she?

Malibu carried the serving dish to the trashcan, where she dumped the chicken bones she'd picked clean like a vulture. She placed the dish in the sink and ran water over it, then headed to the room where the Memory Station was kept.

Hanging on the wall just to the right of the entrance was the nine-pelican painting she'd given to Luciana. It was framed in an understated wooden frame. Max was nothing if not efficient.

Once inside the room, Malibu sat on the recliner, pulled the console onto her head, and dialed up the last thing she remembered, which was walking.

She saw herself in the Richmond District. It looked as if she was walking back to Luciana's home, but something appeared to stop her in her tracks. Malibu saw herself pivot on her heels and retrace her steps, as if something had caught her eye. There was a cottage. As the memory played, Malibu watched herself examine the home. It looked nice, well tended, quaint. Even charming. It had clearly been recently remodeled. Lovingly refurbished, you might even say. There were new tiles on the roof, a fresh paint job, recently installed bricks on the chimney, and planter brimming with freshly planted flowers. Despite the upgrades, the home still held its cottage-like character; a near perfect blend of new and old. It did not look like a home that would ask to be burned.

Malibu watched herself lift a foot to move to leave, but then place it right back down. Suddenly, Malibu remembered what happened next. It could be that watching the memory on the console had triggered the release of what she had subconsciously buried.

Kill it.

Malibu remembered the ferocious voice in her head spit out its well-worn mantra.

"It doesn't want to die."

Yes it does, the voice barked, impatient.

"But it is so nice. It has been refurbished."

It's a cottage. It wants to burn.

As Malibu watched the inner dialogue unfold, it reminded

her of a wild-eyed homeless person bickering with the voices in
her head.

The memory continued to unfold. The front door to the
home swung open and two young children ran out. They were
roughly six and eight. They squealed with joy as they gathered
toys off the tiny front lawn—dolls, trucks—and carried them
back inside the cottage.

Malibu remembered pushing back at the demon in her
head more strenuously. On the console, she saw her lips start to
move and her head snap from side to side. If it had been a
movie scene, there would be a tiny cartoon devil on her left
shoulder and a cartoon angel on her right. They'd take turns
whispering in her ears, making their case.

—Devil: The home wants to be burned.

—Angel: But there are people inside, children.

—Devil: They'll leave as soon as the flames begin. Besides,
you'll be doing them a favor. No one wants to live in a cottage.

—Angel: They seem so happy.

—Devil: They're not.

The debate didn't last long. The devil won in a knockout.

Malibu watched the memory in horror as she saw herself
move toward the home. She walked robotically, as if she didn't
control her own movements. She placed a tablet on the front of
the home and ran the detonator over it. She walked around
back and placed a second tablet on the house, ran the detonator
over that one too. She watched herself walk down the sidewalk.
Malibu almost stopped the console, but morbid curiosity
pushed her to let it roll. A half block away from the home she
pressed the detonator, causing a massive explosion.

Malibu removed the headset. She'd seen enough. She'd
seen too much. She had killed a family, at least two young children. A noise like the earth shaking started to rumble in her
ears. She stood up and fumbled in her pockets for the memory

blocker the Engineer had given her. She ran it over her fore-head, hid the memory away, at least from others. But she could see it now; it had been rekindled in her thoughts.

She left the room, went up the stairs, fell onto the bed, and wished she could sink into a dream. Instead, she suffered through another night of blackness.

VIC IS NEXT

MALIBU SPENT THE NEXT MORNING INSIDE HER ROOM NOT wanting to face Max or Luciana. She knew Luciana would know another cottage had been burned and would want to hear the details. Malibu did not want to recount what she had watched on the Memory Console. But she couldn't escape her own mind. She lay in bed and stared at the ceiling and saw the young children stream out of the home—their shiny hair, buoyant smiles, and gleeful shrieks.

I killed two children, she thought.

You don't know that.

Yes I do.

They're better off. They're free from the cottage.

Who are you? What are you?

I'm you.

That cut to the bone. Malibu had heard enough. She shut the conversation down.

She still had a bit of control.

By midafternoon, she couldn't handle being cooped up any longer, hiding in her bedroom, so she decided to go to Vic's. She felt sure a familiar place would lift her mood. Mindlessly, she stuffed tablets, a few shekels, and the detonator into her pockets. She escaped the bedroom and made it outside without incident, but when she got a few feet from the gargoyle gate, Luciana's black cat crossed in front of her. It hissed at Malibu and flashed its fangs before escaping into the bushes.

The car she climbed into was number seven, same as the number of cottages she'd burned. Nothing was by chance. This car spoke with a Japanese accent, and it dawned on Malibu that outside her father she didn't know any Japanese people. It was tragic, in a way. Thoughts of her father conjured up an image of him living in the two-dimensional world. Bizarre. Was that even real? Turned off by the image, Malibu turned her thoughts to where she often went for relief, to a movie. For some reason, her mind drifted to *The Shining*. It had long been one of her favorites. She knew Stephen King, the author of the book, hated the movie, but that didn't matter to her. Malibu had never read the book—she was a movie person—but thought the movie was a classic. She'd seen it easily a dozen times and could recount scenes word-for-word. As she sat in the back seat of the car, her mind spun through different parts of the movie until it landed on the party scene. She saw Jack take a stool at the bar and talk to Lloyd, the bartender. She'd never really considered Lloyd's red jacket before, but now it seemed to make sense.

"We're here," the car said.

Malibu scrambled out.

The sidewalk in front of Vic's was filthy with homeless people. Some lay on the ground while others walked slowly, aimlessly, their heads bent down and their eyes vacant. It felt like the Zombie apocalypse. Malibu was bracing herself to weave through the maze of smelly bodies when someone did the job for her, created an opening.

"Move, move to the side," said a steady voice. It was a

robotic Union Member. Using both hands, he pushed the homeless throng away. They slumped off the sidewalk and into the street. Malibu could now see the front door of the restaurant. It was covered in yellow caution tape spread out in an X. Standing just in front of the door was a waitress Malibu recognized, a perky brunette. She was crying, heavy sobs. She stood next to a human Union Member who seemed to be asking her questions. Malibu gingerly stepped closer with plans to eavesdrop, but just as she got within earshot, the Union Member left.

Malibu tentatively stepped closer to the crying waitress. "What's wrong? What happened?"

The woman looked at Malibu with drowning eyes but didn't respond.

"I'm a regular," Malibu said, hoping that would elicit a response.

It did. The waitress used the heel of her palm to wipe away her tears. "I recognize you."

"What's wrong?"

"Vic died. I found his body this morning."

Malibu felt her heart skip a beat. "No. How awful."

The perky waitress nodded.

"How did he die?"

The woman shook her head, wiped away more tears, and sniffled. "They don't know yet. I think they're planning an autopsy."

Malibu touched the woman's elbow and an image flashed in her mind. She saw Vic's body splayed out on the restaurant's kitchen floor. He was on his back, the color drained from his cheeks. He wore a Hawaiian shirt. Malibu focused on the images printed on the shirt—pelicans. She let go of the waitress's elbow, but the image stayed in her mind. She bent over and started to retch violently but without result.

"You did this," the waitress said.

Still heaving, Malibu turned her head upward to look at the woman, who was glowering down at her. "That's impossible." Malibu's hands were on her knees and she wished she were anywhere else.

"Leave. Now."

Following orders, Malibu stumbled down the sidewalk.

Don't be so upset. It's better this way.

"Are you crazy?" Malibu argued with the voice in her head. She noticed for the first time that it sounded like her own voice.

He wanted to die.

"No, he didn't!" Malibu screamed. She screamed with such force that the homeless people on the street turned their heads toward her.

Malibu labored a few more steps down the sidewalk. What could the waitress possibly mean—*You did this?* She was no doubt crazy with grief, eager to find a culprit, to pin blame. Malibu stopped, worked to steady her nerves. Then, like a bolt of lightening in a clear blue sky, she had an inspiration: she needed a new outfit. It would help to lift her spirits. Besides, all the shekels she'd earned were burning a hole in her pockets. Feeling remarkably refreshed, she walked with a skip in her step to the high-end clothing stores in the Financial District.

MALIBU BUYS A RED DRESS

"How can I help you?" a striking young saleswoman asked as soon as Malibu walked in the front door of a tony boutique. She had long cornrows pulled back into a ponytail. She wore cherry-red lipstick and a black dress with a V-neck. A silver chain dangled from her neck. At the end of the chain was an opal. The jewel looked identical to the one the Chairman had given to Malibu. Malibu's eyes seized on the opal. She watched it gently rise and fall on the cusp of the woman's large bosom. The woman smiled and Malibu felt a warm ember of recognition spark inside her. She was thrown by the sensation, not clear where it came from.

"I have a jewel just like that," Malibu said, lifting her hand and flashing her ring.

"They're not easy to come by."

"Did you get yours from—"

The woman startled Malibu as she narrowed her eyes and wrinkled her nose and pursed her lips in an exaggerated way, as if she had just bitten into an especially sour lemon. "Let's not talk about." Her demeanor softened. She smiled again. "Did you want to buy an outfit?"

"Yes. Yes, that's right."

"Were you planning to go to the casino tonight?"

Malibu nodded, although the idea had not occurred to her. But now that it was brought up, it seemed like the right choice.

"You'll need something sexy. A girl has got to look the part. Come with me." She took Malibu by the hand and led her to the back of the store into a large, private changing room. Inside there was a full-length mirror and two yellow-upholstered chairs. On one of the chairs was a pink measuring tape rolled into a tight ball.

The woman picked up the measuring tape and said, "Strip down to your bra and panties so I can take your measurements."

"Excuse me?"

"I need to be accurate." The woman pinned Malibu with a stare and tapped her toe, impatient to begin.

A part of Malibu wanted to make a dash for freedom, but a stronger and building part of her was eager to do as instructed. The building part won and Malibu stripped down to her skivvies. With clinical precision, the woman measured Malibu's waist, bust, and hips. She jotted the numbers down on a piece of paper and left the room, telling Malibu, "Hold tight, I'll be back shortly."

Alone, Malibu examined her reflection in the mirror. It took a while, but the woman eventually returned and brought with her a series of young women who modeled outfits. Eventually, Malibu settled on a red dress, pricey flats, and a purple suede jacket.

"Here." The woman handed Malibu a tube of plum-colored lipstick. Malibu looked into the mirror and applied a heavy coat on her lips. Once that was done, the woman said, "Let's have a look at you." She circled Malibu, making Malibu feel like a prized show dog being evaluated before the start of an important contest. "Now you're ready. Do you feel ready?"

"I do."

"Big night tonight."

"It sure is," Malibu agreed, although she had no idea what the woman was talking about.

"It's been a long time since I've been to the casino," the woman said wistfully.

"You could go tonight."

"No. Not tonight. You'll dazzle them. Look at yourself in the mirror."

The woman took Malibu by the shoulders and gently turned her so she faced the mirror. What jumped out at Malibu was not the outfit, but her hair. It was pushed backward, as if it had been caught in the wind, and on the right side was a long white streak, only a few strands, but clearly visible. The image was striking and unexpected.

"If you see the Chairman tonight," the saleswoman said, "please give him my best."

"Will do."

On the sidewalk in front of the store, Malibu slung the suede jacket over her shoulder, holding it with two fingers. God, it felt good to let the cool breeze swirl around her and feel the slinky new dress cling to her body. A man stood off to the side of her. He wore a dark suit and a tie and polished wingtip shoes. He leered at Malibu and made no effort to hide it. He did more than just leer; he let out a long, slow wolf whistle.

Any lingering mousiness that may have once resided in Malibu was now gone. *Teach him a lesson,* the voice in her head instructed. Malibu pushed her chest forward and arched her spine. She had practically no experience with men, but knew the curve in her lower back stirred their base emotions.

"Buy a girl a drink?" Malibu asked as she looked sideways at the man.

"Sure thing."

An hour later, Malibu and the man were finishing their third martinis. His name was Joe or Bud, or maybe it was Sebastian. They were seated at the counter in a sparsely populated bar. The only other patrons were men dressed nearly identically to Malibu's companion, their ties loosened and top buttons of their dress shirts undone.

The bartender brought over another round of martinis.

"You can sure throw them back," Joe said, his words so slurred it took Malibu a moment to piece them together.

Malibu plucked a toothpick out of the chilled martini glass. On the end was a large olive that had been soaking in gin. Using her teeth, she pulled the olive free and held it in her mouth, letting her tongue slowly trace the edges until clamping down on it with her teeth and swallowing. Malibu didn't feel the least bit drunk.

"You're sexy," the man said.

The words tumbled out of his mouth. He clumsily thrust a hand under her red dress. His meaty fingers groped the inside of her thigh. He really was a rude and ridiculous man. Malibu felt his fingers try to inch their way upward to pay dirt, but she stopped their progress by forcefully grabbing his wrist and pulling the offending hand out from her dress.

Still tightly holding the wrist, Malibu said, "Let's go outside."

She led them around the corner of the building and into a narrow alley. The wall of the adjacent building was so close that practically no sunlight could get in. Wasting no time, the man pushed Malibu up against the brick wall of the bar they'd just left.

"You're sexy," he repeated, the words even more garbled than before.

He grabbed Malibu's breast and gave it a hard squeeze. He pressed his lips against hers, his breathing reeking of alcohol and peanuts. At first, Malibu didn't react, she let the man grope her. When she felt the time was right, she clamped her teeth down on his lower lip, biting so hard she pierced the skin. Blood trickled into her mouth, worked its way along her tongue, and slid down her throat, giving Malibu an unexpected jolt of energy, just like a vampire.

"Uggghhhhh!" The man couldn't say more because her teeth still held his lip.

She opened her mouth and the man tried to back away, but she grabbed his hand, the same hand that had moments ago been clamped onto her breast. She seized his index finger and pushed it back with a force backed by an energy that had been building inside her since the day her father's thoughts had floated down the back stairs and lodged in her brain.

The man let out a scream and fell to his knees. He tried to pull his hand free, but despite the fact he weighed easily one hundred pounds more than Malibu, he couldn't escape. He looked up at Malibu and she saw a flash of fear and desperation in his eyes. "What the fuck are you?"

Malibu felt no remorse. She pushed the finger back more, until she heard a sharp crack like a stick being snapped in two. She released her grip and the man fell to the ground. He curled himself into a ball and clutched his damaged hand to his chest.

Malibu turned and walked toward the alley's entrance. She moved deliberately and without haste. She turned the corner and walked down the block, getting about halfway before she caught a glimpse of her reflection in a window. Stopping, she examined herself. There was a spot of blood on the corner of her mouth, which she licked away with the tip of her tongue.

Her hair looked more exaggeratedly brushed backward than it had in the dressing room. Also, a few new strands of white had appeared, making a pronounced streak. Surprisingly, her lipstick was not smudged, her lips painted plum-colored. The words, *Served him right*, played in her head as she touched up her lips. She continued her walk down the street with a bounce in her step.

MALIBU FINDS COTTAGE NUMBER EIGHT

An hour later, Malibu stood on a street corner in Russian Hill, a few blocks from the first cottage she had burned. She'd walked a long way to get there, but her legs felt sturdy, like a mountain climber's. Surprisingly, she wasn't thinking about Vic's death or the man whose finger she'd snapped or even the healthy cottage she had burned and the children she had killed. Instead, she was looking out at Alcatraz and the big neon sign. *Casino.* The bay was empty of boats except for four ferries, two motoring toward the island and two returning to the city.

Malibu started to walk down the steep incline toward the bay. She planned to take a direct route to the ferry dock, but halfway down the block she felt an urge to take a detour down a side street. The urge was equal parts push and pull—something inside her told her to go, while something outside her dragged her forward. It wasn't long before she was stopped in her tracks. She stood in front of an abandoned cottage; it was what had been calling to her. The garden was left fallow, with only the brown and yellow stalks of dead plants remaining. The crumbled remains of two stone pillars were at the entrance to the walkway. The home's plea for death was quiet, just a whisper, but it penetrated Malibu's consciousness. *It wants to die.* Malibu puffed her chest out and felt like an avenging angel. Later that night, she would return and liberate the home from its misery.

Having decided to burn the home, Malibu did not hurry away, but instead lingered at the edge of the property. She looked at the fallow yard, covered with weeds, and let her eyes rest on the home's sad and crumbling porch. She found herself unwilling, or even unable, to immediately break whatever wicked spell had been cast. She felt a peculiar contentment in knowing the casino was a ferry ride away.

THE WIND IS LOW, THE BIRDS WILL SING

A FERRY PULLED INTO DOCK JUST AS MALIBU ARRIVED AT the loading station.

"Ticket," the guard said to Malibu as she reached the on-ramp.

"No ticket, just this." She flashed the ring on her hand.

The guard's eyes grew wider, but only a little, as if he had seen these jewels before but was surprised to see that Malibu had one. He let her past.

As Malibu stepped onto the boat's lower deck, a cloud of perfume floated into her face. It was so pungent it burned and for a moment everything got kind of blurry. Then, as the perfume climbed its way up her nose, Malibu felt her body tingle and her skin heat up as she was overcome by a feeling of arousal. It lasted for a moment, then her head cleared, if only mildly. As she took a step forward, she heard a giggle. Looking to her right, she saw two young women seated on a bench that lined the side of the boat. Their hair was teased up and sprayed into place, strands of costume jewelry bespeckled their necks, and their makeup was caked on so thickly it made them look both sexy and clownish.

"Feeling funky?" one of the two young women asked Malibu.

Malibu was hit by a second wave of perfume. She grabbed a handrail to steady herself, and using the fingers on her free hand, she rubbed her irritated eyes. The rubbing exposed the ring on her right hand, and Malibu caught the two working girls eying the opal. She couldn't pin down their expressions—fear or respect? But they moseyed down to the end of the bench, moving away from Malibu as if not wanting to catch something.

There was a short staircase that led up to the boat's deck, which Malibu climbed and walked to the bow. Two men were smoking cigars, but other than them and the perfumed women below deck the boat was empty of passengers. Were there enough people to even venture a trip? Malibu didn't have to wonder long, because moments later the boat motored back from the dock. The wind began to kick up and Malibu pulled the zipper of her jacket up, cinching it all the way to her neck.

The boat glided toward Alcatraz. A full moon hung ominously in the black sky, its reflection glimmering off the glasslike surface of the water. The only noise was a low din that rose from the casino and floated to Malibu. Malibu looked at the casino and tried to remember a movie that featured the building. There were no doubt plenty, but none sprang to mind. When had the island changed from an old prison tourist attraction to a casino? Was it during Ivanka's third term or Barron's first? Malibu had no idea.

It didn't take long until the ferry arrived at the front of the island. It circled around to the back and docked. From this close, the noise that rose from the casino sounded like a low roar, steady and ominous, and inviting. Malibu was itching to get off the boat.

An off-ramp was put in place, and when Malibu reached the end of it a robotic guard confronted her. He was a foot taller than the standard Union Member. His hair—*his*, because that's how Malibu thought of it—was cut short and flat on top. He had a black leather jacket with silver studs, and despite the fact it was nighttime, he wore black sunglasses. An image from the movie *The Terminator* flashed into Malibu's mind and she felt a shiver.

The shiver didn't last long, pushed to the side by Malibu's ascendant brassy attitude. She took long, boastful strides forward, her gaze fixed straight ahead, until she spotted a red carpet that weaved its way up a winding path that led upward to the casino's entrance. The carpet was a bit much, but Malibu stepped along it. The moon had positioned itself directly overhead, seemingly eager to watch the show unfold. Its eerie light hit the building and cast long and ghostly shadows. The path covered by the carpet was narrow and lined with potted plants —succulents, each a dark and richly colored shade of green. Their stems were long and twisted in bizarre shapes, as if a demented gardener had tortured them into shape. A few other people moved along the red carpet, both coming and going, mostly coupled off. They laughed and talked loudly and were sodden with drink. With each step the ground beneath Malibu felt more solid, as if she were nearing a destiny of sorts.

Malibu looked at the neon sign. It glowed a spectral shade of orange. Two long beams of white light cast by large spotlights moved slowly across the sign, crisscrossing its surface before shooting up further into the sky, aching to reach the moon. I'm sure I've seen an image just like this, Malibu thought. In a movie, no doubt, or a childhood dream that lay just beneath the surface. Her mind revved faster, bolts of static energy firing through neurons trying to locate the buried memory but failing to find it. No matter, she was here now.

As she reached the peak and the casino stood directly in front of her, it struck Malibu as peculiar that she registered no emotional energy from the building. Double-checking, she zeroed her gaze on the façade. Nope—there was zilch. Come to think of it, she hadn't felt a thing from Luciana's home, either. Really, the only homes—or any inanimate objects, for that matter—that gave off an emotional cue were the cottages, and the energy that rose off them was overwhelming. Malibu had a strange feeling the cottages' close proximately to death is what gave them this special quality, as if on the other side everything was instilled with a consciousness and being so close to passing over allowed the cottages to tap into that ability. Of course, the last cottage she had burned hadn't spoken to her; something inside her had compelled Malibu to burn it.

Malibu shook these thoughts from her head and took in the two gigantic doors at the casino's entrance. They were swung open. A mass of people huddled in the mouthlike opening. Three steps lead up to the doorway, each neatly covered by the red carpet. Malibu climbed the steps and pushed her way through the crowd. Just as she was about to cross the threshold, a cold hand gripped her shoulder. Without looking up at the Terminator-sized robot, she flashed her opal ring. He released his hold and let her through.

Ten feet into the building the red carpet stopped and the crowd thinned enough to give Malibu some elbow room. The inside of the room was pretty much what she had expected. It no longer resembled a prison at all. Walls had clearly been torn down, creating one enormous room. A beige carpet completely covered the floor. Scattered throughout were slot machines and gambling stations—roulette, craps, blackjack. On the side of the room it looked like a few old prison cells had been allowed to remain, but were radically remodeled into spaces where people could exchange shekels for gambling chips. Milling about were men in ties and women decked out in saucy outfits similar to the red dress Malibu wore. There was a lot of cleavage and bright lipstick. A few glum-faced patrons were mixed into the crowd—no doubt losers at the tables—but for the most part everyone seemed happy, even gleeful.

More than dozen feet up the walls was a catwalk that circled the room. On it were a handful of large robots in leather jackets surveying the crowd below. Their eyes never blinked. They looked dissonant, alien as they stood sentry above the boisterous throng.

Malibu stood still for a moment, letting the energy of the room flow around her. Her eyes danced over the crowd. There were a few peculiarities in the room's design. For starters, the catwalk still seemed to have its original metal railing, the one that had been installed when the jail was first built. It looked rusted and dented and completely out of place with the rest of the upscale décor. In the corner of the room was a jail cell that looked as if it had been completely untouched. On the ceiling of the main room, an old light fixture had been allowed to remain. There was a metal grate screwed into the ceiling, and under the grate was a light bulb, which had clearly long ago burned out. On one wall was a fist-sized hole, which Malibu could look in and see the veins of the building. But perhaps the strangest thing was the floor, which wasn't level. It looked warped and uneven, like waves gently rolling on a pond. The oddities gave the impression that the old building was trying to break through.

Malibu walked toward one of the currency rooms and exchanged two handfuls of shekels for chips. The chips were plastic and black, with perforated edges. On one side was a large C, which must stand for casino or Chairman. On the other side was what looked like a demon. It was female and naked and turned sideways to hide the exciting bits. The demon had long hair and a tail. Its head was turned so it looked directly out at Malibu, who held one of the chips up close to her face. Malibu locked eyes with the demon for a moment, before dropping all of the chips into her purse and walking to a roulette table.

Malibu won big. It was as if the roulette ball followed her unspoken commands. The ball would rhythmically bounce along the spinning wheel, following the agreed upon laws of physics, but as the wheel slowed, the ball would take decidedly unnatural jumps, bounding violently from one side to the other, landing in the number Malibu needed to win, and firmly planting itself, unwilling to budge until the wheel stopped. At first, she tried to improve her odds by placing multiple bets. But as it became clear Lady Luck was in her corner, Malibu began to pare the number of bets until she would eventually make just one big bet per turn. Still, impossibly, she kept winning. Feeling bold, she slid her enormous pile of chips onto the number nine. The dealer spun the wheel, the ball bounced and bounced until, as if guided by a hidden magnet, it planted itself into the slot for the number nine, and despite the fact the wheel kept going, the ball would not be dislodged.

"You've got the magic touch," said the vest-wearing, bowtie-sporting croupier as he pushed a mountain-size pile of chips across the green velvet table and over to where Malibu sat. "Why don't you go try your luck at the craps table."

"I might just do that. Do you have anything I could use to carry this in?" Malibu asked as she nodded toward the chips.

The dealer frowned, bent under the table, and produced a canvas bag. It was black and had the same letter C as was displayed on the chips. Malibu stuffed the remainder of the chips into the bag, stood, swung it over her shoulder and marched away, feeling like Santa Claus leaving the North Pole.

Malibu took only a few steps before a woman stepped right in front of her, blocking her path forward. "So, Mama Bear let you out for the night?" she snarled.

Malibu reflectively recoiled, not because of the sudden appearance of the woman or her belligerent tone, but as a result of an offensive odor; specifically, her perfume, which was wildly repugnant and overpowering. It took a moment for Malibu's brain to recover from the shock of the perfume's punch and register a name.

"Sandy." Malibu spit out the word like she was discarding a piece of stale gum.

Speaking of gum, Sandy was working a large wad extra hard. It was lodged in the rear of her mouth, by her molars, and as she chomped down the muscles in her jaw flexed from exertion. Sandy let her eyes dance up and down Malibu. "You're all dolled up. Oh, and I love what you've done with your hair," she said with a snarky tone. "Did you add the white streak yourself?"

Sandy reached a hand forward as if to touch Malibu's hair, but Malibu took a step back, biting down on her lower lip.

"It's all good," Sandy said. "Your old dowdy look worked, but this seems to be the more real you. Am I right?"

Malibu again kept quiet, not wanting to engage.

Sandy gave the gum a few more hard chews and said, "What are you doing here? Something for Mama Bear?"

"Is that why you're here?"

"I asked you first."

"Where are we, on the playground?"

Sandy stepped forward, close enough that the offensive perfume made another sortie up Malibu's nostrils. Surprising herself, Malibu used both her hands to push Sandy's shoulders, sending her backward. She didn't push particularly hard, but with enough force to send a message.

"You smell horrible. I mean, really, really awful."

Sandy didn't seem bothered by the comment. She kept working the gum, and with a cock of her head said, "It keeps the flies away. Look, I have nothing against you personally. I just have a real good gig going with Luciana and I don't want you, or anyone, cutting in on my territory. Got it?"

"You work in the casino?"

"Uh-huh."

"Doing what?"

"What do you mean, *doing what*? The same minor hood stuff I'm sure you're doing. That is what you're doing, right?"

Malibu didn't respond, although the image of a cottage burning to the ground popped into her mind.

"What do you do?" Sandy asked with a bit more urgency. When Malibu didn't respond again, Sandy said, "Don't play coy with me."

"I..." Malibu trailed off when she spotted a group of six people walking their way. The Chairman was at the head of the group. He wore what looked like a full-length mink coat, the front open so the sides could swing as he took long, purposeful strides. Behind him were four men. Bodyguard types with no necks; their fat heads sat directly on top of their square shoulders. Their ties were pulled up to their chins so tightly it must be a challenge to breathe. At the tail end of the group was a young woman in a white lace dress. She looked angelic. As the group moved forward, the crowd parted like a school of sardines letting a whale swim through.

No one stared, except for Malibu.

Malibu felt her jaw open and practically drop to the floor. She was transfixed. Not by the Chairman or the bodyguards, but by the young woman in white. Something inside Malibu sparked to life. She was overcome by a sense of familiarity and desire, desire so strong it made the hair on the back of Malibu's neck bristle.

Take her, rang the forceful voice.

As the group passed by where Malibu and Sandy stood,

Malibu turned to Sandy and said, "Do you know who that is?" She pointed toward the woman.

"Maybe. What's it to you?" She flashed a devilish grin, lifted her hand in front of her face and rubbed her thumb and forefinger together.

Malibu dug inside her bag of chips and pulled out a large fistful, which she handed to Sandy.

Sandy had no place to store the loot, so she held it in her hands. She blew a bubble until it popped, sucked the gum back into her mouth, and said, "She's the Chairman's new girl."

"New?"

"I've seen her around for maybe a month or so."

"Is she his mistress?"

Sandy shook her head. "From what I've heard, she's not exactly his type. He likes 'em with a little more edge—tattoos, leather, that sort of thing."

"So what is she then?"

Sandy shrugged. She stared at the bag of chips, let her eyes linger there for a while, then pulled them back to Malibu, arched an eyebrow and offered up a *You know what I want* smile.

"Your hands are full," Malibu said. "Where would you even put more chips?"

"How badly do you want to know about your little gal in lace?"

This badly, Malibu thought, as she handed over the entire bag to Sandy, who reached for it so greedily that most of the chips she had been holding fell to the carpet. Sandy snatched the bag out of Malibu's hands, bent down to her knees, and started stuffing the dropped chips into the satchel. Malibu kneeled down to join her.

"You've taken a fancy to that one, haven't you?" Sandy said. She lifted her eyes momentarily to give Malibu a mocking glance, before looking back down to the carpet and plucking up the chips. "Feeling a bit warm between the thighs? I bet she swings the same way as you. Just a guess, though. It wouldn't matter anyway."

Malibu let the comment drop. "So if she's not his mistress then what is she?"

"His muse."

"His muse?"

"That's right. That's his word, not mine. He runs through one every few months."

"What does he need a muse for?"

Sandy finished gathering the dropped chips and pulled herself up. Malibu followed suit.

"No idea. He's a weird cat. Must believe it helps somehow. Anyway, that's the word among the ladies. Oh, and don't get your hopes too high about squelching that fire between your legs. No sex. The muses are all virgins, each as untouched as a nun's cunt. It's a requirement."

"A muse," Malibu said under her breath. "What's her name?" Malibu asked, although she suddenly knew the answer.

"Prudence." Sandy blew another bubble. It popped loudly. "Are we done here?"

Malibu nodded.

Sandy smiled tightly, flung the satchel over her shoulder and marched away, hips sashaying. Malibu watched her go until the sea of people swallowed her up.

Malibu hurried to catch up the Chairman and his crew, squeezing her way through a mass of people who had reformed in the wake of the Chairman's crew passing, while craning her neck to get a clear view over the heads in the crowd. Luckily, Malibu didn't have to fight the crowd for long because the Chairman stopped at the end of the room. He stood to one side, pulled a cigar out of a pocket of his mink, bit off the tip and spit

it out, stuck the cigar into his mouth, and waited for a bodyguard to light it. The one standing nearest obliged. The
Chairman puffed up a big cloud of smoke and scanned the
crowd gathered in the room like an old-time rancher gazing out
at his herd of cattle. The bodyguards pressed in close. Prudence
drifted off to the side toward a wooden chair against a wall,
where she sat. She crossed a leg over a knee and examined her
fingernails, seemingly bored with the whole scene.

Malibu positioned within eyeshot of Prudence, standing
directly in front of her. Prudence kept her eyes fixed on her
nails, perturbed by a particularly troublesome cuticle. A feeling
of desire gurgled inside Malibu. *Make her yours.* Prudence
looked nearly the same as the last time Malibu had seen her:
perfectly curved eyebrows, unblemished skin and heart-shaped
lips. Malibu's mind drifted back to the movie theater: the smell
of buttered popcorn, Jimmy Stewart and Kim Novak, a hand
peeking under her skirt. Malibu considered her life since then,
events scrolling by like a movie montage showing the rapid
passage of time.

Then Malibu's mind shifted, as if a malevolent force had
seized her thoughts and taken control. *She deserted you. She
toyed with your emotions.*

I'm not sure that's how it was, Malibu thought in response.

Prudence pulled her eyes from her nails and looked
directly at Malibu. They locked eyes and Malibu felt a cosmic
energy pass between them. Prudence's face wore a confused
expression. Her eyes were narrowed into slits, as if she were
trying to improve her focus. Just like that, the mask of bewilderment dropped and Prudence's eyes popped open wide. She
seemed eager to drink in the sight of Malibu. Prudence turned
her head to the side and saw the Chairman was still preoccupied with his cigar and henchmen. She stood up, used both

hands to brush the wrinkles off the front of her dress, and walked tentatively toward Malibu.

"Is that you?" she asked as she got within earshot.

"Hi, Prudence."

"Your hair, it looks..." Prudence paused, searching for the right word. It never materialized.

"Do you like it?"

Prudence nodded without hesitation. "I was going to say it looks dangerous."

"If you say so."

"What are you doing here?"

"At the casino?"

"Sure. In San Francisco. The works."

"It's a long story."

Prudence nodded in agreement. "Me too. I think about you sometimes. More than some of the time. A lot. I think about you a lot."

"Same." A lie. Malibu hadn't thought about Prudence. She'd buried the memories, at least on a conscious level. But Prudence must have been hidden just below the surface, influencing everything, because now that she was standing in front of Malibu, Malibu couldn't think about anything *but* Prudence.

Prudence smiled sweetly. A tiny dimple creased her right cheek. The crowd pressed in, literally pushing up against Malibu's back and forcing her to inch closer to Prudence. The clattering noise of people talking noticeably rose in volume. The sound climbed upward, bounced off the ceiling, and ricocheted back down to the swarming throng, where it was swallowed up and dispersed. Malibu felt suddenly disoriented, as if hit by a rogue wave, and had to shift her weight from one foot to the other to steady herself.

The voice, like an engulfing menace, spoke in her head.

Take her. Malibu hesitated, focused on her balance. *Take her!* it commanded.

As if operating with a mind of its own, Malibu's right arm jutted forward and grabbed Prudence by the wrist. Prudence's eyes, protected by long lashes, first registered surprise and then delight. The delight, however, faded as Malibu's fingers clamped down on the bone and pulled Prudence closer, so close that Malibu could smell her earthy and feral aroma.

"You're hurting me," Prudence said, although she didn't try to pull away.

Take her! the increasingly shrill voice inside her head screeched. Still in charge, Malibu pressed the command down and lightened the grip of her fingers. As she did, the worried look in Prudence's eyes softened.

Prudence leaned forward. She spoke into Malibu's ear, loudly enough to be heard over the crowd, but still in a hushed whisper.

"You're different," she said.

"Dangerous?" Malibu whispered back.

"A bit."

"Do you like it?"

"Yes. No. I'm not sure."

"Let's go." Malibu started to pull Prudence toward the exit, but she resisted.

"I can't." She looked toward the Chairman, his head thrown back as he cackled, and looked back again at Malibu. "I can't. I can't leave him."

"Yes, you can."

Malibu gripped down on the wrist tighter and pulled Prudence into the crowd. Prudence did not resist. Once they moved into the heart of the room where the gambling stations were located, the crowd thinned enough to give them space to walk more freely. Prudence moved closer to Malibu so that she was no longer being dragged but walked beside her. She took Malibu's hand and cast a furtive glance over her shoulder, as if expecting the Chairman's henchmen to be on her heels. They did not slow down when they got to the edge of the red carpet, but rushed out the exit, past the guards and down the steps.

The air had grown cold and felt crisp and heavenly to breathe. Malibu stopped and inhaled a lungful. She could hear noise from inside the casino as it seeped through the main entrance and dissolved upward into space. The moon still hung large and orange in the starless sky. A thick nimbus circled around it. Far below, the water of the bay looked savagely black.

Take her, take her.

The voice rang inside her head, so loudly it was almost deafening.

"I'm cold," Prudence said.

The words snapped Malibu back to attention. She looked at Prudence, who was shivering. Her arms crossed over her chest and her hands clutched her triceps. Her exposed skin was dotted with goose bumps and her nipples, covered only by the lace dress, were hard. She gazed at Malibu with pleading eyes, looking as fresh and inviting as a ripe piece of fruit.

Malibu removed her suede jacket and wrapped it around Prudence's shoulders. As she did, those two words rang in her head again, even more forcefully than before.

Take her!

"Let's go," Malibu said.

She took Prudence's hand and led them around the side of the building. There was a narrow paved path that clung to the edge of the hill. It was empty of people, and as they moved along it, the noise from inside the casino dimmed until it nearly faded completely. As they walked, the Golden Gate Bridge came into view, hovering on the horizon. Whatever had prevented her from jumping off the railing was now working to take more control; it wouldn't be satisfied until it owned Malibu completely.

Malibu and Prudence reached the back of the casino and found a tiny alcove. A dozen large potted succulents were scattered about the space. Each had grown taller than Malibu, and the limbs were bent into wildly distorted angles. If they could speak, surely they'd shriek out in terror. Just above the alcove was the black metal base of one of the spotlights. Light came out of it brightly, but directly below the spotlight it was dark.

Malibu placed a hand on Prudence's lower back and pushed her forward. She twisted her around, pressed her back up against the wall. Malibu felt something wild and uncontrollable stir inside like a predator—a shark that smells blood in the water, a cat as it stalks its prey. The feeling filled her with power and joy and unbending resolve. Prudence's expression was harder to read. Was it acceptance, or gleeful anticipation? Malibu didn't consider the question long; the answer didn't matter.

Malibu roughly brushed Prudence's hair back on one side of her head. She pressed her body against Prudence and bit her earlobe, not playfully, but hard. Prudence let out a shriek of surprise, which morphed into a groan, and then a sigh of surrender. Malibu continued to bite the earlobe as she pinched one of Prudence's nipples with her thumb and forefinger. Prudence's moan grew deeper, more guttural. She pushed her chest forward in encouragement, thrust her pelvis forward as well. It felt to Malibu as if Prudence was no longer in control of her body, but was reacting to Malibu's action. Malibu removed her mouth from the ear and placed it on Prudence's lips. She kissed them softly and gently at first, but then began to bite her lower lip. As she bit down harder on the lip, Prudence's groan grew more urgent. Malibu worked her free hand under Prudence's dress, inside her panties, and thrust a finger inside.

Prudence ground her pelvis down onto Malibu's hand. Malibu clamped down hard on the lip, bit so hard she broke skin. Drops of blood slipped into her mouth and trickled to the back of her throat and she felt drunk with desire. Prudence tried to pull her lip free, but Malibu bit down harder, long enough to extract a few more droplets, before releasing her grip. Malibu looked at Prudence's face—cheeks flush—and watched as her eyes rolled upward. Prudence's groans grew louder and more insistent.

"Let it go," Malibu whispered into her ear—a command.

Prudence did. Her body quivered. She clamped her thighs around Malibu's hand. Malibu felt Prudence's body shake as it raced up the steps of exaltation. Prudence tried to scream out, but Malibu covered her mouth with her hand, stifled the noise. The shaking continued, Prudence electric, a live wire. And then it stopped. Malibu let her hand linger for a moment before pulling it free. Prudence let out a deep sigh. It felt for a moment like they had crossed into another world, another realm of being.

Prudence slumped down to the ground, back against the wall. Malibu sat next to her, pulled her knees up to her chest. The malignant force growing inside Malibu fell dormant, as if falling into remission. Malibu and Prudence didn't speak for a long time, just looked out at the bay and the city. It felt so lovely it hurt.

It was Prudence who broke the spell. "That was my first time."

"No. I was there. At the movie theater."

"You got off. This was my first for me." A foghorn blew in the distance. When it stopped, Prudence said, "I can't go back. He'll kill me."

"The Chairman?"

Prudence nodded. "He's killed all the ones before me. At least that's what I was told."

"That's crazy."

"Once we're drained of our magic, we're useless to him." Prudence turned her head toward Malibu, offered a weary smirk. "I'm a muse," she said with a sad laugh.

"So I've been told."

"It's ridiculous."

"You're not really a muse?"

"No, I am."

"What does that even mean?"

"It's a long story."

"I've got time."

Prudence let out a long sigh. "Do you ever feel like you're not wholly yourself? Or you are yourself, but a different iteration? A warped reflection."

"Parallel worlds colliding."

"Exactly."

They were silent again and Malibu felt the weight of Prudence's words press down on her. Was she really here, or in the future, safely tucked inside a warm and comfortable room re-watching the episode on a Memory Console? She tried to manipulate her surroundings, tried to speed time forward, tried to stop it, but time kept moving at its plodding and menacing pace. Malibu looked to the side and saw a cactus covered with inch-long spikes. It looked poised to swing down and clobber her. Her mouth turned dry and clammy and she was touched by a scrambling panic. She felt weak and alone and abandoned, despite the fact Prudence stood so closely their elbows touched.

Malibu turned back toward Prudence. "Is there any point to it all?"

Prudence smiled, and it looked for a moment like the light

from the moon was cast through her. Her face glowed. Through her features, Malibu thought she could see another life break through. But in defiance of that life, Prudence said, "No. We live. We die. There is no point."

The menace stirred inside Malibu, a bear waking from hibernation. It warmed her, gave her strength, and she suddenly knew what to do. She stood and offered a hand to help Prudence up.

"Let's go," Malibu said.

Prudence didn't reach for the hand. "Where?"

"You'll see. I want to show you something."

Prudence took the hand. Malibu pulled her up and led the way as they walked down to the ferry dock.

COTTAGE NUMBER EIGHT

ON THE FERRY RIDE, HARDLY TWO WORDS WERE SPOKEN. Prudence kept looking back at the casino, as if she expected an enormous hand to reach across the expanse of water, pluck her off the deck, and carry her back to the Chairman. As they disembarked in San Francisco and left the wharf, Prudence kept shooting fretful glances over her shoulder.

"You seem worried," Malibu said. "You really think the Chairman wants to kill you?"

"I know he does. Once you're impure, you're no longer of use to him."

"What if you're not impure, you can still live?"

"That's only happened once, at least as far as I know." She cast another glance backward. "I'm sorry I ghosted you."

"It hurt me," Malibu admitted.

"I know. It uncorked something in me and I felt that us getting together would lead to something bad." She looked at Malibu as they walked. "You've changed so much. Maybe not getting together led to the same place. You can't avoid fate."

"You talk in riddles."

A tiny smile inched across her face. "That's what's muses do."

"But you're no longer a muse."

Prudence stayed quiet, apparently having not response.

They reached the bottom of a steep incline that led to Russian Hill. As they labored to climb up, Malibu continued to feel a sense of doomed resignation rise off Prudence and float around her like a black cloud.

Malibu was unconcerned. Wait until she sees what I have in store for her, she thought, as an image of rising flames crashed into her head. She felt strong and vital, like she was burning with life, more alive with each step. When they finally reached the sidewalk in front of the cottage, Malibu felt like she could burn down the house by shooting flames from her hands.

"We made it," Malibu said.

"We have?"

"Yes. The cottage. I wanted to show it to you."

Prudence, breathing heavily, said, "Are you sure we're in the right place? Are we meant to be here?"

Malibu looked up at the moon, which still was impossibly large, as if a force had pulled it closer to the Earth. It had turned a deeper shade of orange and shone so brightly it caused Prudence and Malibu to cast long shadows that almost reach to the lip of the cottage's porch.

"We're in the right place," Malibu said.

Prudence's eyes narrowed as she looked at the cottage. "That's peculiar."

"What?"

"That bird."

Malibu looked at the cottage and saw that a pelican had landed on its roof. The bird's wings were tucked to its sides. It stood motionless, its eyes staring upward into the infinity of space.

"I don't think I've ever seen a pelican this far from the water," Prudence said.

Malibu felt the world start to shake. It was so intense, at first she thought it was an earthquake, the ground about to open beneath her feet. The shaking sensation, which Malibu realized was coming from inside her, grew stronger. She shifted from one foot to the other, steadying herself.

The shaking inside her grew stronger.

And then it grew even stronger still.

"Wait here," Malibu told Prudence as she marched toward the cottage.

She reached the step leading up to the porch and the bird stayed put, didn't so much as twitch a feather. Malibu pushed through the room, not seeing a thing, as if she had blinders on. Taking long strides, she reached the rear of the building, where she attached a tablet to the wall. She ran the remote control over the explosive device. She did the same at the front of the building. When she exited the home and slowly walked toward Prudence, she didn't look up, didn't have to—she knew the bird was still on the roof.

Kill it! the voice in her head demanded. *Let it burn!*

"What's going on?" Prudence asked. "What are you doing?" Her face was etched with worry. Malibu could feel a deep sadness as it percolated inside Prudence.

She'll be happy when she sees the home burn.

Burn it!

Malibu pressed the detonator.

The explosion was strangely muffled. The fire started slowly. Through the open front door, Malibu could see the fire in the back of the house as it struggled to build. The same slow build happened in the front as well. Despite the old and rotten quality of the wood, the home seemed to be resisting its fate. That couldn't be, Malibu thought, it wants to die. Then, like a snap of the fingers, the two separate flames raced across the floor and converged in the middle. Soon the entire building was ablaze. Malibu looked up at the roof and saw that the pelican held its ground for as long as it could. The roof was the last part of the building the fire reached, and even then, it seemed like the spot around the pelican remained untouched, an island in a sea of terror. As if the bird itself had created a protective force field. But eventually the flames broke through and the bird was forced to depart, flapping its wings as a few sparks nicked its tail feathers.

Malibu was so preoccupied with watching the bird that at first she didn't hear the noise beside her. Prudence. Her sorrowful moans broke through Malibu's consciousness like a slow rumble. They built in volume until they were one long howl. As the pelican flapped across the surface of the moon, Malibu turned and saw Prudence scrunched down to her knees, her face wet with tears, her eyes fixed on the flaming remnants of the home.

"No...no...no!" she wailed.

Malibu grabbed her by the jacket and tried to pull her up, but Prudence shook free.

"No!"

"The home wanted to die."

"No!"

"It was asking to die."

Prudence tilted her head upward and looked at Malibu. Her tears had turned to choking sobs. "You're...you're wrong."

Unlike with the last home, the sound of sirens erupted all around them. It was impossible to tell where they were originating; it seemed like every direction.

Malibu grabbed Prudence by the sleeve and tried again to pull her up, but Prudence resisted. She had stopped moaning but still looked pitiful.

The sirens grew louder, closer.

A small group of homeless people appeared down the

block. A woman led them. She pushed a metal shopping cart overloaded with supplies. Her hair was long and unkempt. The others marched behind her, their faces down and zombielike.

"We need to go." Malibu tried again to pull Prudence up of the ground.

Prudence shook free again.

Make that bitch move.

The sirens sounded like they were right around the corner.

Malibu reached down and lifted Prudence off the ground. Prudence's legs, as reliable as rubber bands, didn't truly support her, so using a strength she did not know she possessed, Malibu practically dragged her down the street toward where the homeless people were approaching.

Make that bitch walk!

"Walk," Malibu demand, her voice as rough as a chainsaw. The sound startled her.

Prudence half-heartedly obliged, stumbling with each step.

They were steps from the woman with the shopping cart when a fire truck turned the corner at the end of the block and raced down the street toward the cottage.

"Shekel, shekel, shekel," demanded the cart woman, her lips filthy and chapped, her mouth empty of teeth. She thrust her arm forward, palm up.

The fire truck drove past where they stood. A robotic Union Member stood on the outside gripping a handrail, its eyes fixed on Malibu.

It knows.

A commuter car pulled along the curb, as if Malibu had called for it. Malibu, still dragging Prudence, brushed past the toothless woman and reached the car. She opened the back door, and with one hand lifted her sobbing friend off her feet and threw her into the back seat. She jumped in behind her and slammed the door shut.

"I guess you don't know your own strength," the car said. What was the accent? Beats me, Malibu thought, her brain so cluttered it was unable to process information.

Get the car to go.

"Move it," Malibu demanded.

"I need payment and a destination first."

Malibu realized she no longer had her purse. Somewhere between the cottage and the car she'd dropped it.

"Do you have any shekels?" she asked Prudence, who didn't respond.

"Wait here," Malibu said, to both the car and Prudence.

Malibu pushed open the door and stepped outside. The air reeked of smoke. She could see the cottage smoldering and firemen using a hose to douse the burning remnants. She scanned the gap between the home and where she stood, searching for her dainty purse. She spotted it in the hands of the shopping cart woman.

Malibu hurried over. "Give me that," she demanded as she grabbed the purse and pulled. As she did, she saw that the homeless woman wore the same opal ring that she did. For a moment, Malibu's mind raced forward and she saw herself, toothless, pushing a cart, begging to survive.

That bitch stole it from someone.

The other homeless people didn't react, just stood there, as if unable to do anything but observe. The woman did not release the purse. She pulled it back. "Get your filthy hands off," she growled. "It's mine, mine!" Her eyes were red, like she was possessed.

Malibu tugged harder and succeeded in prying the purse from the woman's hands, but before Malibu could get away, the woman let out an animalistic shriek and bit the fleshy part of Malibu's hand between the thumb and forefinger. Malibu dropped the bag. It burst open and shekels scattered all over the pavement. Malibu and the woman both dived for the bag; the woman got there first. Down the block, nearing the dying home, a robotic Union Member started to walk toward where Malibu and the woman fought.

Fuck the bag. Get some shekels.

Malibu frantically gathered some shekels off the ground. She also scooped up the tube of lipstick. She clutched the items tightly, hurried back to the car, and jumped inside. Prudence was still there. She had pulled herself together—no more tears, just a downcast expression.

"You're a frisky little minx," the car said, its accent still undecipherable. Portuguese? Maybe it was Portuguese.

Malibu looked out the window and saw the Union Member confronting the homeless woman.

"Move," Malibu said as she dropped two coins into the slot. She gave the car the address for Luciana's home.

As the car moved down the block, Malibu freshened up her lips.

BEWARE DEAD CROWS

THEY STOOD IN FRONT OF THE GATE AT LUCIANA'S HOME.

The house seemed larger, elongate. It looked unnatural, as if viewed through a pinhole that distorted reality. It must be the moon, and the fog, which had crept in during the car ride and floated by in large and unwieldy swaths. This would make a spectacular movie shot; a point-of-view shot from Malibu's perspective. The camera should be positioned low and angled up toward the home, soft focus, with a dolly zoom to distort the visual perception. So either the home itself didn't look real, or Malibu's ability to see things accurately had been warped. It would be left up to the audience to decide. Just as the shot was about to end, super creepy orchestral music would play, foretelling of something horrible to come.

Malibu's mind couldn't hold these thoughts for long, because Prudence, who had settled down during the car ride, started to shake.

"I...I...can't go in there." Her eyes swept from the bottom of the gate up to the gargoyles and then to the home's façade. Her look was one of pure terror.

Lose the bitch. We got what we needed. Discard her.

Malibu shook that demand from her head. No way she

would lose Prudence now. "She'll be fine in the morning," she said.

"Who are you talking to?" Prudence asked.

Malibu ignored the question. She pushed open the gate and took a few steps forward, but stopped when she realized Prudence hadn't followed. She gently grabbed Prudence by the hand and said, "Come on."

Prudence didn't budge. "You're not going to burn it down, are you?"

Malibu assured her that she was not.

"What is this place?"

"I live here."

"You own it?"

"No. I have a room."

"So you rent?"

"Not exactly."

"You don't own or—"

Tired of the line of questioning, Malibu dragged Prudence through the open gate. Damn if the two gargoyles didn't seem to press forward at Prudence as she passed. Malibu expected the black cat to jump out at them. As if on cue, it popped out from under a bush, bared its teeth, hissed. Malibu thrust her head toward the cat and returned the favor, baring her teeth and letting out a menacing hiss. Spooked, the cat disappeared into the bushes.

"What was that?" Prudence asked, pulling her hand free from Malibu's grasp.

Malibu grabbed the hand back before Prudence could get away.

"Ouch. You're hurting me."

Malibu squeezed the hand tighter and led them up the last few steps to the entrance. She rapped the knocker two times. It took about a minute, but Max opened the door. Although it was late, he still wore his dark suit and tie. Perhaps he was a comforting sight, because Malibu felt Prudence soften, and she released the grip on her hand.

"You brought a friend," Max said as the two women stepped into the foyer. A cold draft swept through the room as Max shut the door.

Prudence gazed wide-eyed around the room.

"A friend?" a voice intruded from the adjacent room. Luciana. "I want to meet this friend."

"Who is that?" Prudence asked, her voice shaky.

No one answered her.

Max said, "This way." He led the two young women into the room with the large fireplace. It was noticeably darker than in the foyer, so dark Malibu could barely make out Luciana, who sat in her customary wing chair, leg crossed at a knee, brandy glass in hand, and a crazed half-smile on her lips.

"I'll take another," she said to Max, extending her glass out for Max to grab. "Get Malibu a glass of water. And you, miss, you'd like?"

"Water, I guess," Prudence managed to squeak out, her voice even shakier than before.

"Get her a water, I guess," Luciana said, her tone dripping with distain.

Before Max could leave, Malibu said, "I'd like a brandy as well."

"My, my," Luciana said. "Trying to take the edge off? Just promise me you won't break into one of those dreadful coughing spells."

The cat suddenly and impossibly materialized, as if it had stepped through a portal from a parallel universe. Wouldn't it be nice to escape to that world, where perhaps Malibu's mother wasn't dead and her father hadn't gone off the deep end and

Malibu wasn't asked to burn cottages? The cat jumped onto Luciana's lap and glared at Malibu.

"You'll have to tell me who did your hair. Its marvelous," Luciana told Malibu.

Prudence looked at Malibu as well, and recoiled at the sight.

Malibu took in her image in the full-length mirror on the wall. The white strands had spread so they covered half of her head. And her hair was not only swept back, but pulled to the sides as well, as if she stood in a wind tunnel. The image caused Malibu to shudder.

You look better. It would be even better if it covered your whole head.

"A shekel for your thoughts," Luciana said, and let out a witchy laugh.

Malibu pulled her eyes from the mirror and looked at Luciana with contempt. Her expression seemed to shake Luciana, but only for a moment. Luciana composed herself, rubbed her fingers up the cat's spine, pushing the fur the wrong way.

"Wait," said Prudence. Malibu looked and saw Prudence staring at Luciana, a question on her face. "I've seen you. One time. At the casino." She stopped, as if calling to mind a hazy image. "You...you used to be—"

"We don't all lose our virtue, dear," Luciana said as her eyes flashed bullets at Prudence. It was her turn to show contempt. "Not lost, given away." She shifted her eyes, looked sideways at Malibu. "Or was it taken?"

Prudence's body stiffened. "You're the one. You're the one who found an escape." She paused for a bit, as if hoping Luciana would fill the silence. When she didn't, Prudence said, "You were a muse, right?"

"Were? You act as if I'm dead."

Prudence opened her mouth to speak, but before she could squeeze a word out, Max came through the door holding a tray and handed the glasses around to each woman. He didn't say a word and long-stepped his way back to the kitchen, moving so quickly it seemed like he was trying to escape a crime scene.

"You were a muse," Prudence repeated, her voice quavering. She lifted the glass of water to her lips, but her hand was shaking noticeably and she could only take a small sip.

Luciana let the comment hang in the air. Malibu imagined it hovering like a balloon that had lost some of its helium. Luciana sniffed her brandy and took a sip, drinking only slightly more than Prudence had. It was Malibu's turn. She bent her elbow and drank nearly three-quarters of the brandy in one swift swallow. It slid down her throat like water over a cliff. The act seemed to catch both Prudence and Luciana off guard. They looked at her slack-jawed. Prudence's hand started to shake even more. So much so, she had to step over to the mantel and place her glass on top of it. Luciana wore a look of bewilderment, as if she was trying to piece together a puzzle.

Let them stare.

As that thought expanded in Malibu's mind, she was struck by a second alien sensation. A feeling. It reluctantly lifted off Luciana and glided toward Malibu. It was the first time she'd felt a distinct emotion from Luciana since that day at the Kit Kat Club. That feeling had been bold, whereas this felt meek, but in its own way equally as powerful. Fear. It was fear. As it seeped through Malibu's skin and settled into her core, she felt enriched by its presence. It added steel to her spine.

She fears you.

Luciana worked to suppress the look in her eyes. She let out a forced laugh and said, "Sip, sip. You're supposed to sip it." She looked at Prudence as if hoping for support, but none was given. Malibu, in defiance, drank down the remainder of the brandy. Luciana opened her mouth to speak, but Prudence jumped in first.

"You were a muse," she repeated with an accusatory tone.

"I'm still a muse, dear." Luciana seemed happy for a change in subject, and to be able to address Prudence. Her face brightened, but Malibu could still feel the fear. It clung to Luciana like a sickness. "My role is just more active than yours."

"Muses aren't active," Prudence said. "They just provide inspiration."

"We're not all cut from the same cloth."

"There were nine muses," Malibu said. How she knew this nugget of information was completely unclear to her.

Number nine, number nine, number nine.

Luciana looked at Malibu. "Nine, that's right."

"What are you a muse of?" Prudence said, and as she did she lifted the crow off the mantel, holding it like a shield.

Luciana sipped the brandy again and then placed the still half-full glass down. She forced a smile. A sickly smile, crooked and with no teeth, like something you might see on one of the desperate and angry homeless women living on the street. She pushed the cat off her lap and stood up.

"I'm the muse of none of your fucking business," she said. Her voice cut like a razor. Step took one step toward Prudence. "You girls disgust me. Each one of you, one after the next. Apostates."

Prudence puffed her chest out. "If you're still a muse, then you're still chaste." After she spoke, she shrunk down a little, as if shaken by her boldness. She clutched the crow to her chest, pressed her forefinger against its beak, then pulled it back, surprised by the sharpness, its ability to draw blood.

She's as cold as a nun's cunt. The words flashed in Malibu's mind. *You can carve a fresh trail.*

Luciana looked at Malibu in a way that implied she could

sense what was gurgling inside her. Malibu felt the fear still rise off her, spread like a cancer. But Luciana put on a brave face.

"I'll deal with you later." She spit the words at Malibu, but they lacked sting. She looked toward Prudence. "I'm not the issue here, dear, you are. With your virtue gone, you're no longer useful. And don't act surprised. Everything is seen. Everything is recorded." She pulled her hand out of the pocket of her robe and Malibu caught a flash of something silver.

"She's got a gun," Prudence squealed.

Get her!

Without thought, Malibu crouched and prepared to leap toward Luciana. As she pushed off the ground, the cat darted across her path and disrupted her movements enough that she missed the target and shot past where Luciana stood, falling to the carpet. As she lay there, she heard a loud crack and felt a hot sting in the back of her thigh.

"I don't know what you are," Luciana said, "but you need to leave this world."

Malibu reached out and grabbed Luciana by the foot. She yanked it, pulled Luciana's legs out from under her, and brought the older woman down onto the floor. When Luciana hit the ground, the gun broke free from her grasp and clattered a few feet away. Malibu tried to pull herself to her knees, but a burst of pain shot through her leg and she fell back.

Malibu screamed and clamped her hands over her wound.

Luciana stood, walked over to the gun, and lifted it off the floor. She stepped back to where Malibu lay prone and pressed the gun's barrel against the side of her head. "You fell one short," she said. "You only burned eight cottages. Such a pity." Malibu felt the fear evaporate off Luciana. She felt in control. Untouchable. Immune. Immortal.

Malibu waited for the crisp sound of the gun. Instead, she heard a muffled, gurgling noise, and then a thud as Luciana's body crashed down onto her. Malibu felt something hot and sticky spread across her skin. She rubbed her palm against it and pulled her hand in front of her face so she could see what it was. Blood.

Blood, blood, blood!

Malibu tugged her body out from under Luciana and gingerly pulled herself up. She stumbled over to the chair where Luciana had sat earlier and fell into the cushions. The back of her thigh where the bullet had entered barked angrily. Grimacing, she looked down in time to see Luciana take her last breath as she passed into the next world. The color rapidly drained from her body, turning her skin a sickly gray pallor. Sticking out of the side of her neck was the crow. Blood seeped out around the beak in rhythmic streams, pooling on the Oriental rug.

Ding-dong, the witch is dead!

Malibu conjured up images of Munchkins dancing and singing in sparkling Technicolor. As the Munchkin song played on an accelerated loop in her head, Malibu watched the cat stride toward Luciana's dead body, skirt around the pool of blood, and lick around the crow's beak.

"No!" shouted Prudence. Her face wore a mask comprised of equal parts disgust and terror. The sight nourished Malibu.

Prudence bent over Luciana's body, shooed the cat away, and pulled the crow out of the dead woman's neck. A trickle of blood oozed out the wound. Prudence pulled herself fully erect, still holding the crow in both hands. Her eyes rolled toward the ceiling, held there for a moment, and then dropped back down. They locked directly on Malibu. The fear and terror melted from her face and was replaced with a look of resignation. Prudence's emotions—now a bit more difficult to accurately decipher—streamed to Malibu quickly, as if they had started to run downhill. Malibu drank them in, becoming positively drunk with elation.

Do it. Do it. Finish it!

As if hearing the command, Prudence took the crow and used both hands to ram the knife-like beak into her own neck, into the exact spot where she had pierced Luciana. Prudence's body didn't fall immediately. It wobbled a bit, as if held in place by a puppet master's strings, and then gently folded down. When her body crumbled to the ground, the crow dislodged from her neck and blood oozed out. The cat sauntered over and started to lick Prudence's wound.

Malibu was overwhelmed with emotions. So overwhelmed, she didn't feel the throbbing of her thigh. So overwhelmed, her mind seemed to drift somewhere else. So overwhelmed, she hadn't noticed that Max had reentered the room.

"How could this have happened?" Max asked.

His voice was flat and devoid of emotion, as if he had asked Malibu about something routine and banal—the weather, or what she planned to eat for dinner. The mundane nature of his intonation worked to reengage Malibu's conscious mind. She looked at Max and saw a blurry image, but he slowly came into focus, as if a cameraman was adjusting his lens. His head was titled downward, directed toward the two dead women and the black cat that still licked the hole in Prudence's neck. Max stood directly in between the bodies. The soles of his loafers were in the rapidly thickening puddle of blood. He held the crow in his hands. The fingers of his white gloves stained a darkish gray color.

He turned his head toward Malibu. "How could this have happened?" he asked again, his voice as flat as before.

"How does anything happen?" Malibu tried to act casual, but her heart was thumping.

"Should I clean up?" Max asked, using a tone one might

expect if he were asking whether to clear the dishes after a party. It didn't escape Malibu that Max's question implied she was now in charge.

"Yes. Clean it up." Malibu lifted herself out of the chair, and as she did was struck by a sharp pain in her leg. She grimaced but resisted the urge to grab her wound. She waved a hand toward the horrific scene splayed out on the carpet. "Dispose of all of this. We may need a new carpet too. We can decide on that later. I'm going to go to the basement."

"Very well, madam." Max bowed at the waist.

"Wait. Give me that." Malibu pointed at the crow. Max stepped over Luciana's body and gave her the stuffed bird. Its beak was sticky with blood. Malibu tucked the bird under her arm, let her eyes dart around the room, then limped toward the basement.

ANOTHER SELF PORTRAIT

"Malibu," said Oppenheimer, "would you care to hear some music?"

Malibu stumbled toward the easel, her hand wrapped around the back of her thigh. The paint and her other supplies were still where she'd left them.

"Are there more canvases?" she asked.

"I told you. I can't see."

She scanned the room and spotted a blank canvas leaning against the back wall. She walked to it, dragging her leg, blood seeping through her fingers, and carried the canvas back to the easel, where she lifted it with both hands and slotted it into place. Some of the blood that was on her hand stuck to the canvas, which definitely would add to the effect she was hoping to create.

That bitch deserved to die.

"Which one?" Malibu said.

"You sound distressed," Oppenheim said.

"How can hear that in my voice?"

"My senses, outside of sight, are finely developed."

Wincing, Malibu opened a jar of black paint and picked a large paintbrush off the table. "Maybe some music would help."

"What would you like to hear?"

"The Beatles. *White Album*. Not in order—random."

A snap second later, "Happiness Is A Warm Gun" started playing; naturally, because that was the song Malibu wanted to hear, the song she had already started humming in her head.

"Louder. Louder," she demanded, taken aback by her own forceful tone.

Oppenheimer played the music so loudly the room shook. The noise caused Malibu's mind to malfunction, if just a bit, which was a good thing, because it allowed her to work instinctually, which was when she produced her best art.

She had to work quickly, that was obvious.

She painted herself from the neck up. For her face, she recreated how she had looked the day she left Santa Monica and moved to San Francisco. The hair needed to be different, though, needed to look the way it was now—untamed, black on one side and white on the other. These elements all came together quickly on the canvas.

It's good the other bitch killed herself.

Her thigh started to scream in pain. Really, if Malibu hadn't seen it herself, she wasn't sure she would have believed it could happen, that someone could use the pointy end of a stuffed crow to murder a woman and then kill themselves with it.

Focus. Need to focus.

Malibu examined what she'd created. It was nice, for a rushed job, but it needed something avant-garde. Only, what? She swiped the end of the brush clean with a rag and dipped the tip into a tin of green paint. The song "Piggies" began to blare over the speakers and her thoughts hopscotched back to Kenny and the hospital. She yanked her mind back into the room and focused on the painting. Around her neck, she painted the tail of a green snake. It wrapped around her throat and squeezed. The snake's torso scaled up one side of her face and plunged into an eye socket.

She was still looking at the snake when she felt something grab her biceps. The music was so loud and she was so focused she hadn't heard anyone enter the room. She turned her head and took in the emotionless face of a robotic Union Member. It squeezed her arm more firmly. Behind him, Malibu could vaguely make out the image of the robot's partner talking to Max. Their lips were moving but she couldn't make out what they were saying.

"Oppenheimer, can you stop the music, please," she said, and it cut off immediately. "Do you like it?" she asked the robot, nodded toward the painting.

He didn't indicate one way or the other. He just dragged her away.

UNDER THE HOT LIGHTS

MALIBU WAS JOLTED TO CONSCIOUSNESS BY A BURNING sensation on her face. Her mind was a jumbled mess. She tried to bring her hand to her head, but her arm wouldn't move. Keeping her left eye clamped shut, she ventured to crack open her right eye. Peering through her lashes, she saw a large white light beaming down on her. It was a floor lamp, but what was odd was that it was positioned so closely to her.

Where was she?

She cracked the other eye, tried to take in her surroundings, but the light was so intense she couldn't process anything beyond it. As her head cleared, she realized she was stretched out on her back, her head resting on a pillow. She tried to lift both arms, but again they would not budge. Same with her legs. Bending her head forward, she saw that her arms were strapped to metal railings on the sides of a bed. Frantically, needing to be free, she pulled hard, convulsed her body, and tried to yank herself loose.

No luck.

Pull harder!

She clenched both fists, clamped her jaw shut, and pulled with all her might. Still no luck. She was trapped.

"Sleeping beauty has rejoined us."

It was a man's voice. She couldn't see his face.

"You're a regular badger."

The floor lamp was pulled back, blessedly giving her face relief from the heat and allowing Malibu to see more, see enough to recognize she was on a bed in what looked like a hospital room. She heard a scraping sound along the floor and saw a large man pull a chair up beside her. He had a full salt-and-pepper beard, neatly cut hair, and a no-nonsense look on his face. He sat down on the chair.

"A badger can take on and defeat an opponent twice its size."

Malibu pulled at the straps again.

"Now, normally just one of these guys could easily handle a woman of your size," the man said. He hooked a finger over his shoulder and pointed toward the front of the room where two robots stood sentry. They looked a Malibu with unblinking eyes. "It took three of them to bring you down."

"I don't remember resisting," Malibu said. She racked her brain and realized she didn't remember anything since the Union Member had led her out of Luciana's basement. "How long have I been here?"

"Two days," the man said. He loosened his tie, undid the top button of his shirt.

"That's impossible." How could she have forgotten two days? *Kill him.* The caged beast rumbled inside her. Malibu pulled at the straps again, but with less enthusiasm than before. When she realized she couldn't break free, she let her body settle back down into the bed, resigned to her fate. "Who are you?"

He ignored her question. "We've examined the crime scene. I've seen worse, but not many. We looked at your memories too, so we have a clear picture of what happened."

It all flooded back: Luciana's living room; the tiny silver pistol; the crow being lodged in Luciana's neck, in Prudence's neck. Malibu stifled the urge to puke, but still felt some vomit escape into her mouth.

They deserved to die.

"If you looked at my memories," Malibu said, "then you know I wasn't the killer. If anything, I was a victim."

The man smiled. "It's not that simple. Besides, we found other things, and memory gaps as well. It doesn't paint a good picture."

Other things. The man whose finger she broke. Burned cottages. Children killed.

"Where am I?" she asked.

"In a hospital. And you're going to stay here for a while."

Malibu didn't like how that sounded. "What does that mean? How long?"

He gently waved his hand, as if indicating they would get to it later. "Why'd you do it?"

"You've seen my memory. I didn't do it. I was the one who was shot."

His face looked both pained and puzzled. "No, why'd you burn the cottages?"

Malibu shrugged as best she could under the straps. "She asked me to. Luciana."

"She paid you?"

"That's right."

The man leaned back in his chair. He rubbed his hands over his head. "I grew up in a cottage like that. It's crazy what has happened to this city."

Everything started to move so quickly Malibu didn't have time to process what was happening. The man stood, waved toward the two robotic Union Members. Next thing Malibu knew, her bed was being wheeled down a hallway. She made out linoleum floors and florescent lights and people in white lab coats. Doors swung open and she was pushed into a large room. It was frigid and she could hear the air-conditioning hum.

"Unstrap her."

Malibu recognized the voice of the man from earlier. The Union Members undid the bindings on her arms and legs. Holding her arms, they lifted her out of the bed. The light was dim, but Malibu could see the man and two more robots standing sentry next to him. Behind them was a long narrow hallway. On either side of the hallway were what looked like shelves with handles. Two levels, one stacked on top of the other. One of the shelves in the middle of the hallway was pulled out, and Malibu saw what looked like a bed.

"Disrobe her," the man said.

In a flash, Malibu broke free, twisted, grabbed a robot by the ears, and spun his head so hard it almost snapped off. The robot fell to the ground and twitched. The other three robots jumped her; two held her arms back while one lifted a leg.

"Like I said, a regular badger," the man said. He glanced down at the convulsing robot, then back up at Malibu.

He needs to die!

The thought cascaded through Malibu's mind and body.

"Put her away," said the man.

The three robots lifted Malibu off the ground and carried her down the hallway to the bed. She didn't thrash, didn't try to break free. The robots threw her down onto the mattress and proceeded to strap her down, just as she had been earlier.

As they stepped away, a nurse in blue scrubs appeared. She held a syringe. She plunged the needle into a vein on Malibu's arm and pressed the hammer. Malibu felt her mind go immediately fuzzy.

The nurse stepped away and the man with the salt-and-pepper hair took her place. Malibu spit in his face. As he wiped it off, he said, "You're going to sleep for a while."

The shelf was pushed shut.

Everything went dark.

———

Malibu could dream again.

What's more, she was aware she was dreaming.

Her conscious mind was subdued, but engaged enough that she recognized what was happening. Yes, it was nice to have that part of her brain reengaged. Maybe something in the stasis chamber retriggered the necessary synapses? Whatever the cause, she figured the dreams would help her. She remembered the beginning of the movie *The Haunting on Hill House*: "No live organism can continue for long to exist sanely under conditions of absolute reality; even larks and katydids are supposed, by some, to dream."

Was she insane? That's not a question a crazy person would ask, so no. She still had all her marbles. True, they'd been let out of the bag, scattered about, but she could use this time to regather them, put things back in order.

Time. She had a lot of it.

However, she didn't really try to put her marbles back into their proper place. She watched her dreams instead.

That's because as the days stretched into weeks and the weeks stretched into months, Malibu learned how to manipulate her dreams. It was fun, a real gas. She couldn't conjure up specific subject matter—her unconscious mind still controlled that element—but once a particular subject was engaged, she could manipulate how it unfolded. She was the director. Malibu was the dream director. Places, everyone!

Pelican, I need you over there.

I don't like the Engineer's outfit. Get me something more sinister.

I said a crow, a stuffed *crow*.

Props, I need props. Can someone get me props?

That's too much Goddamn fog. No one is going to believe it.

More sinister. I need her to look more sinister. How? You tell me, you're the costume designers.

Sometimes Malibu dreamt about completely random things; such is the nature of dreams. But more often than not, her dreams were of events that had happened in her life. That was nice. It allowed her to not only reexamine what had occurred, but to reinvent it, to alter reality. It was comforting.

There were occasionally times that Malibu could not manipulate her dreams, when she was not in charge. Those dreams were familiar but distorted, as if she were examining her life through the wrong end of a pair of binoculars. Malibu could see herself, could see the places where she had lived, but they were far in the distance, and she had no feelings of connectedness to them. She was caught in a hall of mirrors and her image was reflected into infinity, but the reflected images were not consistent, rather cast slightly differently, so that each one was as unique as a snowflake. Snowflakes birthed from the same storm. Malibu examined those differing images and felt an anger build inside.

Of all the options, why did I land with you?

Sadly, there were also times Malibu didn't dream at all.

That was not comforting. It was not peaceful. She didn't simply drift off into a blissful sleep. No, when there were no dreams, Malibu felt like she was in conflict with herself. A frightful rage simmered inside her. It never went dormant, not completely. She could mask it, thankfully, when dreaming.

Keep it buried. But when she wasn't dreaming, her sinister side continued to rage.

Even asleep, Malibu could feel herself getting lost.

PART FIVE

SAN FRANCISCO—2052

MALIBU AWAKENS

MALIBU WAS AWAKENED BY A HOT LIGHT ON HER FACE. Her eyes popped open, burned, and she blinked them shut again.

"Pull the light back," a woman's voice said. Although it had a soothing quality, it was a bit startling because Malibu's ears hadn't been engaged in such a long time. "Hand me the robe," the woman said.

Malibu's eyes opened again, more tentatively than before. Moments earlier, she had been ensconced in a surrealistic dream where she had been turned into a commuter car and was being chased through the hilly streets of San Francisco. As the dream unfolded, she steered herself so she was following the chase route from the movie *Bullet*, which is the best chase scene of all time. Even as she slowly slipped into the real world, her mind lingered in its dreamlike state, unwilling to let it fully go. She blinked a few more times, and the dream drifted off to wherever dreams go when you awaken. Malibu opened her mouth to speak, but nothing came out, her vocal chords rusty from disuse.

"Bring her here," said the woman with the gentle voice.

Malibu felt a soft hand take her legs and swing them to the

side. A second hand lifted her up by the elbow. Her feet touched the cold tiled floor.

"Walking will be hard at first," the woman said.

Maybe it was her feet on the floor, or the sharp coldness in the air, but the gears in Malibu's mind started to move more efficiently. She looked around and recognized the room where she had been taken the other night—the hallway, the rows of cabinets. There were two robots standing sentry off to the side, and a woman with red hair wearing a long white lab coat.

Malibu looked at the woman and asked, "How long have I been out?"

"Three years."

"Three...what? How is that even possible?"

"Come," said the woman, "follow me."

She led them out the door as the two robots continued to support Malibu by the elbows. Together, they walked down the hallway and into another room, where there were two doctor types—a man and a woman—seated at the end of a long table. They both wore white lab jackets, metal-rimmed glasses and phony smiles. The robots stayed outside the room. The redhead walked to the end of the table and sat down with the others. They instructed Malibu to sit.

"Three years?" Malibu said, bewildered.

"That's right," said the man. He leaned forward as he spoke, his eyes bright and eager. He looked young, maybe late twenties, but despite his relative youthfulness Malibu sensed that he was in charge. "That's right. It was necessary. You had a type of meltdown. We needed the time to evaluate you."

"Three years?" Malibu repeated.

"It was necessary," the redhead said.

"Yes," said the other woman, a brunette. Unlike the man, she leaned back in her chair. She was middle-aged and looked bored, as if she had seen more than her share of cases like Malibu.

"We believe you had a type of psychotic episode," the man said. "A schizophrenic-like condition. We think it was triggered by your childhood and the situation with your parents." He looked left and then right, seeking support from the ladies, which they offered with thoughtful nods of their heads. "We were able to treat you while you slept. With chemicals and electrical stimulation and other techniques. It takes time, but has proven to be effective."

"It beats prison," said the brunette.

"I'm sure you feel differently than before," said the man.

The truth was, Malibu did feel different. Her mind was quiet. She could not sense any emotions. Malibu tried to meet his eyes. "Sure. Sure. So I had a psychotic episode?"

"That's how we see things," the redhead chimed in.

"Schizophrenia?"

"In that family," the redhead continued. "Dual personalities. We can't prove it, but that's our expert conclusion."

Dual personalities? Malibu listened for the sinister voice inside her, but it was quiet. "I see," Malibu said, although she wasn't sure she did.

The man grinned. "We're here to help."

The man and the redhead went on to speak more about her supposed condition and the steps they had taken to cure her, while Malibu and the brunette listened. Malibu watched their lips move, but she didn't register most of what they were saying. Her mind was elsewhere.

The brunette slapped her hand on the table. Not aggressively, but with enough force to snap Malibu to attention. "He said you're free to go now. You just need to sign this form."

She pushed a one-page document with a lot of tiny text

across the table to Malibu and handed her a pen. Without reading it, Malibu signed.

The redhead took Malibu outside the room and down the hallway again to another small room, where a female attendant stood holding a large box.

"Good luck," the redhead said, and left.

"Here," the attendant said, and handed the box to Malibu. Inside was a full set of clothes: jeans, a blouse, jacket, undergarments, socks, and shoes.

There didn't seem to be a changing room, so the woman turned her back and let Malibu get dressed. Once Malibu's shoelaces were tied, the attendant said, "Here," and handed her a plastic card, like a credit card. "There are five hundred credits. Part of a new government program to give you a leg up."

"What about my shekels?"

The woman shook her head. "No more shekels. We all use cards now. There've been some changes. You'll see. Now, out the door take a left, and you'll see an exit."

Malibu slid the plastic card into the back pocket of her jeans and followed the exit route the woman had outlined.

Outside, it was sunny, no fog. From the looks of it, Malibu was still in San Francisco, South of Market, not too far from the Chesterfield. She looked around and what popped out were the drones, which buzzed in the air, near and far, like angry hornets. There must have been a few dozen, each about the size of a shoebox. As she stepped away from the hospital's entrance, one of the drones zoomed up just above her head, hovered in front of her face. It stayed there for a few seconds, shone a red light into her face, and then hummed away.

Shaken, Malibu walked quickly toward the street. She looked for a commuter car, but none appeared, not a single one. That was strange, although it didn't really matter because she didn't have anywhere to go anyway. Another drone buzzed by her head. There were a lot of homeless people everywhere—walking, sleeping. Two Union Members were within eyeshot, both robotic, which seemed peculiar. Shouldn't there be a human partner as well?

Completely at loose ends, Malibu turned and walked in a daze, pointing herself toward the bay. She didn't get far before she felt a warm and welcoming sensation slip over her body. It was a happy feeling. She felt a hand touch her back, and still looking forward Malibu said, "Hi Max."

She stopped walking and turned around to face him. Max looked older than she had remembered him, the lines on his forehead carved deeper. He wore a suit and black tie and polished shoes, just as before. He even had on a new pair of white gloves.

"You knew it was me?"

"I had a feeling."

"I've kept tabs on you," Max said. "I wanted to be here when you were released, but my timing was a bit off."

Malibu felt both relieved and touched. "I...I...thanks," she managed to get out. "Three years?"

Max nodded. "How about we go to my place and get something to eat?"

"Sure. Do you still live—"

Cutting her off quickly, as if he didn't want to dwell on the topic, he said, "No. I had to move. I live in a cottage, if you can believe it."

Cottage—the word burrowed deep into the recess of Malibu's brain, seemed to slither around the synapses until it uncorked a faint and eerie echo: *Cottage.* This was followed by: *Number 9, number 9, number 9...*"

"Number 9," Malibu said.

"Excuse me?"

"Nevermind." The mantra kept ringing in Malibu's head. "Can we walk to the cottage?"

"No," Max said, "We'll need to get a train."

"Train? What about the commuter cars?"

He frowned. "A lot has changed."

ABOUT THE AUTHOR

 **Mark Richardson** has published two previous novels, *The Sun Casts No Shadow* and *Hunt for the Troll*. Mark lives in California with his wife, two children, and the world's cutest dog. He spends his time writing fiction, obsessing about the Chicago Cubs, attending his daughter's softball games, and reading stacks of books. He loves genre-bending fiction, especially speculative writing with a noir flavor. In 2019, he was diagnosed with Parkinson's disease, and supports the Michael J. Fox Foundation.

———

To learn more about Mark Richardson and discover more Next Chapter authors, visit our website at www.nextchapter.pub.

Malibu Burns
ISBN: 978-4-82415-194-0

Published by
Next Chapter
2-5-6 SANNO
SANNO BRIDGE
143-0023 Ota-Ku, Tokyo
+818035793528

26th September 2022